APOCALYPSE MISSION 3

A DEMON, A DUNGEON, A DEN OF EVIL

MARK E. FISHER

Apocalypse Mission 3: A Demon, A Dungeon, A Den of Evil (Apocalypse Mission, #3), by Mark E. Fisher

Extraordinary Tales Publishing, LLC
@ExtraordinaryTalesPublishing.biz
First Extraordinary Tales, LLC edition: October 2025. Version 2.1: 11/25
Copyright © 2025 by Mark E. Fisher

Print Book ISBN: 978-1-950235-30-8
eBook ISBN: 978-1-950235-31-5

Cover art created with ChatGPT
Cover design and eBook formatting by Booknook.biz
Print book formatting by ExtraordinaryTalesPublishing.biz
Editing by Deirdre Lockhart of Brilliant Cut Editing

To learn where to buy this book or for more information about this and the author's other books visit: MarkFisherAuthor.com

Scripture marked HCSB is taken from the Holman Christian Standard Bible®, Copyright © 1999, 2000, 2002, 2003, 2009 by Holman Bible Publishers. Used by permission. Holman Christian Standard Bible®, Holman CSB®, and HCSB® are federally registered trademarks of Holman Bible Publishers.

Library of Congress Cataloging-in-Publication Data:
Fisher, Mark E.
Apocalypse Mission 3: A Demon, A Dungeon, A Den of Evil (Apocalypse Mission, #3) / Mark E. Fisher 1st ed.

Printed in the United States of America

Contents

CAST OF CHARACTERS

THE PRINCIPALS

* Aurora Carter—Aurora's cousin, Drew Carter, bequeathed her a notebook in which he dictated prophecies given by an angel with missions meant only for her and her brothers. After witnessing the prophecies come true and reading the book of Revelation, she accepted Christ. She and her brothers then escorted the holy man, Eli, from Minnesota across the Atlantic to Israel. There, a rogue faction of the Unitum Imperium captured her.

* Brett Carter—Brother to Aurora and Tyler, Brett became a believer after seeing the notebook's prophecies come true and Eli preach against the Antichrist. He, Tyler, Lisette, and Maeve hope to discover where Unitum Imperium agents took Aurora.

* Brooke Barkley—Girlfriend of Nick Carter who moved with him to Jerusalem where Nick is working for the Ministry of Truth.

* Lisette Bellini—Tyler's girlfriend, but not a Christian. After learning that Aurora was taken prisoner, she vowed to do everything she could to get her back.

* Maeve McNeil—The Carter siblings' friend, she acted as their yacht pilot during the Atlantic crossing. An Irish firebrand, she developed a close friendship with Brett and has joined in the search for Aurora.

* Nick Carter—Father to Aurora, Brett, and Tyler, Nick worked for Turner Enterprises. But when that merged into Davato's Ministry of Truth, Nick found himself trapped, working as part of the feared Central Security Agency with no way out. With Brooke, he lives at the Clal Center, Davato's headquarters in Jerusalem.

* Tyler Carter—Before the Rapture, Tyler abandoned his degree and skills as a computer programmer and dreamed of writing novels. After seeing the Bible's prophecies and the notebook's predictions come to pass, he became a Christian. Now, he and his companions are on a mission to find and rescue Aurora.

THE UNITUM IMPERIUM

* Adam Turner—Adam is the director of the Ministry of Truth. Formerly, he was CEO of Turner Enterprises, one of the largest security and internet providers in the world, until Davato folded it into the Ministry of Truth under the Unitum Imperium.

* Davato—Davato is the Antichrist, also called the son of destruction, the man of lawlessness, and the beast. He is now the Imperator, the sole ruler of the Unitum Imperium, the old Roman Empire resurrected, with plans to unite the entire world.

* Finn Foster—Finn is a lieutenant colonel in Davato's Imperium Dark Service with wide-ranging powers to investigate whatever he wants. He is cousin to the Carter siblings, but after their grandfather shorted his mother on her inheritance, he changed his name and nurtured a grudge and a vendetta against all the Carters.

* Greyson Ross—Greyson Ross is the reclusive mogul who created Universal Networks and was hired by the Unitum Imperium, integrating his proprietary algorithms into a surveillance network. Tyler Carter has taken over his identity after finding him and his crew dead aboard a ghost ship.

* Hugo—Hugo is Finn's muscleman for wet work. He left a master's degree program in archaeology to join the League of Abaddon. Now, he's a lieutenant in Davato's Imperium Dark Service.

* Sebastien Rey—Sebastien is known as the Prophet. He is the second part of the unholy satanic trinity that includes Davato and the Dragon.

CASTLE DANGER

* Dr. Albert Creig—The premier researcher in charge of the Decency Inquiry Project under the Ministry of Virtue.
* Fergus McDuff—The director in charge of Castle Danger. He answers to Sebastien Rey of the Ministry of Virtue.
* Ewan—The head guard at Castle Danger.
* Wallace Sloan—A special agent of the Ministry of Virtue assigned to Castle Danger, Scotland.

PREFACE

The signs of the end converge as never before, and the tribulation casts its shadow before us.

So where do we find our hope? Is it in the promises of men or governments or a new leader, even if that leader charts a course away from the egregious, sinful ways of the past?

Or do we place our hope in the unchanging, eternal promises of a perfectly holy, infinite, ever-present, all-powerful, all-loving God? From Psalm 62:5–9 (HCSB):

> Rest in God alone, my soul, for my hope comes from Him. He alone is my rock and my salvation, my stronghold; I will not be shaken. My salvation and glory depend on God, my strong rock. My refuge is in God. Trust in Him at all times, you people; pour out your hearts before Him. God is our refuge. *Selah*
> Men are only a vapor; exalted men, an illusion. Weighed in the scales, they go up; together they are less than a vapor.

Our characters now face obstacles they cannot overcome on their own. They are confronted by forces of satanic evil too powerful for mere mortals to stand against without divine help. Their enemies' minds are captured by ideologies and beliefs that have blinded them to the truth. Their souls commune—perhaps unwillingly and even without their knowledge—with demons.

How much are they like so many of our friends and neighbors today!

So here, in these pages, we follow our characters into the heart of darkness, into the valley of the shadow of death itself, as they strive and fight and try to overcome a world ruled by an enemy of all that is true, right, and holy.

But in the end, it's only by relying on the God of light, truth, and justice that anyone can stand against the darkness.

This novel brings our characters through February and March of the tribulation's third year. And as the pen and the Spirit led me, the book ended up going in a different direction than I'd planned. The reader may find it more of an adventure story and a bit different from the others in the series. But know that our characters will eventually find their way back into the meta-narrative of the great biblical end-times story, back into the center of the prophecies that the apostle John revealed in the book of Revelation. So be patient and keep reading.

Once again, this novel contains scenes where some of our characters visit Hell. For those with delicate sensibilities, also know that they were based, not purely on my imagination, but on real-life reports from near-death experiences. Let them stand as a stark warning for all who do not know Christ.

I hope the reader enjoys the tale.

But above all, I hope the reader's eternal fate is secure, resting solely on Jesus, the Lord of lords and King of kings.

Mark E. Fisher, MMin
Rochester, Minnesota
June 2025

P.S. For those who have read the preface and the "Mark's Books" sections of Apocalypse Mission 1 and 2 before their updates in May 2025, note that I have extended this series to six books. At the risk of being compared to Jerry B. Jenkins and Tim LaHaye's endless series, Apocalypse Mission now encompasses the entire seven years of the tribulation.

NEWSLETTER INVITATION #1

The shadow of the Tribulation already darkens our world.
Stay true to the faith and seek refuge in Christ.

Subscribe and keep abreast of new releases and receive these free gifts:

1. 10 Reasons Why the End Times Could Come Tomorrow
2. How the Green Agenda Prepares the Way for Earth Worship and the Antichrist
3. Prophecy and the Book of Revelation: What Is Its Blessing?
4. The Rapture of the Church: Time Is Running Out. Are You Ready?

To sign up, go to: www.MarkFisherAuthor.com/newsletter

PART I
CASTLE DANGER

Revelation 6:9–11 (HCSB):

When He opened the fifth seal, I saw under the altar the people slaughtered because of God's word and the testimony they had. They cried out with a loud voice: "Lord, the One who is holy and true, how long until You judge and avenge our blood from those who live on the earth?" So a white robe was given to each of them, and they were told to rest a little while longer until the number would be completed of their fellow slaves and their brothers, who were going to be killed just as they had been.

CHAPTER 1

A CELL OF STONE

Castle Danger, Scotland ~ February, Year 3

Micah 2:1 (HCSB): *Woe to those who dream up wickedness and prepare evil plans on their beds!*

Someone was leading Aurora down stone steps, and her feet descended, seemingly of their own accord—down, down, down—into a dark and cold place. The slapping of many shoes echoed off the rock walls and ceiling, hammering her ears and jerking her out of a drug-induced stupor.

She opened her eyes and cringed. The creature who'd made a home inside her skull woke and, with apparent glee, began methodically banging a maul against her temples.

The stairs ended, the path widened into uneven cobbles, and she nearly tripped. A row of cells carved from rock opened on her right. She passed into a circle of bright light, shining down from a shaft above, too harsh upon waking eyes.

Special Agent Wallace Sloan walked ahead of her, and she winced as she followed him through the light.

She glanced back. A thin man with a black goatee and tattooed arms waved a truncheon as if to say, "Keep going, woman." She kept going.

The cell doors beside her contained thick iron bars. From the shadowy interiors, faces pressed up against the bars and peered out, eyes shining yellow in the dim light.

"Protect us, Lord," came the whisper from one cell. "Save us from this evil place."

"Dear Jesus," came the cry from another dark chamber, "get us out of here."

The guard with the goatee rushed forward and rattled his truncheon across the bars. "Be silent!" he shouted. "Or it's the pit for you."

Silence followed, and the yellow eyes withdrew into the darkness.

A blast of cold air dropped down from the ceiling shaft. On the rock wall to her left, a faint trickle meandered down a gray granite slab. The cells ended, and a flat stretch of rock shelf opened to her right.

As they continued, she sensed evil, weak at first, then stronger. Massive horizontal bars lay across a deep hole. She peered through the cracks into the darkness beneath, and a heaviness weighed upon her chest.

Here, in the presence of whatever lay in the pit below, it was as if she'd entered an unearthly realm where right and good and hope and even love itself had been banished.

Two large green eyes peered up from the deep. Then came a guttural, primal snort. The foul scent of sulfur and rotting flesh rose up around her, and she gagged.

That sense of great evil, as of some enervating, airborne poison, drew the strength from her muscles, flesh, and bones, and her hands groped for her wildly thumping heart.

Sloan grabbed her shoulders and shook her. "Never stare into the maw of the demon beastie, lass. For your own sake, look aside and keep walking."

Shaken from her trance, she tore her gaze away and kept walking.

The further they went, the more its presence diminished, and she drew a deep, comforting breath.

"What was that?" she asked. "Why did you call it a 'demon beastie'?"

"The less you know, the better." Sloan shot her a backward glance. "Who can understand the nature of that which comes from below, from the distant, dark realms beyond our ken?"

A shudder rippled through her, and she followed her captor.

The cells resumed, and the tunnel turned a corner. More ceiling shafts let in more circles of light. The passage continued, and, some meters ahead, it turned again.

Sloan stopped them before cell number 52. "This one's yours." He pulled a device from his pocket, punched a button, and the lock clicked open. He waved her inside.

She gazed into the dark chamber, but her feet refused to move.

"Go in, lass." He shrugged. "You've really no choice."

She stepped inside.

A bed was carved from the rock. It held a blanket and a pillow with a coverlet, stained, stuffed, and leaking straw. The cell's three stone walls had no recesses or shelves. Twelve feet above, the shadows of the door's grillwork striped a rock ceiling.

A shiver began in her shoulders and crawled down her back.

How had this happened to her? How had she ended up in—what? A dungeon?

Hadn't the notebook been guiding her and her brothers on divine missions? Or was that now finished? Had the others delivered Eli, their holy man, to his appointment? Or had they failed?

Her vision blurred with moisture. One hand rose and wiped a tear from a cheek.

Had God abandoned her to rot in this foul prison?

Sloan stood in the doorway, holding the door open and watching her. "I–I am truly sorry." He began closing the bars. "Maybe it will go better for you than for others?"

"Wait!" She gripped the bars and held them. "Where are we? Is this Scotland?"

"Aye, lass, as I said earlier."

"Why am I here? What do they do in this place?"

He shook his head. "What I am allowed to say is that we are associated with the Highlands Regional CSA office, but with broader, higher-level authority. I can also say you are now a subject of the Decency Inquiry Project run by Director Fergus McDuff. Eventually, the director meets with all new arrivals."

"What kind of project? What does it do?"

"Though we wear CSA-type uniforms, we are a special unit of Minister Sebastien Rey's Ministry of Virtue."

"Decency? Virtue? You're not making sense." When he began closing the door again, she held it open. "No. Please. I don't understand."

He eased up his pressure on the door. "Please, lass. I don't like this any more than you do." His fingers grasped hers and gently peeled them, one by one, off the iron. Then he closed the door, and the lock clicked shut.

She stared at him through the bars, and he remained. He held her gaze with eyes in which—was it possible?—she sensed pity and mercy. Maybe even regret?

After an awkward silence, he turned on his heels. His footsteps echoed away across the stone.

Gradually, her eyes adjusted to the twilight, but her mind was reeling.

She was clinging by her fingertips to the edge of a deep pit, grasping for some bare branch or fragment of root, anything to keep her from falling into the murky depths below.

Then she thought of Eli and what he was always telling them. She fell to her knees. A chill from the stone seeped through her kneecaps and up her legs. She lifted her hands to the ceiling.

"Dear Jesus, please help me. I don't know why I'm here in this place so far from my brothers and my friends. I feel so alone and abandoned. Here I am, in the valley of death itself. Enemies surround me on all sides. Please give me the strength to endure whatever I may face. I ask this in your holy name. Amen."

She started to rise but dropped again to her knees. "And please, dear Jesus, is there some reason, some purpose, for why I am here?"

Satisfied she'd left nothing out, she stood. But she'd taken only one step toward the bed when she stopped. Was it her imagination, or had someone just spoken?

It was a word, a single word punctuating the stillness. And it was—

"Yes."

CHAPTER 2
SEARCHING FOR CLUES

Tel Aviv, Israel ~ February, Year 3

It was late afternoon when Tyler left the taxi with Lisette, Maeve, and Brett. He paid with one of Greyson Ross's credit cards, and they crossed the street to the Mashya Restaurant at the Mendeli Street Hotel, scene of Aurora's capture. But a metal grille blocked the entrance, and a sign on the window told him the place was closed. He faced his companions.

"Now what?"

Lisette pointed to the hotel entrance beside the restaurant. "Maybe they know something?"

"Aye, lass," said Maeve. "I see someone inside."

Tyler led them through the glass door to the counter.

"May I help you?" asked a young, black-haired woman.

"I was wondering"—he showed her his ring—"does anyone here have a ring like this one?"

Her eyes widened, her forehead crinkled, and she nodded to a bench in the foyer. "Wait there."

They settled onto the offered seats and waited until a middle-aged woman with brown hair and a face carved in stone approached. "What can I do for you?"

Again, Tyler showed the ring and asked his question.

Frowning, she glanced at him and at the others. "I was warned about someone like you, coming to me with such questions. Fortunately for you, the authorities know nothing about that ring. If you seek the manager and the employees involved in the illegal activities at the Mashya Restaurant, I can't help you. This hotel stays open only because I convinced the authorities we had nothing to do with the affairs over there." She waved toward the door. "You'd best leave."

They stood, but they hadn't taken two steps before Brett turned back. "What became of the manager? Do you know where he is? Our sister was captured that night. Do you know if the CSA took a young woman?"

Scowling, she crossed her arms. "I saw the whole thing through the window. There were two groups of CSA, one of which I didn't recognize. The CSA I know captured two people who worked at the restaurant. They sent them off to who knows where. The rest escaped. They questioned me for hours, discovered nothing, and then I pestered them. They gave me the names of their prisoners, and they didn't get Benyamin, the manager. But they wouldn't reveal a thing about the other organization, only that some other group took a customer, a woman who didn't work at the restaurant. Maybe she was your sister."

"Did they mention her name?" Tyler's heart sped up.

"No."

"If we could find this Benyamin," said Brett, "maybe he could tell us how to find our sister?"

"Unlikely. I was surprised he got mixed up in this. He once mentioned a family farm in Sicily. When he moved here and took over the restaurant, he changed his name from Beniamino to Benyamin. I don't know his Italian last name. And where that farm is or whether he's there now, who knows? I liked the man, and I hope that after this, he stays on the right side of the law."

"Thank you," said Tyler.

She held up a hand. "A word of warning. I'm supposed to inform the authorities if ever someone like you shows up asking questions like yours." Her scowl deepened. "But if I do, they'll interrogate me again, taking hours away from my duties. Why should I do their dirty work for them? So just save me the trouble and don't come here again."

Tyler nodded, and they returned to the street. But after a few meters, they stopped.

Maeve laid hands on her hips. "Now what? We can't just go wandering around Sicily. We don't even know if this Benyamin went there. And we don't have his last name."

"You're right." Tyler scratched his chin. "Who has the notebook?"

Brett patted the backpack behind him. "I've got it."

"Have you checked it lately?"

"Twice since we left Jerusalem." He removed the pack from his back, fished out the notebook, and looked again. "Nothing."

The notebook's prophecies had been guiding them since Aurora returned from Cousin Drew's funeral in Buffalo. Tyler still marveled that God had chosen him and his siblings to receive its cryptic messages, dictated by an angel and recorded by Drew before his death. They'd been undertaking its missions for over two and a half years, even before the Vanishing, and when the next message would appear, the last one would vanish.

"Maybe we should go to the ship and wait. God has been guiding us through the notebook so far. Maybe he'll tell us what to do next?"

The others agreed, and they took a taxi to the marina. At the entrance, Tyler withdrew the maximum amount of cash from an ATM. The CSA could track him whenever he used Ross's cards, and soon, he'd have to stop relying on them.

At some point, they'd have to go dark. But he had another option for getting cash, one he hadn't disclosed to the others. Meanwhile, he'd get cash at every opportunity.

* * *

DUSK HAD ALREADY FALLEN WHEN they arrived at the ship. Fortunately, it was the same as they'd left it a few days ago.

Tyler then realized no one had yet informed Father of the bad news. He pulled out his phone and punched the number. When Father came on the line, Tyler related all that had happened, ending with Aurora's capture.

"Oh no! This is bad, very bad. . . ." Then came heavy breathing before Father spoke again. "I've told you what they do with rebels and Christians. We can only hope they didn't send her to that German internment camp."

"The woman at the restaurant said there were two groups of CSA, one of which she didn't recognize. They're the ones who took her."

"Two groups? How odd!" Silence at the other end. "Perhaps it was the IDS, and she didn't recognize their uniforms. Or maybe it was a new group in opposition to the others. It's possible. Power corrupts, and if some new faction wanted to take power from the rest, I could believe it. This might actually work in our favor."

"How so?" asked Tyler.

"If the forces of the Antichrist are fighting for control among themselves, it could open up opportunities for us. Think about it."

"You could be right. But what are *you* going to do now?"

"I'm temporarily back in Jerusalem with priority-file access. I should also tell you that while I'm away, I've hired Dante Marino to watch the villa in Italy. He worked for us before Antonia, when you were quite young. I'll start searching for information about this second group, but inquiries like that might create suspicion. If I find something, I'll call you back."

"Okay." Tyler gripped the phone tighter. "We must do everything we can to find her and get her out."

"If she's in that German camp, from what I've heard, there's little chance of helping her."

"I hope you're wrong." He took a deep breath. "Let's pray she's not there."

"A word of warning. If you must take the ship out again, there have been reports of piracy in the Mediterranean. Lawlessness is spreading everywhere."

"Thanks. But we don't know where she is. We don't even know if we'll need the ship."

They ended the call, but nothing Father had said left him with much hope.

CHAPTER 3

A NEW MESSAGE

Tel Aviv, Israel ~ February, Year 3

To save supplies, they decided to take their evening meal in a restaurant beyond the marina. It was already dark as Brett and the others strolled to Shtuspak where a beaming waiter seated them at once.

"So few patrons these days." He shook his head. "It's good to see paying customers."

Brett set his knapsack with the notebook and Bible on the floor beside him. Why he'd brought it along, he didn't know, only that it seemed like the right thing to do.

The menu held a selection of salads and seafood dishes, and he ordered pasta with grilled sea bass. The others followed his lead, ordering the same, and the waiter brought them a bottle of white wine to share.

"What if the notebook tells us to go somewhere in Europe, not in Israel?" asked Lisette. "How will we get there?"

"We'll take the ship," answered Tyler. "It's the best way to avoid the CSA."

Brett frowned. "But they can track the *Carpe Diem*. They know it belongs to Greyson Ross."

Tyler rubbed his chin. "What if we changed its name?"

"Then you'd need new registration papers." Maeve swished the wine in her glass. "Without those, if anyone stops us, we'd be stateless. That would be trouble. We'd also need a travel pass."

"With some cash on the table"—Tyler raised an eyebrow—"maybe the harbormaster will agree to both?"

After they'd eaten and the waiter removed empty dishes, they sat and finished a second bottle.

Brett brought the knapsack to his lap. "This has been bothering me all day. I don't know why, but it's been telling me to keep looking."

"Might our Brett now be communing with the Creator?" Maeve shot him a wry smile and laid a hand on his. "Is he becoming a man of God?"

"And so what if he is, Irishwoman?" Brett smiled back, brought her fingers to his lips, and kissed them. Removing the notebook, he placed it on the table and flipped to where the next message should be.

"There's something here!"

While he read, the others craned their necks toward the book.

Go where you have gone before, where friends await, and seek their counsel. But know that sometimes the desires of friends must come before yours. Psalm 40:1.

He passed the notebook to the others then brought out the Bible and flipped to the passage. He read, "'I waited patiently for the LORD, and he turned to me and heard my cry for help.'" He glanced up. "That's all."

"It's telling us," said Tyler, "to return to the inn and restaurant at San Felice Circeo."

"But what does that second sentence mean about the desires of friends?" Lisette scowled.

"Who knows?" Brett stuffed the Bible and notebook into his pack. "But at least now we know where we're going."

"Right." Tyler called for the waiter, he paid, and they started back.

But as they headed down the marina toward pier number 5 and the *Carpe Diem*, Brett stopped. At pier number 2, a harbor patrol agent was posting a notice on a ship in a nearby berth.

Brett waved the others ahead and approached the man. "What's going on?"

"The owner died in the hospital, and the ship's for sale, cheap. He lived onboard, and we can't find any relatives. But inside, it's a total disaster. There was a fire, and the harbormaster is desperate to get rid of it."

"All right. Thanks."

The ship, *Lady of the Lake*, was much like the *Carpe Diem*, maybe a few feet shorter. It also had a main and a mizzen.

He hurried to catch up with the others waiting on the deck.

After Brett related his find, Tyler smiled. "What if we bought this ship and stole its name? If it's similar to ours, we can use its registration papers for the *Carpe Diem*?"

"Do you have the money to buy it?" asked Brett.

Tyler's smile widened to a grin. "I've been saving some news for a special occasion, and this is it. Ross had another account using an alias. It's at a well-known bank, and there's a branch here in Tel Aviv."

"You dog, you!" Brett beamed. "Do you suppose . . . ?"

"If it's literally a fire sale, I'll buy the ship, tell the harbormaster I want it for parts, and then ask him to destroy it. We can paint a new name on the *Carpe Diem*'s hull and give it a new registration."

"Sounds like a plan." Brett slapped his brother on the shoulder. "If it all works out, we could be sailing to Italy tomorrow."

CHAPTER 4

FINN'S ARRIVAL

Edinburgh, Scotland ~ February, Year 3

Airport personnel rolled a squeaking stairway to the Learjet's passenger side door. It clanked open, and Finn Foster rushed down the steps onto the tarmac.

Carrying both their bags, Hugo hurried to catch up.

Shivering from the cold, Finn entered the hangar he'd rented, his feet echoing through the empty space. "Anyone here?" he called. He'd phoned ahead, so someone from the Edinburgh CSA headquarters had better be here to meet him.

"Coming," came a voice from the back corner.

Hugo stopped and handed Finn his heavy jacket. "It must be forty degrees here."

"Scotland in winter," said a short, balding man striding toward them. He had a pudgy face and wore a disheveled CSA uniform. Smiling, he held out a hand. "You must be Lieutenant Colonel Finn Foster?"

"I am." Finn took the offered hand and introduced Hugo. "Now tell me what's going on with the prisoner Aurora Carter."

"Yes, yes, all in good time. I am Bagby Creel, your liaison while you're here in beautiful Caledonia, the land of cakes." He uttered a short laugh. "But perhaps we should discuss things over a bite of lunch?"

Finn checked his watch. It was past noon, and he wanted to get down to business. But one glance at Hugo's nodding head told him he'd appreciate food. "Yes. Lunch. All right."

"Good. I've got a car around back."

They followed him to an Audi SUV, and the waiting chauffeur drove them to the Guildford Arms. Finn was anxious to question the man on the way. But much to his annoyance, Creel answered a call from his daughter and spent the entire trip on the phone.

The driver dropped them off, and they entered a pub adorned with plush carpets, brass rails, crystal chandeliers, and round mahogany tables. Rich, dark wood paneled the walls and ceiling. Creel led them to an isolated table in back.

They'd barely sat when a waiter arrived with menus and a pint of dark ale he set before Creel. "Good afternoon, Bagby. The usual?"

"Aye, Tom." Creel glanced at his guests. "What'll you have?"

Finn gave the menu a cursory glance, chose fish and chips, a mug of Caledonia's Best, and ordered. Hugo asked for the same.

The moment they were alone again, Finn slapped both hands on the table. "Now tell me, Bagby Creel, what about my prisoner, Aurora Carter?"

A smiling Creel brought out a pipe, stuffed it with tobacco, and lit it with a match. "Patience, my friend. We have all the time in the world. I find it's always best to have a few drinks and relax before we dive into work."

His frustration rising, Finn glared.

"Yes, yes, my friend." Perhaps sensing Finn's impatience, Creel set down his pipe and leaned forward. "As I said, there is no rush. Aurora Carter is in custody, but, unfortunately, not by us."

"What do you mean? Who has her?"

"Some group on an isolated peninsula in the west. And, unfortunately, their authority comes not from the Ministry of Truth, but from the Ministry of Virtue. They have a compound up there we have tried to infiltrate, but so far, our efforts have failed. They're overly secretive." He shook his head. "We're all supposed to be working for the Imperator, are we not? But these people think they're above the rest of us." He chuckled as if at some private joke.

"Perhaps not." Finn's beer arrived, and he pushed it aside. "The authority of the Imperium Dark Service supersedes all others. They will hand her over to me or face the consequences. When can we go there?"

Creel gave him a knowing smile. "In this situation, my friend, you may find your authority means little."

"And why is that?"

"A man by the name of Fergus McDuff is in charge. The Decency Inquiry Project is what they call their mission, and it's under the auspices of the Department of Decency under Sebastien Rey's Ministry of Virtue." To the sounds of crackling, burning tobacco, he sucked in on the pipe, held the smoke, then blew out. "There's also some doctor working with them. For some time now, they've been stealing prisoners out from under the noses of the CSA, and none of them have ever been released. We don't know what they do up there, but twice now, we've sent agents to investigate, only to be stonewalled, returning empty-handed. But that's not the worst of it."

"There's more?"

"They pretend to cooperate. They give our men a tour of the facility. There are cells of prisoners, but the one thing that our agents return with that impresses them the most is the demon."

"A demon?" Few things could surprise him, but now Finn's eyes widened. "Explain!"

"Somehow, they've trapped a demon in their dungeon. And the rumor is that this Fergus McDuff, and maybe the doctor also, talk with the thing." Creel shrugged. "Now, whether this is true or not . . . ?"

"Demon or not, they will release her to me." Finn pounded a fist on the table. "The IDS has supreme authority. Does this place have a name?"

"They call it Castle Danger. It's remote, in the civil parish of Lochbroom, and to get there, one must travel by boat then hike through brambles, moors, and mountains. There might be another way, but we know not of it."

"When can we leave?"

"It's too late to travel today." Creel sipped his ale. "So patience, my friend. Tomorrow is soon enough."

Finn sat back. Creel didn't understand the urgency or the importance of this mission to round up the Carter family. Did anyone? But when Finn stood before this Fergus McDuff, the director would hand over his prisoner to a lieutenant colonel in the uniform of the dreaded Imperium Dark Service.

Or the man would pay dearly.

CHAPTER 5

THE HARBOR INCIDENT

Tel Aviv, Israel ~ February, Year 3

The morning after the notebook's message, Tyler took a taxi to a branch of the local bank where Greyson Ross had an account under the name of Gavin Roberts. Tyler had already created an alternate ID with his picture. With that ID, he withdrew the amount of the purchase and more than enough cash to take them to the ends of the earth.

Wearing Ross's best, Tyler approached the harbormaster. Aldo Fontana was a short man with thick glasses and a wide brown mustache. He was obviously happy to find a purchaser for the ruined boat and get it out of his marina. Tyler gave the excuse that he wanted to cannibalize a few items from the ship for his own vessel, expected in port next week. Fontana nodded and agreed on a dirt-cheap price.

After signing the ship over to Gavin Roberts with a new, official registration, Fontana assumed the transaction was over and started to rise.

But then, Tyler steeled himself and asked for a travel pass.

Fontana sat again in his squeaking chair and frowned. "I have authority to grant travel passes only in special situations, and yours is not one. For what you want, you must contact the CSA."

"Another harbormaster helped me out in this way. In Naples."

As if to dismiss his visitor, the man waved both hands. "Maybe when given to persons of great importance and authority, but that situation does not apply here, does it?"

For some moments, Tyler held the man's gaze. Then he opened his wallet. One by one, he placed hundred-euro bills on the desk until he reached a thousand. He lifted his gaze. "Would this help with the paperwork?"

Fontana stared at the pile of cash, glanced at Tyler, then turned his right hand so that his thumb pointed up.

Tyler counted out another five hundred and sat back.

"Sì." A smiling Fontana collected the pile and dropped it in a desk drawer. "I have reconsidered. Perhaps, in this instance, we might just have a special situation." He withdrew a form from another drawer, wrote for several minutes, stamped it, and handed it over.

Tyler thanked him and left with the pass.

By the time he'd returned to the ship, it was late afternoon, and Brett had painted *Lady of the Lake* over the *Carpe Diem*'s name.

"How did it go?" asked Maeve.

"Great! We've got what we need."

"Good. But now we'd be seeing a strong wind stirring up the bonny waves. No rain. Just wind. Should we wait?"

Tyler gazed beyond the shelter of the harbor at the whitecaps and dark skies. "Eli and Moses declared a six-month drought, so it can't be a storm. If it's only a windstorm, we should go. We have no time to waste."

"Aye. In that case, let's be off."

* * *

THEY LEFT THE CALM HARBOR waters for the heavy seas. But no sooner had the buildings of Tel Aviv sunk over the horizon than a coast patrol boat appeared on the port side, flashing its lights and whirring its siren.

"Now what?" asked Brett.

"Probably a routine inspection of papers," answered Maeve from the wheel.

Before it arrived, Tyler went below and secured his pile of cash in the new safe they'd installed while in port. The safe lay hidden in a panel behind a salon closet. But when he returned to the deck, both Brett and Maeve bore looks of concern.

"Something's wrong." Maeve pointed. "Look at their uniforms."

Tyler squinted at four men standing on the ship's deck about two hundred meters away. "They're wearing keffiyeh. And they're carrying AK-47s."

"Right. Who are they?" Maeve's hand went to the throttle.

"Arabs?" Brett's hands balled into fists. "Pirates?"

"Can we outrun them?" asked Tyler.

"We'll see." Maeve increased the throttle. The ship crashed through the heavy surf. Behind them, the patrol boat followed, lights flashing, siren blaring.

But their pursuer began closing the gap. When the other ship was within fifty meters, one of the dark-skinned men fired a round at the *Lady of the Lake*, and a bullet punctured a hole in the pilothouse above Maeve's head.

"We can't outrun them. They'll kill us all." Tyler waved to Maeve. "We have to stop."

"What do they want?" Lisette crowded in.

"I don't know, but I'm not going down without a fight." Brett patted the holster under his shirt where he kept his Glock.

"Right, boyo. I'm with you." Much to Tyler's surprise, Maeve revealed a hidden pistol of her own under her shirt. When had she gotten that?

The other vessel motored closer. A tall, dark-haired, dark-bearded man with an AK-47 slung over one shoulder raised a bullhorn. "Cut engine and come on deck. Then we board."

Maeve put the engine in idle. Slowly, they filed out of the pilothouse.

On the bucking deck, as Tyler waited for the pirates to cross the gap between the ships, the wind drove stinging salt spray against his face. The sea beyond heaved and surged.

While one dark-skinned Arab stood on deck, pointing his gun across the water, three others lowered a dinghy off the stern. They climbed in and began rowing toward the *Lady of the Lake*. But the seas were rough, and their progress was slow.

"Look behind the pilothouse." Brett pointed at the patrol boat. "Is that a reserve tank?"

"Aye, laddie. Probably diesel. And if you'd be thinking what I'd be thinking . . ."

"Wait!" Tyler held up a hand and walked back inside the pilothouse to the aft wheel. He looked up and nodded.

"On my count," said Brett to Maeve.

"One . . . two . . . three." They drew their weapons from their hidden holsters. They aimed. And they fired.

The gunshots blasted Tyler's ears. The tank exploded, throwing flaming diesel everywhere across the patrol boat's deck.

Tyler put the controls in gear and rammed the throttle all the way forward. The ship lurched and crashed into the waves.

Behind them, the three Arabs in the dinghy aimed their AK-47s and fired. Everyone ducked as bullets whizzed overhead. A few punched holes in the pilothouse.

But the dinghy was flotsam in a turbulent sea, and the three men had all they could do to aim and keep their craft afloat.

The fourth Arab on the ship was now covered with flames. He jumped off the doomed vessel into the water and began swimming toward his companions.

As the *Lady of the Lake* distanced itself from its pursuers, the Arabs turned the dinghy back toward their mate, thrashing in the water.

Minutes later, the *Lady of the Lake* left the burning ship in the rear.

Still facing backward, Lisette squinted at the smoke drifting up. "Do you think they'll make it to shore?"

"It would serve them right if they didn't," answered Tyler at the wheel. "But I wonder if the coast patrol would like to know that the pirates who'd captured one of their ships are heading their way. I'll radio the harbormaster. If they do make it to shore, that will ensure a nice reception."

Brett grinned. "Aye, laddie."

Tyler shot him a puzzled glance. "Are you turning Irish on us?"

Standing beside Brett, Maeve planted a kiss on his cheek. "Better watch out, Tyler. It might be contagious."

CHAPTER 6

UNDER SUSPICION

Jerusalem, Israel ~ February, Year 3

Following a request from another department, Nick Carter trailed the tall, mustachioed IDS agent into a fourth-floor interrogation room of the Clal Center. Someone probably wanted his advice on a subject under suspicion. It had happened before. But after he sat on the table's far side, the man left the room, and Nick found himself alone. How odd. What was going on?

Ten minutes later, the agent returned with a short, bald, clean-shaven man.

They sat across from him, and the bald man cleared his throat. "I am Agent Endrizzi, and my partner here is Agent Fontana. We have invited you here today to ask a few questions of concern to the IDS."

"Of course, and what is the nature of your concern, Agent Endrizzi?"

"It's, ah, of a personal nature." The man's gaze dropped to the table. "Having to do with your family."

Nick's heart sped up. Were they making him the subject here today? "What do you want to know?"

"For some time, the CSA had been monitoring an eating establishment in Tel Aviv known for its association with the underground. Recently, your daughter, Aurora Carter, was caught up in the operation and taken into custody. She is suspected of colluding with the Enemy. Another unhappy aspect of the event is that we don't have her. A different group took her from us."

"Who has her?" Nick's eyes widened. It was best if he feigned surprise. Yesterday, he'd tried to find out where she was and who had taken her but came up with nothing. If they knew about his search, surely, they would have mentioned it. "Where is she?"

"We don't know." Endrizzi waved a hand. "I wish we did."

"So that's what this meeting is about? To inform me of this?"

"Not exactly." The man scratched his neck. "Some time ago, the Chicago CSA also took your son, Tyler Carter, into custody. He was accused of aiding and abetting a man known to be an extreme threat to the Unitum Imperium. But your son . . . escaped. His whereabouts are unknown."

"So why are you telling me this?" By the hesitation in Endrizzi's manner, Nick could see the man was uncomfortable. "What do you want from me?"

Endrizzi leaned forward. "Do you know where we can find Tyler?"

"I do not."

Then the tall Fontana folded his hands and spoke. "It appears, Nick Carter, that your family is involved in seditious activities that threaten the Unitum Imperium. What do you have to say to that?"

Nick breathed deeply and braced his elbows on the table with his fingers locked. It was time to stop this before it went any further. "Agents Fontana and Endrizzi, do you have children of your own?"

Both shook their heads.

"When and if you do, you may find that they have independent lives and are no longer under your control. No matter what you tell them, how you warn them, they will ignore your wishes and go their own way. And there's nothing you can do about it." He speared each of them with a glance, raised his voice, and slammed a fist on the table. "I am not my children! I am not responsible for their conduct!"

Fontana jerked back, and Endrizzi shot a glance at his partner.

"You must know of my position and my longtime association with Director Adam Turner, the head of the Ministry of Truth, the agency to which you report. Regardless of what my children have or have not done without my knowledge, I would suggest you tread carefully before you cast doubt on my character or my loyalty to the UI."

"Yes, yes." Fontana sent a glance to his partner and pushed back from the table. "We were supposed to ask. There's no need to go any further."

"I guess that answers our questions." Endrizzi stood and laid a hand on Fontana's shoulder. "I think we're done here."

"Good." Nick stood, walked around the table, and left the room. But as he headed for the elevator and pushed the button for his floor, he tried to slow his racing pulse.

Tyler's and Aurora's and Brett's activities were exposing him to scrutiny. But if he were in their position, wouldn't he do the same as they?

His heart was not with Davato, the Unitum Imperium, or his work here. Every day was a struggle to hide his true feelings and loyalties.

How long before they caught up with him?

He was trapped in this job, in this city, in this building, and escape seemed impossible.

CHAPTER 7

BAGBY CREEL'S ADVICE

From Edinburgh to Ullapool, Scotland ~ February, Year 3

For forty minutes, Finn paced and checked his watch until Bagby Creel finally arrived outside the Hilton Edinburgh Carlton where he and Hugo had spent the night. Swallowing his irritation, Finn plopped into the front seat, Hugo sat in back, and Creel drove.

Around noon, despite Finn's eagerness to continue, Creel insisted on a leisurely lunch at The River House in Inverness where he downed two glasses of ale, a plate of Sicilian seafood pasta, and droned on and on about nothing and everything.

Another hour and a half of slow driving brought them to Ullapool in late afternoon where Creel parked at the Caledonian Hotel. He was about to exit the car when Finn held up a hand.

"What are we doing?" he asked. "Is not the prisoner across the bay? Why aren't we going there now?"

Creel faced him with a startled look. "I made reservations here. I suggest you stay at the Caledonian tonight, eat a fine meal, and cross to Alltnaharrie tomorrow. The rumor is that it was once a nice place until new owners took over. I'm not sure it's ever been reopened."

"But must we not go there first before going to the castle?"

"It's the only route I know of, aye. But the sun will set in fifteen minutes, and—"

"Then let's go there before the sun sets."

"I doubt we can go further than Alltnaharrie today, but if that's your wish . . ."

"That's my wish."

Shrugging, Creel drove them to the docks and parked. It was dusk when they left the vehicle and donned their jackets.

Creel approached a black-bearded man just stepping onto the dock from a fishing trawler. He wore a wide-brimmed hat, rubber pants, and jacket.

With much waving toward the inlet and a shaking of heads, the two carried on an animated conversation. As Creel returned, the fisherman behind him stood with a scowl on his lips and hands in his pockets. "He says he's packed up for the night, and no one goes to the peninsula anymore. He says it's cursed. He's the only boat out here now, and he's just not interested."

"How much does he want?"

"He says he won't go. My advice is to stay here and try in the morning."

"I don't care how much it costs. Give him what he wants. I want to be there tonight."

Creel cocked his head, kept Finn's glance for a moment, then approached the man again. After longer negotiations, Creel handed the man a wad of cash then returned. "He says it's foolishness. But he took your cash, and he'll take you over."

Finn and Hugo grabbed their bags and left the dock for wet seats beside some coiled rope and a pile of nets in the trawler. But Creel still stood on the pier.

Finn cast him an annoyed glance. "Well? Aren't you coming?"

"Nay, my friend." Creel waved a hand toward the bay. "This is your venture, not mine."

"What kind of liaison are you?"

"The kind who enjoys a night in a warm bed and a good meal in a decent restaurant before running off half-cocked." He smiled, saluted, and turned on his heels.

Finn nodded to the trawler captain. "Let's go."

The man mumbled something under his breath and started the engine, and the ship motored into the inlet. Dusk had already covered the water with an inky blanket of fog.

"Fool thing," muttered the captain, "to go to Alltnaharrie in the dark."

The crossing took less than half an hour through an oppressive black mist. On the far side, the trawler motored up to a wooden dock.

Holding their bags, Finn and Hugo left the ship.

Without another word, the trawler captain piloted the ship into the bay's dark mist. The fog quickly swallowed the puttering of the engine.

"Boss?" Hugo shone his flashlight toward where the end of the dock should be, now obscured by fog.

"Right." Finn also switched on his flashlight. "Lead on."

Hugo led them into a fog that hovered only feet above the dock's surface. And when Finn wiped a hand across his jacket, the mist left no trace of moisture or dew.

The boards creaked under their feet. Where the dock ended, a stone path began. Following that took them up a rocky trail to a one-story building. But the windows were dark. Finn's flashlight shone on the door's wooden sign:

Lochbroom Ministry of Virtue
Outpost #2
No Trespassing! Violators Will Be Shot!

Below the sign was a phone number.

"Not a very friendly welcome, boss." Hugo frowned. "Why would they give a phone number if they shoot visitors?"

"I don't know, but I'm calling it."

Finn punched the numbers into his phone but received no answer.

He called several more times, but no one picked up.

"Doesn't look good." Hugo rattled the locked door.

Finn followed Hugo over a creaking wooden deck around the side of the building. He peered through a window into darkness. Pulling out his phone, he tried again to reach someone. But there was still no answer.

Finn returned to the front door and pointed. "Break the glass. We need to find shelter."

Nodding, Hugo smashed an elbow through the window then picked out enough broken glass so he could reach inside and unlock the door.

Finn switched on a light and shivered. "It's cold in here. We need heat." He waved to a brick fireplace occupying an inside wall. Beside it was a metal rack with logs.

"And I need food," said Hugo. "I'm starving."

The room held two dusty tables with four chairs each. A panel on the wall flashed a red light, and Finn approached. "This is the control panel for an alarm system. Maybe we set off an alarm?"

"Good. Maybe that will get someone's attention?"

The next room held a primitive kitchen with a propane stove. Hugo opened all the cupboards. They were empty except for boxes of cereal, crackers, powdered milk, and a jar of peanut butter. The refrigerator was also empty. A twenty-liter water dispenser was half empty.

Hugo turned from the cupboard. "We should have stayed with Creel. Looks like it's crackers and muesli for supper."

Finn shrugged then continued down the hall. He found two bedrooms and beds without sheets. Back in the dining room, Hugo was creating milk from powder.

Finn started a fire from the logs. Then they sat down to eat a bowl of muesli, crackers with peanut butter, and reconstituted milk.

"Can I ask you something, boss?" Hugo stopped a spoonful of cereal halfway to his mouth.

"What?"

"I understand why Tyler and Aurora Carter are threats. But why are you so intent on capturing the rest of their family?"

Finn lowered the cracker with its load of peanut butter and regarded the initials someone had carved in the wooden table. "The whole bunch of them are a threat to the Unitum Imperium. They are all in league against us."

"But isn't finding Christians our highest priority?" Hugo spoke around a mouthful. "Are these Carters Christians?"

"I don't think so. At least, they didn't used to be." Finn shoved his bowl aside. He wasn't in the mood for cereal or crackers. "You don't understand. I know, deep inside, that these people are a menace to all we are doing, and they must be put under lock and key."

Hugo wiped cracker crumbs from his shirt. "I'm worried, boss, that you have made this Carter thing a personal vendetta, that in this matter, you are taking us far beyond our directive."

"It's my prerogative." Finn scrunched his brows and pushed back from the table. "They are threats to the Imperator, and we will pursue them wherever they are, even if it takes us to the ends of the earth."

Hugo set down his spoon and returned Finn's stare. "If that's what you want, boss . . ."

"Yes, it's what I—"

The whirring of helicopter blades passing overhead stopped him. Then the chattering receded into the distance, followed by silence.

"What was that?" asked Hugo.

"Whoever they are, they didn't land nearby. Maybe too much fog." Finn stood from the table and went to the fire. "I'm going to warm myself then turn in."

Hugo finished eating and joined him by the fireplace.

Perhaps thirty minutes passed before the door crashed in, and two masked men, wearing body armor and carrying automatic weapons, spread out inside the room. Black scarves covered their faces.

Finn and Hugo shot to their feet.

"Raise your hands! You are under arrest!" ordered the tallest among them. "This is restricted property, and you have no right to be here."

CHAPTER 8

FERGUS MCDUFF

Castle Danger, Scotland ~ February, Year 3

"I have every right to be here!" Finn tried to reach for the badge on his belt.

But the group's leader shook his head. "Don't move, or I'll shoot."

"Do you not see my uniform and its rank?" Finn's voice rose. "Can you not see I am a lieutenant colonel of the Imperium Dark Service?"

"If it were not for that uniform," said the taller man, "you'd already have a bullet in you. Then you'd be headed for the bottom of the bay with a rock tied to your leg."

"How do we know you're legitimate?" asked the second man. "Let me see your IDs?"

"That's what I was trying to do." Finn pulled his out, as did Hugo. The tall leader examined them and handed them back. "Maybe you are who you say you are, but it doesn't matter. You have not cleared your arrival with the director. You will come with us."

"Good. That's why we're here. And now, you will lower those weapons and treat us with the respect we deserve."

The masked leader turned to the man beside him, and they held a whispered conversation. Then they lowered their weapons. "Very well. Now come with us."

With their noses and mouths still hidden under scarves, the two men led Finn and Hugo onto a dark and foggy trail by flashlight. For most of forty minutes, they climbed a rugged, rock-strewn path up the side of a mountain, until they reached a wide, flat space out of the fog where waited a helicopter.

The men waved them inside, the rotors whirred, and they rose into the night. They crossed a field of rocks and heather bordered on both sides by pine forests and mountains. Then they dropped into a valley covered with mist. They landed in a compound lit by floodlights, in the center of which rose a castle surrounded by low outbuildings. Five towers punctuated the perimeter of the battlements.

The helicopter's blades stopped spinning. The masked men ushered Finn and Hugo along a stone path leading to a drawbridge where stood a tall man with a strong jaw, a weathered face, and thick, brown hair falling over his forehead. He crossed his arms and frowned. "My name is Special Agent Wallace Sloan, and you are . . . ?"

Finn raised himself to his full height but still had to look up to catch Sloan's glance. "I am Lieutenant Colonel Finn Foster of the Imperium Dark Service." Then he introduced Hugo.

"Yes, well, the IDS doesn't carry much weight around here. You were caught breaking into one of our outposts, a violation you will now have to explain to Director McDuff."

"I called, but no one answered. I also texted."

"Before you enter restricted space, you need prior permission from the Ministry of Virtue. Follow me." Sloan turned on his heel, and Finn followed.

They crossed under a portcullis into a cobbled courtyard. In the center was a circle of dwarf pines with benches surrounding a fountain. One side of the yard was devoted to a cobbled area with benches facing two upright posts supporting an empty crossbeam.

Sloan led them to one of the towers. Inside a circular staircase, they climbed, their footsteps echoing up and down the stone tower.

On the third floor, Sloan took them along a hall and knocked on a heavy wooden door.

"Come in," came a deep voice from within.

They entered a room lined with books on two walls. An oak table with four chairs occupied one corner. More books surrounded a window on a third wall, with a counter holding glasses and bottles of scotch, whiskey, brandy, and wine.

Before a roaring fire, a gray-haired, middle-aged man, weathered of face and without beard or mustache, rose from an armchair then gripped the seatback for support. "So these are the intruders?" he asked Sloan.

"They are, sir."

He fixed a stern glance on Finn and Hugo. "I am Fergus McDuff, director of this facility. Who are you, and why did you break into one of my outposts?"

Finn was indignant, but he tried to suppress his anger. Again, he introduced himself and Hugo. Then he added, "I am here to relieve you of Aurora Carter, a prisoner in your possession whom the IDS has been seeking for some time."

A thin smile lifted McDuff's lips. "The woman in question is in our custody and will remain so. I have no reason to release her."

Finn felt his face warming. "Do you not understand that I am a member of the Imperium Dark Service? My authority supersedes yours, and if I order you to release this woman, you must comply. Or face the consequences."

McDuff laughed. "I've heard that kind of bluster before. All of you IDS types seem to think quite a bit of yourselves and your organization. But the Prophet initiated the Decency Inquiry Project, and the Imperator himself has decreed that we have supremacy, even over the IDS. In the morning, we will escort you back to the mainland where you may contact your superiors. They will verify everything I've said."

He turned to Sloan. "Give them rooms for the night and make them comfortable. Escort them to Ullapool tomorrow."

Finn stood motionless, disbelieving what he'd heard, his anger rising. "You will regret this, you—"

McDuff turned his back on them and returned to his seat by the fire and a glass of wine on an end table. Only then did Finn see the cane resting beside the man's chair.

"Follow me," said Sloan.

Having no other options, Finn complied, with Hugo behind him.

Sloan led them down one floor into a room holding two beds, a fireplace, a wardrobe standing in the corner, and a closet with a WC. "You should be comfortable here. Have you eaten? Where you were taken is not much for amenities."

"A decent meal would be appreciated," said Hugo.

"I will have something brought to you. We had haggis at dinner, and there should still be some left. Some ale too."

"Much appreciated," answered Hugo.

But after Sloan left, there was a loud click from the door lock. Finn rushed over and tried the knob. The door wouldn't open.

Then he went to the window and opened the frame. In gushed cold air that felt damp but held no moisture.

But iron bars separated him from the night beyond.

Tonight, it appeared, the IDS were prisoners of the Ministry of Virtue.

CHAPTER 9

DR. ALBERT CREIG

Castle Danger, Scotland ~ February, Year 3

When footsteps echoed down the walkway, Aurora stood and glanced through the bars at two approaching shadows. It was her second day here, and her eyes had become accustomed to the weak light. At night, a handful of LEDs cast enough illumination for the guards to keep an eye on the prisoners. During the day, the shafts in the ceiling shone a dim light outside her cell.

The figures stopped before her door, their faces in shadow. It wasn't mealtime, so why were they here?

Breakfast had been a gruel of oatmeal and milk. Last night's dinner was boiled fish, a potato, and a slice of bread. Lunch was an apple and a sandwich with cheese and barley bread. Not great fare, but they weren't starving her. To drink, they had only water.

"I'm to take you to Dr. Creig today," came the voice from the tall one. She recognized it as belonging to Wallace Sloan. But did she detect regret in his tone? Beside him stood a short, burly guard wearing a pistol on his belt.

With his pocket device, Sloan opened her cell door and waved her out. She followed him into the aisle and around two corners. As they passed the "demon beastie", she clung to the far side of the passage and looked away. Even though she avoided its glance, the thing's presence still left her chilled and shivering.

They walked up the stairwell, entered the courtyard, and crossed to one of the towers.

Their footsteps reverberated off the stone as they climbed round and round up a spiral staircase. On the fourth landing, Sloan led her down a dark hallway.

He pointed to a wooden bench, and she sat. He knocked on an oaken door then held a whispered conversation with someone inside.

As Sloan sat beside her, their burly escort entered, leaving Sloan and Aurora in the hall.

"Apparently," said Sloan, "the doctor is not quite ready."

For some minutes, they sat in silence, until, from the room beyond, came a scream.

Aurora whipped her gaze to Sloan. "What will he do to me in there?"

"Today? I don't know." As if avoiding her glance, he dropped his elbows onto his knees, his chin to his hands, and his gaze to the floor. "That's Sarah with him now. She's been here for a year."

"Why is she screaming?"

"You'd have to ask Creig." Then he sat up straight and caught her glance. "A man came here last night. He was from the IDS, and he was quite insistent he must take you into custody. I shouldn't be telling you this, but I didn't like him. He was arrogant and full of himself. Do you know why an IDS agent would want you?"

"What did he look like?"

After he described Finn Foster, she closed her eyes. "I know him. He's been after me for some time. He has a personal vendetta against me and my family. But I haven't done anything to him. Are you going to give me to the IDS?"

"It's rare, and it's happened before. But if Dr. Creig finds you an interesting subject, he won't give you up."

She frowned. "I don't like the sound of that. Am I a subject in some kind of experiment?"

"You could say that."

The door opened, and their burly escort led a thin and haggard woman into the hallway. Her eyes were wild, and tears streamed down her cheeks. When her glance found Aurora, she winced. "I'm sorry for you, miss," she whispered.

Then the guard shoved the woman toward the stairwell, and their footsteps descended the tower.

A short man with wire-rim glasses, a thin, black mustache, and sparse black hair peered out from the open door. "You can come in now."

Sloan ushered her along, and Aurora entered a room smelling of carbolic acid, electricity, and cigarette smoke. A chair much like one would find in a dentist's office occupied the center—except it was all metal.

Against one wall, a counter held bottles of colored liquids and trays of metal instruments, syringes, and electronic gadgets. An X-ray machine on wheels filled another wall, and two other electronic devices of unknown purpose were rolled up against it.

With a cigarette dangling in one hand, Dr. Creig waved dismissively. "Miss, you will now sit." He pointed to the chair, but she stared at it and backed up. On the metal arms and below where her legs would go, four metal clasps stood like teeth in an open jaw, as if the chair were waiting for a victim.

"Please." Creig shook his head. "Let us not do this. Or I will have to order our friend Sloan to force you into the chair. Then things will become very unpleasant."

"Wait. I need to use the restroom."

Creig sighed. "Really?"

"Yes, really."

"Sloan, take her to the WC in the hall then bring her back." He waved them away.

Sloan led her out the door and down the hall to the WC. "You won't do anything stupid in there, will you?"

"No." She entered and bent to the ankle bracelet. After Sloan's description of what might happen to her, wouldn't this be the best time to use the green pill that Rosella from the Friends had given her? That one was supposed to dull the pain. But after she pressed on both sides of the anklet, it wouldn't open. She tried again and again, but without luck.

Sloan knocked on the door. "Everything all right in there? Creig is waiting."

"Yes. I'm done." Whatever was going to happen to her, she'd have to endure it without help.

She flushed the toilet and rejoined Sloan, who brought her back into Creig's lab. Without a choice, she sat in his chair.

Creig did something behind her back, and cold metal teeth clamped around her arms and legs, all except for her right leg. Raising her glance to Creig, she narrowed her eyes. "What are you going to do to me?"

"First, I'm going to remove that anklet." He knelt to her right leg and began searching for a way to take it off. When it wouldn't budge, he attempted to pull off her ring. But nothing he did worked. After trying the anklet again, he stood, stared at them, and pulled a cigarette from a shirt pocket. "Never mind. It's not worth my time." Something clicked behind the chair, and a clamp secured her right leg.

Creig lit another cigarette, sucked in smoke, then went to the counter where he lifted a tray with a syringe and a row of small, empty bottles. "Now, I'm going to take some of your blood. We're going to find out what makes you tick—or not, as the case may be. Twist your arm and expose your elbow."

She did as ordered.

He tightened a rubber hose around her biceps and wiped her arm with alcohol. He plunged the syringe into a vein by her elbow and filled vial after vial with her blood.

"You didn't answer my question." She glanced at the sixth and final vial filling with her lifeblood.

He set the tray with the vials on the counter, sucked the last from his cigarette, and rubbed it out in an ashtray. "I owe you nothing."

Next, he grabbed an instrument with two long metal pincers attached to a large circular hub with markings. He brought it to her head and separated both arms. Stretching them wide, he placed them around her skull with one pincer beside each ear. He dialed the pincers tight against her skull. He read something on the device's hub and wrote it down. Then he took a similar measurement with the pincers on her temple and the back of her head.

"Why do you need my blood? Why are you measuring my head?"

Creig made several more measurements, wrote them down, and placed both hands on his hips. "All right, Miss Carter, you might as well know. You are now a subject of the Decency Inquiry Project. Its purpose is to investigate why otherwise ordinary people would give themselves over to the Enemy. It's a mystery beyond my ken why anyone would refuse the pleasures, riches, and security that the Imperator offers. So my job is to collect evidence in support of a theory by Sebastien Rey, our beloved Prophet, that there is some genetic or morphological defect inherent in all

Christians, and possibly in Jews, that makes them susceptible to following the Enemy. For surely, there is something terribly, innately wrong with all of you."

Her jaw dropped. "That's preposterous!"

"Nay, my beautiful subject. Think about it. On the one hand, you Christians are given the option to engage in a smorgasbord of unrestrained pleasures." He sucked in on the cigarette dangling loosely from two fingers. "You are offered the chance to engage freely in bodily union with any partner of any sex, age, or gender. You are given unlimited, unfettered access to a host of pleasure drugs in any amount. You are provided with unlimited quantities of whatever brandy, scotch, vodka, or wine your body craves. But what do you Christians do?" He waved the cigarette, and her next breath sucked in the smoke.

"Instead, you choose to believe in a ghost, a figment of some religious zealot's fevered mind. Because of that, you live lives of abstinence, sobriety, and denial, rejecting our offer of unlimited, unrestrained pleasures, something every member of our species has dreamed of and desired since we first walked the earth." He smiled, and if condescension could be concentrated into a single look, he managed it. "No, my beautiful Aurora, there is something inherently defective with a person believing and living as you people do. And that is why I search for a cause. Because if I can find a reason for your behavior, perhaps I can find a cure."

His gaze wandered to the stone wall, and his voice lowered. "A vaccine, perhaps? Or a drug? A lobotomy to remove infected brain tissue? Whatever is needed to reverse what is obviously a mistake in the human condition."

"And something, maybe," added Sloan from the corner, "to give the good doctor the hefty reward the Prophet has promised if he succeeds?"

Creig shot him a frown. "What you say is true. But for me, only a secondary consideration. I am here purely for the advancement of science."

"Certainly. Of course. Without question, for the advancement of science." But in Sloan's words came a clear hint of sarcasm.

"Dr. Creig, you are so, so wrong!" Aurora's blood pumped faster. She couldn't believe what she'd heard. "You can search all you want, but your search is futile. I became a Christian because I *chose* to, not because something is wrong with my brain or my body chemistry or my genetics. It's your thinking—not my body, my blood, or my genetics—that's defective. If only you could understand! There are spiritual worlds beyond our own, and because I believe in God's Son, he will lead me to an eternity of bliss and joy. More than that, because the Holy Spirit lives within me, I have experienced Jesus here and now. But the demons you serve will only bring you earthly misery and take you deep into the pit of Hell."

"Enough!" Creig went to the counter, grabbed a thermometer, and rammed it into her mouth. "I've heard it all before. Do not spout your poisonous treason. Others have tried before and failed."

She tried to spit out the thermometer, but he pushed it back in, and she winced. "Fight me, woman, and it will go badly for you. Then you will leave here in a drug-induced stupor. I will perform my research, and you will not resist or try to convert me."

From where he stood in the corner, Sloan closed his eyes and nodded. She quit fighting.

For the next hour and a half, Creig prodded and measured and X-rayed various parts of her body.

He set up a camera on a tripod and switched it on. Then he injected her with some kind of clear liquid, and she began to shake all over. It was as if she'd acquired some temporary palsy, and every muscle in her body rebelled. As the camera recorded her reaction, the tremors lasted for more than thirty minutes. When it stopped, it left her drenched with sweat, shivering, and exhausted.

After Creig released her, Sloan led her in silence back to her cell where she plopped onto the bed.

He laid a hand on a shoulder and whispered. "I'm sorry, Aurora, that you are part of this."

He turned to leave, but she touched his arm to stop him. "You don't believe in this, do you, Wallace Sloan? At heart, you are a good person, and everything they do here goes against what you know, deep inside you, is right."

Startled eyes focused on hers, and his mouth opened.

"I can tell." She grabbed one of his hands. "I sense this isn't who you are. Let me tell you about a better way."

"You want to convert *me*?" He pulled his hand from her grasp. "It's been tried before. Forget it."

"But you're wavering, aren't you?"

To that, he had no response. He just stared into her eyes and shook his head. "You don't know what you're talking about."

He took two strides toward the door then turned back. "Say nothing about this conversation to anyone." Then he locked the door and was gone.

As the echoes of his feet receded down the corridor, she smiled to herself.

Wallace Sloan was a lost soul, adrift in a sea of spiritual darkness, searching for a lifeline.

And was it possible? Could he become a secret ally?

PART II
A DEN OF EVIL

Ephesians 6:10–13 (NLT):

A final word: Be strong in the Lord and in his mighty power. Put on all of God's armor so that you will be able to stand firm against all strategies of the devil. For we are not fighting against flesh-and-blood enemies, but against evil rulers and authorities of the unseen world, against mighty powers in this dark world, and against evil spirits in the heavenly places.

Therefore, put on every piece of God's armor so you will be able to resist the enemy in the time of evil. Then after the battle you will still be standing firm.

CHAPTER 10

THE FRIENDS' REQUEST

San Felice Circeo, Italy ~ February, Year 3

Three days after sailing from Tel Aviv, Maeve piloted the yacht into the familiar harbor of San Felice Circeo and glided it to a halt in an empty berth. It was already dark when they secured the ship.

Tyler led the group down the pier to the village and to La Ritirata Della Sirena (The Mermaid's Retreat), the restaurant where they had first met the Friends of Light.

When he entered, slim Rosella approached from the back and greeted them. She threw a handful of long, blonde hair over one shoulder. "My friends, you have returned, and your holy man is not with you. Was your mission successful?"

"Yes," answered Tyler. "He is now preaching against the Antichrist according to biblical prophecy."

Her eyes widened. "I suspected he was important, but never had I guessed that his task might be in the holy book."

Then he explained that Eli was Elijah of the Old Testament and that he was one of the Two Witnesses now passing judgment on Davato and his people in Temple Square.

Her hands covered her mouth, and when they opened again, she gave Tyler the widest smile he had ever seen from her. "Hallelujah! I am so, so blessed to have been a part of your mission."

For a moment, she was silent. "But what brings you back?"

"In Tel Aviv," said Lisette, "we carried out a mission for the Friends, but it went badly. Aurora . . ." Lisette frowned and looked away. "Aurora was captured by the CSA!"

"Oh no!" Rosella shook her head. "I am truly sorry. From the bottom of my heart, I am truly sorry. And you did this for us . . ." Her glance found the far corner of the room, and for a second time, she was silent.

When she next lifted her gaze, her eyes were moist. "Are you and I not like some country—perhaps the world itself?—that's been occupied by some foreign aggressor? But our occupation is far worse than for the Poles or the Belgians as the Nazi jackboots and German tanks bullied their way across their lands. No, for our occupiers are interested in far more than the land they already possess. Their goal is deeper and darker, for they intend to drill down into the very core of what makes us human. They desire nothing less than to conquer the eternal souls of those who stand in their way. Yes, our enemy comes from the deepest, darkest well, from the ultimate source of all evil—from Satan who is the Dragon, the father of all lies, deceits, and accusations." She closed her eyes and pressed her palms to them. "Heaven, help us all!"

"You are right," said Tyler. "This is far, far worse."

"Yes, yes. Forgive me." She reached for a cloth napkin from the nearest table. "Too often have I dwelt on such things, and now I have burdened you with my visions of doom."

"No, Rosella. It's not a burden. It is what we, too, have always believed. You are only reminding us of the truth."

"Thank you. It is good to be among friends." She smiled and wiped a tear from one eye. "But that is not why you came here today. What can I do for you?"

Then Brett spoke. "The manager who ran the Mashya Restaurant in Tel Aviv disappeared after the CSA came after us. We are looking for him, as this man might know where the goons have taken our sister. Since he was a Friend, we were hoping you might know where he is."

"We have greeted no one from Israel recently. What was his name?"

"The woman at the hotel said his name was Benyamin. She also told us that a different group, not regular CSA, took Aurora."

As if in thought, Rosella dropped her gaze to the floor. "I have heard rumors about a rogue faction of the Unitum Imperium. I wonder, perhaps . . ." Now her eyes were alight. "One of our operatives in Rome might know more about this. I will contact him. Until he responds, you are welcome to rooms upstairs. But it's late, and because this happened to you while working for us, the rooms and meals are on the house."

"Rooms would be much appreciated," said Brett. "Especially the excellent food from your kitchen."

"Always thinking about his stomach, he is." Maeve shot him a smile. "'Tis one of the many reasons I fancy him. But aye, Rosella, we thank you kindly for your hospitality."

Tyler always marveled how, even when speaking Italian, Maeve managed to add an Irish slant to her words.

That evening after supper, Rosella informed them that a man was coming tomorrow, in person, with more information and a proposal. Tyler asked her what kind of proposal, but she didn't know more.

But as he climbed the stairs leading to his room, he frowned. The last time they heard a proposal from the Friends, it ended in Aurora's capture.

* * *

THEIR MAN ARRIVED FROM ROME in midmorning. He was clean-shaven and of medium build with piercing brown eyes, black-rimmed glasses, and a mop of brown hair. Rosella grabbed a pitcher of coffee and six cups and led everyone into a private back room.

They sat at a round oak table where she introduced everyone.

Bonifacio was the visitor's name, and his gaze settled on Tyler. "I understand that a woman important to you was captured by the Unitum Imperium, but you believe they weren't regular CSA?"

"That's correct," answered Tyler. "She's my sister and Brett's." Then he related everything they'd learned from the hotel manager in Tel Aviv.

"Interesting." Bonifacio's eyes lit up, and he leaned forward. "We have been looking for a link to solve a troubling mystery, and this may be it. Your situation is not the first where a second group, not regular CSA, was involved. For some time, our spies have heard about some kind of schism within the Unitum Imperium. While the Truth Squads or the CSA are in the process of capturing a group of Christians, another group intervenes and takes a few of their prisoners. Then they spirit them away to places unknown."

"So why are you interested in this?" asked Tyler.

"If we can find out where these people have been taken, maybe there's a way we can free them. Your situation may be the opportunity we've been looking for. Maybe this can help us get the information we need to find, not only about your sister but also about others who have disappeared from the grasp of the UI goons."

"I don't understand," said Brett. "We were told that everyone taken by the CSA ends up in some camp in Germany."

"Normally, that's true. They go either to Germany or to New Babylon. But the German camp is so well guarded that breaking anyone out of it is nigh on impossible. And New Babylon? Well, freeing anyone from that remote desert city would also be difficult. But our spies tell us this group is holding their prisoners elsewhere. If we knew the location, we would know what is possible and what isn't."

"So what is this opportunity you mentioned?" asked Lisette.

"Ah, yes. Our operatives are stretched thin, and this is where you come in."

"You'd better explain." The Friends, it seemed to Tyler, were always asking for their help, help that would likely be dangerous. But if that could somehow free Aurora . . .

Bonifacio cleared his throat. "We have learned of a meeting to be held in Geneva, Switzerland. It will be attended by highly placed Unitum Imperium officials. Davato himself will be there, as will the directors of his ministries. Our plan is to replace two of the waitstaff with our people. Their mission will be to plant bugs in the meeting room beforehand. While we're listening in on so many insider conversations, someone might leak where this group is located. And who knows what other information they might reveal?"

"And you think we could replace their waitstaff." Tyler pursed his lips. "Sounds risky. And dangerous."

"I won't downplay the risk if you're discovered. But here today, I see two men and two women. And helping us in this matter could well lead to discovering the location and nature of this rogue group. If they're the ones who took your sister, you would also be helping her."

"I can't go, and neither can Lisette," said Tyler. "At a dinner in Rome, attended by Adam Turner, the director of the Ministry of Truth, I was pretending to be Greyson Ross, and Lisette was my mistress. If Turner or any of his staff will be there, I cannot attend."

Bonifacio whistled. "That must have been some ruse. And you pulled it off?"

Tyler nodded. "In my guise as Greyson Ross, I told Turner I had to leave on personal business—that's how I got away to help find Aurora."

"That leaves me and Maeve." Brett faced Maeve, whose face appeared to lose all color.

"You want me to serve people like the Antichrist and his staff?" She'd lost her Irish accent, and her glance swiveled around the table. "What an alarming request. And I've never waitressed before."

"Nor have I," added Brett.

"There's nothing to it." Lisette laid a hand on Maeve's. "I can teach you everything you need to know."

"Is that a sì?" Bonifacio was grinning now. "Will you do this for us? And, of course, for your Aurora?"

"I guess that's a yes," said Brett.

"Then tomorrow, I will bring train tickets and travel passes for you two, and—"

"Wait." Tyler held up a hand. "We need to go with them. If we find what you're looking for, all of us must go on from there. But they're looking for me."

"Ah, sì. That is a problem. So I will get travel passes for everyone. But I understand that you, Tyler Carter, have created a new ID under the name of Gavin Roberts?"

"That is so."

"Excellent. You can use that. Lisette, you are Gavin Roberts's companion, but let me see . . ." Bonifacio rubbed his chin. "What if we call you Dafne Venturi? Tyler, can you make a new ID for her?"

"I will." He smiled at Lisette who nodded.

"Tomorrow, we'll give you both a makeover, and, Tyler, if you are able to update those IDs with pictures after we're done with you, you should have no problem at any UI checkpoint."

"Makeovers?" Tyler cocked his head. "Okay. I can update the IDs with new pictures. No problem."

"Good. Then tomorrow, I will provide Brett and Maeve with the identities of the waiter and waitress who are already in our custody. We have infiltrated the agency the hotel uses, and we will hold the real waitstaff under guard until this affair concludes." Grinning, he stood, walked around the table, and shook their hands.

Before he left, he asked Tyler to give him his glasses. "We'll return them tomorrow with lenses that match your prescription, but with new frames."

"If you must." Tyler took off his wire-rimmed glasses and handed them over.

But as he climbed the stairs to his room and Bonifacio left to catch a train back to Rome, Tyler prayed that this new mission, unlike the last one they undertook for the Friends, would not end with someone else ending up in a UI prison.

CHAPTER 11

THE FRIENDS' MISSION

From San Felice Circeo, Italy, to Geneva, Switzerland ~ February, Year 3

The next day, Bonifacio arrived with train tickets and travel passes for Geneva. He handed Tyler a new pair of glasses with tinted lenses and thick, black plastic frames. "I have arranged for you and Lisette to visit a local salon to change your hair color. Tawny for Tyler. Blonde for Lisette, but with a ponytail."

"Wow." Lisette grinned. "I've always wanted to be a blonde. Maybe I'll have more fun?"

Tyler matched her grin then faced their host. "Do the salon folks know why they're doing this?"

"No, and you'll be arriving separately. When you get there, you don't know each other."

"Right."

At the salon, Tyler arrived an hour after Lisette. He put on a smock and over a period of three hours, one of the women worked in the dye. When the stylist tried to engage him in conversation, he was tight-lipped.

Afterward, Bonifacio was parked outside in his BMW. Lisette was already seated, and they drove back to the Mermaid's Retreat. There, Bonifacio led them and the others to the back room where Rosella served coffee with cream, sugar, rolls, and butter. "We can still get coffee," she said. "And a farmer nearby supplies us with milk. But we may not see the rolls again for weeks. Everything is so expensive these days."

"The famine." Bonifacio shook his head. "The result of the third seal."

"If only we had believed before," said Rosella.

"What's done is done." Then, from across the table, Bonifacio gripped Tyler's forearm. "Even though you and Lisette won't be going to the meeting, you'll be staying in the same hotel as the directors of the ministries and their staff. And Davato. If someone sees you by accident, your new disguises should prevent anyone from recognizing you. But we're not quite done." He handed Lisette a set of big, round, rose-colored glasses. "These are for you."

She put them on, glanced around the room, and smiled. "Are you trying to brighten my view of the world?"

Tyler tugged a lock of her now-blonde hair. "It's a plot to make you happier."

She swatted his hand away and flashed him a mock frown.

"See what I mean?" he said to the others while cupping his mouth.

Everyone laughed.

"And we can't forget this." Bonifacio handed Tyler a tube of cosmetic glue and a fake mustache and goatee matching his tawny hair color. "This will turn you into a new man."

Tyler accepted it and thanked him.

Then Bonifacio gave Brett and Maeve IDs with names that matched their other documents. "You, Brett, are now Rocco Moretti. And you, Maeve, are now Michela DeLuca."

"Me head swirls with all me fake identities. What if I develop a split personality?" She gripped her head and shook it, and they all laughed again.

"Your train departs tomorrow morning for Geneva." Bonifacio brought out itineraries with travel passes for their new IDs. "The passes are good anywhere in Europe. Tyler and Lisette, once you arrive at the hotel, you do not know and must not acknowledge Brett and Maeve. You will rent a car at the station, park it in the hotel garage, and check in separately from them. Brett and Maeve, you will take a taxi to the hotel. You will eat separately. And I suggest, Tyler, that you and Lisette should avoid the hotel restaurant. Go down the street for your meals. Or order room service. The exception to this rule is on the night of your arrival. At twenty-one hundred hours, your contact will bring Brett and Maeve to your room to brief everyone on the mission. Her name is Margueritte."

He extended a hand, and they shook it. "Good luck to you all. This mission involves great risk. You understand that, and we are grateful for your help. But if we obtain the information we're hoping to get, the

Friends of Light will do all it can to free your sister and anyone else who's been captured by this rogue IDS faction."

* * *

The train to Geneva took most of the day. Four times, CSA agents passed through the car to check IDs. But the digital cards Tyler had updated for him and Lisette the night before served them well. They arrived in Switzerland without incident.

At the train station, Tyler rented the BMW M135 that Bonifacio had reserved for him under the name of Gavin Roberts. "Where you're going, it's best to appear like you've got money," he'd said. "And you will need the vehicle later."

They drove to the Intercontinental Conference Center and Hotel. When they tried to enter the parking ramp, the garage was full, and they were told they must use valet service. Tyler passed his key fob to the attendant, and they carried their bags to the reception desk.

As they waited in line, Davato and Adam Turner approached with a priority hotel escort. Three meters behind them was a man with bushy white eyebrows and wild gray hair—Bertoldo Donati. Following this entourage, staff rolled carts piled high with their bags.

His heart speeding up, Tyler leaned close to Lisette's ear. "Don't look, but Turner, Donati, and Davato are on our left."

"Oh no!" She whipped her lead toward something interesting on the wall behind the clerk.

But as the line moved closer to the check-in desk, Tyler heard an all-too-familiar voice addressing the clerk in front of him. "Can you send a bottle of your finest whiskey to my room?" he asked in French.

It was Turner.

Adam Turner was standing right beside him.

It was Adam Turner, the director of the Ministry of Truth, the man for whom Tyler had worked as Greyson Ross!

"Of course, monsieur. Right away, monsieur."

Tyler knelt to untie and retie his shoe. But only two feet away were the shoes of the director of the Ministry of Truth. They looked expensive. Probably nine hundred euros worth of Italian patent leather.

49

As his heart raced and his fingers shook, he hoped the man wasn't looking in Lisette's direction. He hoped his fake mustache and goatee and his tawny hair would do their work.

Then the nine-hundred-euro shoes slapped the marble and joined the rest of Davato's group as they headed for the elevator.

Rising and wiping sweat from his forehead, he faced the clerk, presented his ID, and checked in.

Once the bellhops had left the room and he and Lisette were alone, he collapsed into an easy chair.

"He looked directly at me." Lisette's eyes were wide. "For a moment, I thought we were undone. Then he just walked away."

Tyler's gaze fixed on hers, and he shook his head. "That was close. We won't be wandering the halls of this hotel anytime soon."

"I don't like this, Tyler. To be staying in the same hotel as *them*." She shivered.

He pulled her close and kissed one cheek. "We'll be all right. If it helps the Friends to find out where they're keeping Aurora, it will be worth it."

CHAPTER 12

PREPARING FOR ESPIONAGE

Geneva, Switzerland ~ February, Year 3

As Brett ate supper with Maeve in their seventh-floor room, he kept glancing at this woman whom he'd come to admire and, yes, love. For some time, he'd been pondering a certain question to put to her, and now, tonight, before they carried out their risky charade tomorrow, the time was right for the asking.

Yet he hesitated. He thought of himself as brave. But as he went over how he would approach the subject and what he would say, his will weakened with each passing second.

Nine o'clock arrived, and someone knocked on the door. He opened it to a slender blonde-haired beauty whose blue eyes twinkled when she saw them.

"I am Margueritte, your contact for the affair in tomorrow's den of evil." She switched the leather purse she carried to her left hand and extended her right.

Brett took it.

"We so appreciate your volunteering for this mission." She then shook Maeve's hand. "I understand neither of you has waited on tables before? Is that so?"

"Aye." Maeve laid a hand on Brett's shoulder. "Neither has Brett."

"Remember: From now on, you are Michela DeLuca, and Brett is Rocco Moretti. You should begin calling each other by those names, even in private. You don't know who might be listening."

"Aye, Margueritte." A grin played with the edges of her mouth. "I'll call me lad only by his new moniker."

"Ah, yes. The Irish." Margueritte frowned. "Michela, if you do that in public, you'll end up in the camps."

"Yes, sorry." Maeve, or Michela, lost her accent. "From now on, I will speak only proper French."

"Right. Now follow me, and we'll join the others."

They left the room and rode the elevator down two floors, and Tyler let them in.

After fishing in her purse, Margueritte passed Brett and Maeve pin-on badges with their names, photographs, and embedded chips. "These are your agency badges. Carry them along with your other IDs. You'll need them all. The EMV chips identify you as being vetted by the catering agency for high-security work. Tomorrow afternoon, after you pass through security, I will be in the kitchen, and you'll collect the bugs you'll plant in the table decorations. There, you will also meet Frieda König, the chef de cuisine. Beware of her. She has the personality of a cobra. She belonged to the League of Abaddon, and she's always looking for traitors to the cause. She will go over your responsibilities during the dinner, so do whatever she tells you."

"How and when are we supposed to plant these bugs?" asked Brett.

"You should be the only waitstaff under König, and your first duty will be to set the tables with plates and silverware. While you're doing that, you will plant one bug in each table decoration. The place will already have been swept for listening devices. Since everyone passes through a checkpoint before entering the dining area, they won't be expecting the bugs that I've already hidden beneath a layer of shielding on top of the toilet tank in the women's WC. After you get your work uniforms tomorrow afternoon, Michela, you will have to stand on the seat to reach the tank. It's halfway to the ceiling. You will remove the tank lid and set it on the floor. Be careful not to drop it. Then reach inside, get the package, strip off the shielding, and give half of the devices to Rocco. Can you do that?"

"I can," said Maeve. "So you're part of the staff?"

"I will help with cooking."

"I've never waitressed," repeated Maeve. "Nor has Brett."

Margueritte beckoned Lisette from her perch on the bed. "Now, Lisette, or should I call you Dafne? I will watch as you school these two in the art of being a waitress and waiter." She removed from her purse a set of silverware and plates. Using those, Lisette, alias Dafne, began teaching Brett and Maeve the proper way to serve in style:

The purpose of each plate and bowl.

Where to place the silverware beside the tableware.

On which side of the diner they were to serve.

How to allow the patrons the opportunity to sample the wine before pouring.

And when they were finished serving, where they were to stand in the corner, and how they were to watch for a raised hand when a customer needed something.

It went on and on. After Lisette was done, Brett had a new appreciation for the women and men who'd served him in the few eating establishments he'd visited that didn't have a TV on every wall or a pool table in the corner.

"If anything goes wrong," said Margueritte, "I'll be in the kitchen, watching. If we have to flee, we'll meet at the entrance to the Restaurant de la plage Le Reposoir on the Route de Lausanne just northeast of the Jardin de la Paix park. When and if I can, I'll warn Tyler and Lisette that we've fled. Everyone, study the map so you know how to get to that location. If I don't arrive right away, or if you're being pursued, you will go to Paris where you will meet a contact at Napoleon's Tomb. Either I or someone else will be at the tomb's second level each day at noon for thirty minutes. We'll use the usual passwords, of course."

"Wow!" Maeve shook her head. "You've planned everything."

Tyler raised a hand. "If we all have to flee, should we find rooms in Paris?"

"Of course."

"A lot of escape plans." Lisette stood from the bed. "This is risky, isn't it?"

"It is, mademoiselle. But if all goes well, we won't need them."

They nodded, Margueritte wished them good luck, and she left.

Before returning to their room, Brett grabbed Maeve's hand. "Let's take a walk. I have something to ask you."

Eyeing him with apparent suspicion, she nodded.

But as he led her toward the elevator, the thought of what he was about to do brought sweat to his forehead. Was he really ready for this?

CHAPTER 13

BRETT'S QUESTION

Geneva, Switzerland ~ February, Year 3

When they left the hotel behind, Brett was still holding Maeve's hand. They followed the sidewalk beside a hedge as cars passed them on the street. It was cold tonight, and he could see his breath.

He'd been planning this for—how long had it been? Weeks? Months? But the right moment never seemed to come along. Tomorrow, they'd be waiting on tables for the Antichrist and all his staff, and he was no waiter. If tomorrow didn't work out, he might not have another chance at this. Or at anything else in this life.

Tomorrow, they must succeed.

Maeve kept glancing at him, but he just kept walking, saying nothing.

It was easier to face an angry bar patron swinging a pool cue at his head because of some offhand remark taken in offense. With a few quick moves, Brett could disarm such an assailant and put him in a headlock, all without losing his nerve.

But tonight, to say what he was about to say to Maeve . . . ?

Sweat was already beading up on his forehead.

"So, me laddie, are we going to walk all the way to France, or is there something on your mind?"

"I thought you were going to lose your Irish accent?"

"We're alone, far from the hotel." She glanced to the side. "And we're getting farther from it, I might add. And it's cold out here. So what's up?"

"You and I have grown close in the time we've come to know each other, haven't we?" He kept his gaze straight ahead. The words inside him were like steam inside a pipe, the pressure building, pushing against a valve until it rattled.

"Aye, we have."

"And in that time, I've come to like you." No, that wasn't what he wanted to say. "I mean it's more than that. Yes, more than that." It wasn't just liking her, so why couldn't he put it into words? Why couldn't he just come out with it?

He stopped, caught her gaze, and waited for a response. Maybe she would catch his drift and take it from there?

"You're acting strange tonight, Brett. What's going on? What are you trying to say?"

"I don't know." He started walking again. Hedges still holding onto their green leaves bordered the highway, lit by streetlights from above. A few cars whizzed past. "I'm not sure."

His heart was beating fast. His hands were clammy. And the sweat continued to bead up on his forehead.

"Well, Brett, spit it out. What's on your mind?"

He shook his head. "Nothing. Maybe we should go back." As if someone had opened a pressure valve, the tension inside him released, and the breath that came out of him was white mist against the cold air.

"Yeah, laddie. This is odd. Let's go back." She squinted her eyes. "We've got a big day tomorrow."

He hadn't said what he'd brought her out here to say, and now he felt regret. And anger. His fingers dug into his palms until they hurt. Could anyone be more stupid than he was right now?

He'd never thought of himself as a coward. But tonight, that's exactly what he'd become.

CHAPTER 14

REPORTING FOR WORK

Geneva, Switzerland ~ February, Year 3

Still hating himself for yesterday's cowardice, Brett exited the elevator on the second floor where security people had cordoned off the kitchen and the conference dining room. After they showed their agency badges and were frisked head to toe, one of the CSA men led the two to the kitchen and to Frieda König, the chef de cuisine.

The first thing she did was reinspect their IDs. The second thing was to make them stand at attention.

After Margueritte's description, Brett was expecting a portly, busty German matron, but the woman who greeted them was a slender, starkly beautiful, black-haired beauty with high cheekbones. She could have been a model.

"So you are the two replacements the agency recommended for this." She stepped back, laid hands on her hips, and swept a cold gaze over her troops. "I hope you will meet my expectations, for they are quite high. This is the most important dinner I have ever catered, and there must be no slipups. If my favorite waiters had not come down with some kind of flu, I wouldn't even be using you. The agency sent you with good recommendations, but we'll see about that. So let me repeat. I will tolerate no mistakes. Verstehen Sie?"

Until he'd met Frieda König, Brett had never encountered anyone with such deep-black pupils. But now, as the muscles in her face hardened and she speared them with such a darkly menacing stare, he suppressed a shudder. An image arose of a creature he'd once seen in a movie based on Greek mythology. She could have been one of those deadly sirens whose beauty entranced and lured men to their deaths.

"Oui, ma'am," he answered.

She shook her head. "The proper response is, 'Oui, mademoiselle.' Ensure that you never use such slang again in my presence."

"Of course, mademoiselle."

"Here are your work uniforms for this afternoon." She handed them over. "You will have formal outfits for the main event this evening. You can use the restrooms to change then begin by setting the tables. There are bags in the WC for your street clothes. When you're finished, I will inspect each place setting to ensure they are done correctly. Everything you need is already on carts in the room."

Taking his uniform, Brett followed Maeve to the restrooms reserved for the kitchen staff. He dressed, making sure the shirt covered all of his tattoos. When he emerged, Maeve was waiting in a skimpy outfit that exposed her midriff. Her skirt had a single, bulging pocket—filled with bug devices? He winced.

She glanced up and down the aisle then passed him a handful of what looked like nickels with holes attached to metal clips. He shoved them into a pocket, and they returned to the dining room.

The room contained fourteen round tables, headed by one oblong table with a microphone. That's probably where Davato himself would sit, and Brett shuddered. How had he ever gotten involved with this?

But two men in the green-and-white uniforms of the CSA were also there, holding some kind of electronic devices—bug detectors? One of them was waving his device over and under each table. The other was sweeping the walls and ceiling. If Brett walked further into this room with a pocketful of bugs, would he set off their alarms?

He grabbed Maeve's arm and pulled her back into the kitchen. "We have to wait until they leave."

She shot the men a glance, swallowed, and nodded.

Back in the kitchen, the König woman rushed over. "Why aren't you in there, doing your job?"

"I, uh, I have a question."

"What's that?"

"Tonight, will we be the only ones doing the serving?"

"Besides me, only you two. That's why, much to my displeasure, I was forced to beg your agency for replacements. I'm short of help."

"You haven't told us how many courses. What will we be serving?"

Again, she laid hands on hips and speared him with an icy glare. "What kind of question is that? It doesn't matter. Whatever the cooks come up with, you will serve! Now get back in there!"

Nodding, Brett led Maeve back into the dining room where the CSA men were leaving by the far door. He breathed out his relief and headed toward the carts.

From the first cart, he took a tablecloth, black and edged with gold lace. He laid it carefully over the nearest table. Maeve did the same until they'd covered all fifteen tables.

The second cart contained the flower decorations—fresh-cut tulips flown in from Holland, interspersed with lilies. He carried a vase to the nearest table and set it in the center.

Brett shot a glance around the room. Only he and Maeve, or rather, Michela, were present. He brought out the first device, reached inside the flowers, and clipped it to a tulip stem.

Maeve was doing the same. When they'd done half the tables, she whispered, "This is easy. No problem, hey, boyo?"

"Shh. The door is opening."

The König woman entered, strolling slowly and examining each table. She stopped and pointed. "This tablecloth has extra material hanging down one side. Who did this?"

"I did." He sauntered to where she stood, pulled on the opposite side, and evened it out. Then he recentered the decoration.

"I expect better than this, Rocco. Much better." Then, as his heart pounded, she leaned toward the decoration, shifted it a few inches, bent closer, and breathed in. Could anyone looking inside the flowers see the bugs?

But no. She smiled, backed away from the table, and left the room.

They finished with the decorations and the bugs. Then they laid the tables with silverware and tableware. When they were halfway through, Frieda König reentered and began examining his place settings, moving a fork or a plate here, a knife or a bowl there. Then she yelled across the room. "Be more careful with the distance between plates and utensils. They must be evenly spaced. When you're finished, go over each setting again and redo. When you're done with that, vacuum the room again, especially the perimeter. Then you can help by polishing the serving dishes in the kitchen. They're silver and in need of a better shine."

Brett wondered if he should salute and click his heels, thought better of it, and just gave her a nod.

They finished their duties, and at five in the afternoon, she dismissed them.

"You will return here in one hour, a full hour before our important guests arrive at nineteen hundred hours." She headed for the door. "And I hope you discharge your duties better than the shoddy performances I have so far witnessed."

"Oui, mademoiselle." He gave her a crisp salute but refrained from clicking his heels.

Then he strode for the door.

CHAPTER 15

EVIL IN THE HOTEL

Geneva, Switzerland ~ February, Year 3

Luke 10:17 (NLT): *When the seventy-two disciples returned, they joyfully reported to him, "Lord, even the demons obey us when we use your name!"*

The day after their arrival at the Intercontinental, Tyler and Lisette ate a breakfast delivered by room service. That morning, they read the novels they'd brought. At lunch, they again ordered room service. Late in the afternoon, Tyler rose from his chair by the glass table and grabbed his jacket and stocking cap. "I can't just sit here all day. I need some exercise and fresh air. Want to come?"

"No, and I don't think you should go either. What if someone sees you?"

"Once I'm outside, I'll be okay." He opened the door, walked down the hall, and found the elevator. He was on the fifth floor, and he pushed the button for the lobby. But instead of going down, the elevator went up. The numbers climbed until they stopped on the seventeenth floor.

But when the doors opened, the man waiting to enter was none other than Adam Turner. Fortunately, the director was alone, and his nose was in his phone.

Tyler was wearing his black-framed, tinted glasses. His hair had been dyed tawny to match his fake goatee and mustache. Before the director looked up, he slipped into the hallway and made a quick turn to the right.

When the elevator door clanked shut, followed by the sound of a bell, he breathed out. That was the second time he'd narrowly missed being seen. Now he dared not descend for fear Turner would be in the lobby. He would take the stairs instead. That would waste some time. And it would be good exercise. A sign for the stairwell pointed right, and he started down the hall.

But he'd only gone halfway when someone else he knew was headed toward him—wild-haired Bertoldo Donati. Beside him was a woman Tyler didn't recognize, and Donati's attention was on her. Both were laughing and deep in conversation. Was Donati flirting with her?

Tyler glanced to both sides. The door to a room across the aisle was ajar, propped open by a block of wood. He pushed through and entered. It was dark inside, but he didn't turn on the lights. He waited for Donati's familiar voice to recede down the hallway.

He was about to reenter the hall when an icy chill began in his shoulders and trickled down his back. He'd felt the sensation before. Something in this room was wrong.

Curious, he flipped on the lights.

Then he gasped.

The hotel brochures assured the reader that every room in this luxury hotel boasted a view of the lake or the city. But here, the windows were blacked out, and all the furniture had been pushed to a far corner.

In the room's center, almost touching the ceiling, was a bent statue of gold. Its edges were round, it was tilted to one side, and it was more like a featureless phallus than an obelisk.

Waves of evil poured off the thing, and his heart raced. He wanted to turn and run. But something about this crooked statue of gold called to him, for *this* was the source of the cold spider legs that even now crawled down his back.

Then the overhead fluorescents dimmed.

On all sides, dark, vaporous beings materialized. They swirled and hovered above him and around the statue. The bent gold carving began to glow, not with light, but with churning shadows of black flame.

Then it was as if his consciousness were being drawn into a dark tunnel, plunging deep beneath the earth, and the thing transported him out of the room.

He traveled faster and faster. And it swept him to a realm too horrible and strange for description.

In the vision, he landed on a rocky plain where he was naked. On all sides, hot, dark fire leapt from hundreds of crevices. The heat from the rock beneath his bare feet and the tongues of fire rising up all around and licking his body burned his skin with such intensity, he would be incinerated within seconds if he were in his own body. But now—and how could this possibly be?—he was occupying the vessel of some unfortunate, doomed soul. Whose body it belonged to, he knew not.

He breathed in, and the stench of rotting flesh, offal, feces, and sulfur so attacked his nose and lungs that he gagged. How could anyone breathe this foul, heated air and survive, even for one minute?

From the distance came screams of agony, and a glance at the horizon revealed more condemned souls. Thousands, possibly tens of thousands. Also naked, they fled from the misshapen creatures that pursued them. And these demons—yes, they were demons!—were laughing, shouting insults, accusing their quarry of being stupid, explaining how they would rip the limbs from their victims' bodies and gloat as their fingers and toes and arms and legs grew painfully back before the demons ripped them out again.

Again and again.

He was in Hell. The stone idol had brought him a vision of Hell. And now Tyler was clutching his head with both hands and was shaking.

A tall figure stepped through the black flames and stopped before him. It was a man. Or was it? He stood ten feet tall, and when he approached, he appeared as the most beautiful creature Tyler had ever seen. But as Tyler's eyes narrowed and focused, the visage morphed into something else—swirling black shadows. Currents of evil as powerful as surging ocean breakers swept over him, wave after wave, and Tyler cowered.

WHO ARE YOU, INTERLOPER, AND WHY ARE YOU HERE? The words came not to his ears but materialized inside his head. *WHY DID YOU APPROACH THE IDOL OF GOLD?*

"I–I don't know." He took two steps away. "I want to go back."

The creature's eyes were endless black pools. Surely, this was the Dragon, the one the Antichrist worshiped. This could only be Satan himself.

BUT YOU ARE HERE NOW, STRANGER, SO COME HERE AND JOIN ME. FALL DOWN ON YOUR KNEES. WORSHIP ME, AND YOU WILL BE FREE.

Worship Satan? The father of lies? This was worse than his encounter with the Baphomet idol back in Chicago. His heart was a pounding drum, ready to explode. He took another step back.

"No, no, a thousand times no! Dear Jesus, save me!"

Instantly, the vision vanished, and he was back in the hotel room. But he wasn't standing. He was rolled up in a ball on the floor—

Shaking.

Shivering.

Drenched with sweat.

Behind him, the door opened, and two workmen entered, bearing straps for moving furniture. "What are you doing here?" said a man with a mop of curly red hair and a ring through his nose. He turned to his burly partner. "Call security. We've got an intruder."

"An intruder?" answered the second. The man found his phone and punched some numbers. "Everyone in this room is an intruder."

Tyler didn't wait for security. He shot to his feet and dodged past the men. He rushed through the door and turned left. He ran down an empty hallway. At the stairwell, his feet pounded down flight after flight until the eighth floor where he got off. Trying to calm a racing heart, he walked calmly down the aisle to a set of elevators.

He punched the button for the lobby, and the car descended. When the door opened, he checked to make sure no one he recognized was in the vast space beyond.

Striding but not running, he pushed through revolving doors into the street. He'd studied the area map in the room. He would head for the large park a few streets away.

He breathed deeply, slowed his pace, and tried to clear his head.

Was Davato using the gold idol to commune with the Dragon? Did he take the thing with him wherever he went? Again, a shudder rippled through him.

Fortunately, the Dragon couldn't read his mind, and it didn't know who he was. Only by speaking the name of Jesus had Tyler escaped.

How had he ever ended up here in this den of evil?

He just hoped Brett and Maeve could finish their task before the forces of darkness found them. Silently, he prayed that something would come of this affair.

Because if they found out where the CSA had taken Aurora—it would all be worth it.

CHAPTER 16

A DEN OF EVIL

Geneva, Switzerland ~ February, Year 3

Revelation 13:1, 5–7 (NLT): *Then I saw a beast rising up out of the sea. It had seven heads and ten horns, with ten crowns on its horns. And written on each head were names that blasphemed God. . . . Then the beast was allowed to speak great blasphemies against God. And he was given authority to do whatever he wanted for forty-two months. And he spoke terrible words of blasphemy against God, slandering his name and his dwelling— that is, those who dwell in heaven. And the beast was allowed to wage war against God's holy people and to conquer them. And he was given authority to rule over every tribe and people and language and nation.*

Brett and Maeve stood at attention in the kitchen while the German woman glared at Brett. "I cannot stress enough how important this dinner is to me. In the room beyond are the most important people on the planet, and if I see one screwup, one spilt drop from a single serving dish . . ."

So tight were her neck muscles, so red were her cheeks, Brett thought she might burst. The image of a pin approaching a helium balloon rose up, and he tried to keep from grinning.

"Michela has a way to go to live up to my standards." She shook her head. "But you, Rocco! We've served the wine without you, and while we refill the glasses, you will bring out the heavy platter of hors d'oeuvres and begin serving them. Two plates per person at the head table. One plate per person thereafter."

Chafing under her glare, he lifted the platter. Upon it were plates of Almas Beluga caviar spread over toast—fish eggs from the Iranian beluga sturgeon costing thousands of euros per ounce. But after his first step, the platter tilted, and the plates clattered together.

"If you drop that," warned König, "you'll leave here owing *us*!"

Balancing the platter on one hand as though he knew what he were doing, he backed through the swinging doors into the dining room.

Inside, the place buzzed with the conversation of the Unitum Imperium's upper crust.

Behind him, Maeve and König were bringing more bottles of wine. This evening, they'd given Maeve a uniform leaving little to the imagination—a skimpy leather top barely covering her breasts, and a black leather miniskirt ending just above her crotch, revealing a bare midriff.

König wore the same outfit, and Brett had to admit how shapely and attractive was the woman—like some beautiful jungle flower, but one carrying the deadliest of poisons for anyone foolish enough to sniff its scent.

As ordered, he went first to the head table, the one seating Davato. At the Antichrist's table, the guests were lined up on a single side facing the room.

Davato was in the center, flanked on either side by:

Adam Turner, director of the Ministry of Truth.

Gaston Soucy, director of the Ministry of Charity.

Sebastien Rey, the Prophet whom they had twice seen on television.

General Eric Hofmann, head of the Ministry of Peace, commander of all UI forces.

And tonight's special guests—the three richest and most famous CEOs in the world:

Bill Gray, the Australian founder of Daintree, the world's biggest online provider and shipper of merchandise.

Jason Howard, the CEO of Worldnet, owner of the planet's premier search engine and provider of most of the world's software, computers, microchips, and security systems.

And finally—Sam Wainwright, founder of PetroSol, the world's main manufacturer of wind, solar, minerals, pharmaceuticals, gasoline, diesel, and petroleum products.

With one hand, Brett set up a stand. With the other, he placed the heavy platter upon it. He was hoping to hear snatches of conversation, and before he served the first dish, he wasn't disappointed.

Davato's voice rose above all others. "I reject this idea that the Enemy is all-powerful, all-seeing, and present everywhere at once. It's preposterous. Certainly, he ripped the Christians out of the world, but that proves nothing. The Dragon can do as much if not more."

"But, my lord"—Jason Howard turned in his seat—"we were told that aliens took the Christians away in UFOs."

"A convenient explanation for an ignorant populace. No, my friends, it was the Enemy who did the deed. When Sebastien saw the event, he used it to our advantage. He broadcast to the world that the UFOs came from Gaia, the goddess of the earth. He said that she took away those who were not in sync with the planet. And that is partly true. The Christians are not like us, not of us, and don't belong here. We can only thank the Enemy for removing them from our presence. When we find more of them, we will root them out like the cancer they are."

"And when the forces of Russia, Iran, Turkey, and the others came against you?"—Sam Wainwright raised his eyebrows—"Sebastien told us it was Gaia who saved you from destruction. Was that true?"

"Yes, there is no other explanation. Gaia is real." He'd said the words, but Davato was frowning as he lifted his wine glass, twirled it, and held it up to the light. "But so is the Dragon. And the Dragon's power is far greater than the Enemy's, certainly more than any earth goddess."

Brett set two plates before Davato, and the man looked up with a gracious smile. It was ingratiating, that smile, disarming and mesmerizing, and for a moment, Brett understood why he had deceived so many.

"What say you, Sebastien?" Davato glanced down the table. "Who is more powerful? Gaia or the Dragon?"

Brett's glance fell on this silver-haired, pale-faced, green-eyed director of the Ministry of Virtue, and revulsion rose up like a cobra before a snake charmer. On the screen, the man left a good impression. But up close—Brett shuddered.

"My lord," began the Prophet, "without doubt, it is the Dragon whose power is the greater. It is he who grants us the ability to do many things. My friends, a simple demonstration. Watch now and learn . . ."

He picked up a fork from the table, held it at eye level, and turned it this way, then that, shining in the LED lights. After every eye was upon it, he gave the fork a nod, and then—

It burst into flame.

Fire rose from each tine of the silverware, flickering with black and red and yellow tongues of flame.

Gasps arose from all who were seated and from the tables nearest Davato.

Sebastien leaned forward, and as one extinguishes candles on a birthday cake, he blew. And the flame went out.

Applause swept the room, and the Prophet bowed.

"Excellent demonstration, Sebastien." Davato beamed. "Everyone should know that it is the Dragon who bestows such power upon my Prophet."

The event was over, and Brett continued serving the hors d'oeuvres. Close behind him, his German taskmaster followed with more wine. But every time he stole a glance at her, she was watching him.

Perhaps it was the Prophet's disturbing exhibition, or Brett's nervousness at this unfamiliar task. Or maybe it was König's annoying watchfulness.

But as he reached down to set two dishes of Beluga caviar before the CEO of Daintree, the toast slipped off a plate, the fish eggs flipped upside down, and they landed with a splat upon the pristine white linen.

Behind him, König gasped, and Brett shot her a glance. His mistake had so unnerved her, she had poured a goodly splash of Chianti on the tablecloth beside Davato's glass.

And now, Brett couldn't help but smile.

"Oh, my lord, I am so, so sorry." She bowed. "Please forgive me."

Davato waved away the apology. "'Tis nothing, mademoiselle."

"No, no, I apologize for the clumsiness of my staff and myself. Please, please forgive me."

He scrunched his brows. "I said it was nothing. Now move on."

Chastened, she bowed again and stepped to the next dignitary. But first, she sent an icy glare in Brett's direction.

His glance returned to the fish eggs on the tablecloth before Bill Gray, where the Australian stared at a spreading wet stain. "Waiter, I assume you will give me another?"

Brett nodded, removed the empty plate, and handed him a third. When the platter was empty, he returned to the kitchen where König was waiting. "That was exactly what I was afraid of—your stupid, bumbling incompetence. I am reporting this to your agency, and I'll make sure they never use you again. When you leave here, you'll be owing us. And don't you dare make another mistake!"

He grabbed another platter of hors d'oeuvres and headed back into the dining room to finish serving the head table. After setting his load on the stand, he was about to take a dish to Jason Howard when the man leaned toward the centerpiece with his nose in the roses.

Then his eyes widened. And he frowned.

He reached inside the decoration.

And his fingers brought out a bug.

"What's this?" Holding it up, he turned to Davato, sitting three seats away. "Are you listening to us, my lord?"

"What?" A storm crossed Davato's forehead, and his fingers dug inside the centerpiece before him. Then he, too, retrieved another listening device. "Security!" he called. "Where is security?"

Brett had to get out, and fast. But he was serving, and if he abandoned his task before the platter was empty, they'd suspect him. "I'll go tell someone," he announced.

He left for the kitchen where Maeve had just returned for more bottles of wine.

"They found the bugs," he whispered. "We've got to get out of here— now!"

"Righto. I'll go to the WC for my bag."

"And I can't leave without my bag," said Brett. "It has the notebook."

"You brought it with you!"

"Yes."

But as they headed for the back door and the stairwell, König burst through the swinging door with an accusing finger. "It was *you*, wasn't it?"

Brett and Maeve kept walking, but the woman kept coming. "Security!" she screamed. "*They* did it!"

He broke into a run with Maeve close behind.

Ahead, Margueritte was standing by one of the range tops. She saw them coming and nodded. As he passed her, the smell of lobster bisque wafted from the steaming pot in her hands.

Brett kept going.

Then, from behind, a scream split the air. A pot clattered to the floor. He glanced back in time to see lobster bisque dripping from Frieda König's leather bikini, midriff, and skirt.

"You oaf, you burned me!" Shaking and dripping pink soup, she faced Margueritte. "What's worse—you've ruined the next course. You idiot!"

"I am so, so sorry," she said. "Forgive me."

Suppressing a smile, Brett whirled and followed Maeve between burners and counters to the back exit. In the hall, when they approached a security guard, they slowed to a walk. Oblivious to events, he waved them through.

In the WC, Brett grabbed his bag of street clothes with his cell phone and Aurora's notebook and met Maeve in the hall.

From the kitchen came shouting. Any moment now, the CSA would be coming through that door.

At the next stairwell, they descended one flight to the lobby floor. On their left was the entrance to the main floor where a CSA man was listening intently on his phone, probably being advised that two spies in serving uniforms were headed his way.

"Quick!" said Brett, "out the back."

They turned right, then right again into a long, empty hallway where they broke into a run. At the end, they pushed through onto the sidewalk.

A wash of cold air hit them, and Maeve shivered. "It's freezing out here."

"No time to change now," he said. "We've got to get to that restaurant Margueritte told us about."

"Right. But if they're looking for us, this outfit will give me away."
"We'll find a place to change. But right now, we've got to run!"

CHAPTER 17

ESCAPE FROM GENEVA

Geneva, Switzerland ~ February, Year 3

When Tyler's phone rang, he was leaning back on the sofa, eyes half closed, his book lying on his chest. Lisette was on the bed, asleep in her clothes. Sitting up straight, he answered. It was Margueritte.

"It's time for the emergency plan we talked about." Her voice was tense, and her tone sent a jolt of electricity through him. "The others got out. They're heading for the rendezvous point."

"Oh no."

"Oh no is right. If I'm not there in thirty minutes, take everyone to the backup meeting place and wait for me. Remember: Every day at noon for thirty minutes." Then she hung up.

Lisette was already waking up. He told her what was happening.

"Something went wrong?" Her eyes were wide.

"Apparently."

They packed their bags in haste and donned their winter coats.

Then he called the front desk. "We're checking out early, so please have our car brought to the front."

"I will, monsieur," came the answer. "But there's been an incident in the hotel, and anyone leaving the building will have to show their IDs and undergo inspection."

He acknowledged the woman then told Lisette about the extra security.

"I feel like the walls are closing in." She ran to him, and he hugged her.

With their bags in tow, they entered the elevator, and he punched the button for the lobby.

When they exited, the green-and-white uniforms of the CSA were everywhere. At the checkout desk, he paid with the Gavin Roberts credit card.

Then a bellhop approached. "May I carry your bags, monsieur?"

He nodded. It would be good to put someone between him and the men at the door.

As the youth carried their luggage, they headed for the front doors where two CSA agents were checking the IDs of everyone leaving the building. But when Tyler saw who was standing beside the agents, inspecting each departure, he gasped.

It was Adam Turner himself.

It was too late to leave by the back. If he ran, they'd be all over him. There was nothing to do now but depend on his disguise. And they were looking for Brett and Maeve, not Gavin Roberts and Dafne Venturi. He got in line behind an older couple who were talking with the two agents at the door. They presented their IDs, the CSA men waved them on, and Tyler took their place.

At first, Turner was on the phone and didn't look up. "Yes, I'm here at the front," he said. "I know what they look like, so I'll stay here until we catch them. You can take the back."

He hung up. Only then did Turner's gaze fall upon Tyler.

One of the CSA agents was watching him intently. He was short and stocky with rings in his ears and nose, and he stood to the side with a pistol at his belt. A second agent, gray-haired with wire-rim glasses, held out his hand. "IDs, please."

Ignoring Turner and keeping his gaze on the agent, Tyler handed the man their IDs.

"Have we met somewhere before?" asked Turner.

Tyler gave him a quick glance and shook his head.

"You look familiar." Turner scowled. "I can't place it. Maybe at the Imperator's reception in Rome when Davato announced the formation of the Unitum Imperium?"

"No, monsieur," said Tyler in the heaviest French accent he could muster. "I was not privileged to be at that event."

Apparently puzzled, Turner cocked his head. The CSA man let them through, and Tyler followed the youth outside to their waiting car.

Still breathing fast, he tipped the bellhop and the valet then drove onto the Route de Ferney and headed toward the lake.

"He didn't recognize you," said Lisette. "I was on the other side of the bellboy, keeping him between us, but Turner had his eyes only on you. And still, he didn't know you."

"Sometimes, when we see people out of context, it confuses our sense of recognition." Tyler wiped his brow. "And Bonifacio did a good job with my disguise. Even my own mother would have trouble knowing me today. Let's just hope he doesn't remember later."

"That was close." She shivered. "Now what?"

"We are to meet Brett and Maeve at the restaurant entrance. Hopefully, they escaped the CSA goons." He pointed to two men in green-and-white uniforms striding fast on the sidewalk beside the highway. "They seem to be everywhere."

* * *

IT WAS COLD AND DARK, and the outfit they'd given Maeve was more suited to a strip club than a formal dinner. But it fit the ethos of immorality in the den of iniquity behind them. She was shivering so much that Brett gave her his long-sleeved shirt, and now *he* was cold. At least his shirt covered her midriff.

Cars were passing on the street, and Maeve's unusual clothing would surely attract attention. They needed a place where she could change. But where?

From far down the street came the high-low-high-low whine of a police siren. They had just crossed the Avenue de la Paix next to the Parc de l'Ariana. From his study of the maps, a railroad track divided the way on the north, and the section they'd entered was on the west side. In the park, there'd be more places to hide.

He grabbed Maeve's hand, and they entered the high grass under the trees. As the sirens approached, Brett drew Maeve into the shadow of a trunk and held her tight.

"I–I appreciate y–your hugs, boyo." She gave him a smile. "B–but I fear 'tis not enough to k–keep me from freezing to death."

He kissed one cheek then nodded to a grove of leafless trees fifty meters away. "You can change over there."

The police siren dropped in pitch, receded into the distance, and kept going. Brett exhaled.

He left the cover of the tree trunk with his hand still in hers. When they reached a spot far enough from the highway, they stopped.

She returned his shirt, slid her street clothes from the bag, and dressed. "Better. But I'm still cold."

"I'm not sure, but I think a path up ahead should wind back to the Avenue de la Paix where we can cross the tracks."

"L–lead on. B–better to keep moving."

Less than fifty meters later, he found a path leading east, and it brought them back to the avenue. They followed the sidewalk beside the street and crossed the bridge.

But again, a police siren approached from behind.

Grabbing Maeve's hand once more, he broke into a run. Beyond the bridge was the entrance to the Jardin de la Paix—The Peace Garden—and they entered.

But the police had seen them. A vehicle screeched to a stop behind them. Car doors slammed shut, and someone shouted. "Stop and present your identification!"

But they didn't stop. Instead, they broke into a run.

By his reckoning, they had to traverse three-quarters of the park from south to north. The restaurant where they were to meet was northeast of the park on the shores of Lake Geneva.

"Let's go! We've got a good head start."

He sprinted onto the first trail, and when it split, he chose the left fork. A glance behind revealed four men on foot. But they were regular police, not CSA. Two men followed the right fork, probably trying to cut them off. The other two followed Brett and Maeve. But they were a hundred yards behind.

Brett hurried on.

At the next fork, he turned right, and they passed flower beds with dried-up stalks of plants. He took turn after turn, passing dry fountains and empty dirt beds until he could no longer see their pursuers. When a field opened on the north, he led her into it, and the trees swallowed them up.

On the grove's far side, they found the path again, and he veered east. The path led them to an exit and the main road. Beyond was Lake Geneva.

"This is the Route de Lausanne. The entrance to the restaurant is across the street."

He checked both ways. No CSA or police. They crossed the highway to the restaurant's street entrance.

"Over here!"

Brett looked toward the familiar voice.

Tyler had parked the BMW in a small lot inside the entrance. Both he and Lisette ran out to greet them.

"Everyone, get inside!" Brett shot a glance toward the street. "The cops are everywhere, and they might be behind us."

"Right!" Tyler slid into the driver's seat. Lisette sat in front, and the rest got in back.

"Turn up the heat," said a shivering Maeve from the back seat. "You've got a frozen lassie back here."

As Tyler waited for the traffic to clear, another police car passed with its siren blaring. When it was gone, he backed the car out of the parking spot and drove onto the highway, heading north.

"So now we go to the backup meeting place." Tyler glanced aside at Lisette. "That was the plan."

"In Paris?" she asked.

"Yes. We should get there by three in the morning."

"I'll reserve rooms." Brett fished in his bag. "I have my phone and also the notebook."

"Good!" Without looking back, Tyler gave Brett a thumbs-up. "I was hoping you had it with you."

"But we left all our stuff back there," said Maeve. "I'll need an entirely new wardrobe."

Tyler caught her glance in the rearview mirror. "In Paris, you and Brett can shop in style."

"Where are we supposed to meet this contact?" asked Lisette.

"At Napoleon's Tomb," answered Tyler. "Tomorrow at noon."

"Meeting at a tomb?" Lisette shook her head. "Isn't that ominous?"

Brett frowned. "I hope not."

PART III
A DUNGEON

Proverbs 4:14–19 (HCSB):

Don't set foot on the path of the wicked; don't proceed in the way of evil ones. Avoid it; don't travel on it. Turn away from it and pass it by. For they can't sleep unless they have done what is evil; they are robbed of sleep unless they make someone stumble. They eat the bread of wickedness and drink the wine of violence. The path of the righteous is like the light of dawn, shining brighter and brighter until midday. But the way of the wicked is like the darkest gloom; they don't know what makes them stumble.

CHAPTER 18

QUESTIONABLE METHODS

Lochbroom, Scotland ~ February, Year 3

It was time for the meeting, and Wallace's feet reverberated up and down the stone steps of the tower's spiral staircase. On the third floor, he entered the inner sanctum of Director Fergus McDuff.

McDuff was already seated in a stuffed chair before a fire crackling in the hearth. Beside him sat Dr. Albert Creig.

Holding his pipe, the director swiveled in his seat. "Get yourself a drink, Wallace, and take a chair." Both he and Creig held tumblers of brown liquid. Whiskey, probably, for McDuff. Scotch for Creig. As if an afterthought, a cigarette dangled from between Creig's fingers.

At the counter beside the window, Wallace poured himself a shot of scotch. Instead of sitting, he went to the bookshelf and ran a finger over the titles.

The Great Gatsby by F. Scott Fitzgerald.

The Sun Also Rises by Ernest Hemingway.

Death of the Archbishop by Willa Cather.

Anna Karenina by Leo Tolstoy.

Catch-22 by Joseph Heller.

David Copperfield by Charles Dickens.

He also found books in Italian, French, English, and German—all languages that Wallace could speak. It was one of the reasons he'd been admitted as a special agent of the Ministry of Virtue.

He left the shelf, took a seat beside Creig, and sipped his scotch. "You have quite a collection of classics, Director. Aren't you afraid some of them are banned?"

"Rank has its privileges, and none of them advance any agenda of the Enemy."

Wallace sipped his scotch and nodded. "May I borrow one sometime?"

McDuff smiled, set his drink and his pipe on the armrest, and intertwined his fingers before his chest. "You may, but the penalty for not returning one of my books is quite severe."

"And what," asked Wallace, "might that be?"

"Listening to Creig play his violin while strapped in that chair he's got in his lab."

Both Wallace and McDuff burst out laughing, but Creig's stony face told them he found nothing amusing about the joke.

"Yes, well, let's move to the table." McDuff left his pipe. With one hand on his drink and the other on his cane, he stood. "I find the table more conducive for serious business."

The others followed him away from the fire.

"This is a status meeting, Creig." McDuff laid both hands flat on the oak. "When last we met, it was a month ago, and in a few days, I must report to Sebastien Rey on our progress. What do you have for me?"

Creig cleared his throat. "Unfortunately, I have learned little since last month. I have now examined thirty-five subjects, comparing them with my control group. And there seems to be no correlation between placement of the eyes or nose or the width of the forehead or chin or even the size of the brain cavity with a propensity toward false belief."

"Yes, I believe you said the same thing last time." McDuff frowned.

"Last month, I had thirty subjects. My control group holds thirty, and I'm doing the same to them that I'm doing to the Christians."

"And you've heard my objection to your control group, as you call it." Wallace crossed his arms and sat back. "Those are normal people who haven't consorted with the Enemy. They are average citizens whom you snatched off the street without cause, just like you've stolen prisoners from our sister agencies."

Before they sent him to Tel Aviv and he'd captured Aurora Carter, he told them that was the last time he'd go on such a mission. Even thieves should have honor, and regardless of what the Prophet said, stealing Christians from sister agencies was lawless. But grabbing innocent civilians off the streets? That was even worse.

Creig wanted more subjects, but the opportunities to take Christians from the IDS or the CSA in the seconds their operatives completed a raid were few and far between. Once the other agencies discovered what the Ministry of Virtue was doing, they refused to cooperate. Now, they kept their raids secret until the last minute, leaving McDuff to rely on leaked memos or emails or paid informers to discover when the next raid would occur. Even with that, they often missed the moment, arrived too late, and left empty-handed. Now, they were forced to travel as far as Israel for a rare opportunity. But now they could send someone else. Wallace was done with all of it.

"We've been through all this, Wallace." McDuff gave a condescending smile. "The ends justify the means. This project is too important for one citizen's life to get in the way of its execution. When we release them, they will be duly compensated."

"If the good doctor hasn't first turned them into blubbering vegetables."

"Come, come, Wallace." Creig's voice barely rose, but his smile widened. "Let us be civil."

"I'm serious. You or I could have been one of those."

"Anyone who worked for the Unitum Imperium or who had a connection with it was released immediately." Creig's tone was tired. "If it had been one of us, we would not have ended up in a cell below."

Wallace stared. It was useless arguing the point, so why did he feel the need to keep bringing it up?

Creig pulled a pack of cigarettes from a pocket and removed another white cylinder.

"Must you?" McDuff scowled at the cigarette.

"I must." Creig lit a match, sucked in, and blew out smoke. "I have cataloged the blood chemistry for all thirty-five individuals, including the new arrival, Aurora Carter. We are embarked on a great quest, are we not? What is the missing compound they might all have in common? What is the chemical defect in the Christians' blood to account for their behavior? I was hoping for an answer. But so far, I've found only aberrations related to chronic diseases. I have not yet found some abnormality shared by all. In short, that line of inquiry seems to be ending, though I'm not ready to give up on it entirely."

"Not good." McDuff scowled. "We must have something to report to Director Rey. What other avenues are you exploring?"

Creig shrugged. "I have tried challenge tests with various chemicals to see how they react versus the control group."

"Hence, the screams coming from your surgery." Wallace took a long sip of the scotch and scowled.

Creig tapped ash from his cigarette. "Necessary, Wallace. All necessary. But I am about to approach the matter with a promising new line of attack."

McDuff nodded. "That sounds better. What do you have in mind?"

"Instead of finding a cause for the Christians' poor judgment, I will bypass that line of inquiry and go straight for a cure."

"Excellent!" McDuff leaned forward. "When will you begin?"

"This week. It will involve hallucinogens. And light deprivation followed by excessive light. And when the tank I ordered arrives, I'll try sensory deprivation, followed by sensory overload. After each of these challenges to the body and the mind, I will ask my subjects to recant their faith and worship the Dragon. Eventually, I'm convinced that some combination will produce the desired result."

"Yes, yes, I like this approach." McDuff brought a fist down on the table, and his tumbler jumped. "I will inform the Prophet of our search for a cure instead of a cause. I'm sure he will approve."

Creig smiled and lit another cigarette. "I'm told there was an IDS agent here recently, and he demanded to take one of my subjects. Is this anything I should be concerned about?"

McDuff waved away the suggestion. "I sent him and his goon back to Ullapool. He won't be bothering us again." He laughed. "These IDS people are so impressed with their own authority they cannot imagine that anyone can refuse what they ask. He was quite indignant. It's hard enough to get subjects for you. We're not going to release any of them to the IDS."

"I escorted him to the mainland," said Wallace. "But I'm guessing we haven't seen the last of him."

"He can protest and demand all he wants. It will get him nowhere." McDuff grabbed his tumbler and cane and returned to his seat by the fire where waited an open book. "That is all I have for now. Enough for my report. You may return to your duties."

Wallace finished the last of his drink, stood, and followed Creig out the door.

In the hall, Creig turned to him with another of his frowns. "Sometimes, Sloan, you go too far. Especially in front of the director. I would watch myself if I were you."

"What do you mean by that, Creig? Is that a threat?"

"Nothing of the kind. Just a piece of friendly advice." Then he whirled on his heels and preceded Wallace down the tower stairs.

How had he ended up here in this place, working with a monster like Albert Creig?

This wasn't what he'd had in mind when the ministry recruited him. Before that, he was making a living selling and installing security systems in businesses and homes. He was even taking flying lessons with the dream of one day buying a small plane. Then came the Great Catastrophe, his business fell apart, and those plans ended. Even though crime had risen exponentially, no one could afford what he needed to charge, and security system sales dried up. He tried getting a government contract. That might have saved the business. But after his sole employee died in the plague, he couldn't keep going. He searched everywhere for another job. But no one was hiring, and competition was stiff. So when someone at the Ministry of Virtue saw his contract application and résumé, they offered him this job, and he took it.

Now he wondered if he'd sold his soul.

He would do his duty, for that was his creed. But too often lately, the tasks they wanted him to perform at the castle grated on his conscience like a knifepoint dragged across a car hood. It all went to the heart of a question that had been building in him for some time.

What kind of man, deep down, was Wallace Sloan?

Was he, at heart, a good man? Or had he sold himself in slavery to the worst evil on the planet?

CHAPTER 19

THE EVENTS IN PARIS

Paris, France ~ February, Year 3

At three in the morning, the traffic still roared when Tyler pulled into the lot for Hôtel Le Pavillon. Even after the first four seals had removed one-quarter of the population, there were more than enough cars, vans, and trucks to fill the gap.

He had booked two rooms, and everyone was so exhausted, they slept until ten. After Tyler rousted Brett then called Maeve and Lisette in their room, they met in the downstairs restaurant where he used his Gavin Roberts credit card to buy a breakfast of pricey coffee, rolls, butter, and jam. The proprietor was more than happy to find paying customers.

"The famine and then the plague!" The little bald man, sporting an obvious toupee, shook his head. "It's ruined my business. Too many beggars on the street. Too few customers. No one can pay for anything."

Tyler had agreed on the disastrous state of the world, and he gave the man a good tip.

"We don't know if this meeting is dangerous or not." Tyler sipped the last of his coffee and stood. "Maybe Brett and I should go, and you women should stay here."

"You don't think we lassies can handle it?" asked Maeve.

"No sense in everyone taking the risk." Brett laid a hand on her shoulder.

She agreed, and the two men made the short walk from the hotel to the National Hôtel des Invalides, a hospital for wounded French soldiers. They arrived five minutes before the appointed time at the Dome of the Invalides, a massive, columned structure, inside of which was Napoleon's Tomb.

Tyler approached the attendant to pay for their tickets.

"Only six visitors today," said the thin, gray-mustachioed man inside the booth. He handed Tyler their two tickets. "Nobody appreciates

French history anymore. It's all about the Unitum Imperium and how things are going to get so much better."

But by the man's expression, he didn't go along with that.

"So business is slow?"

"Slow? We used to have lines out the door. But now?" He shrugged. "Down to a trickle. Today's young folks, or what's left of them, don't care about history, and they aren't being taught. I've heard them coming in with their parents, and they don't even know who Napoleon was. They have no idea about the glory that once was France."

"Times have changed," said Tyler. "And not for the better."

"You can say that again. Plague. Famine. Earthquakes." The man lowered his voice. "And Truth Squads."

Tyler nodded.

"You can look all you like, but—a warning." The man waved past the turnstile. "The last two men I let in were government snoops. Plainclothes spies in suits. They're everywhere nowadays. But you didn't hear me say that."

"Of course, monsieur. Thank you." Then Tyler followed Brett through the turnstile into the tomb.

"Plainclothes squaddies?" asked Brett. "Here? Today?"

"Maybe it's coincidence."

"I don't like it."

Inside the cavernous space were one elderly couple and a man with a shaggy mop of blond hair in workman's clothes. Neither Margueritte nor the squaddies in suits were in sight. But there were two levels, and anyone could be hidden behind a pillar.

A circular balustrade surrounded the tomb on two levels, and Margueritte was to meet them on the second floor. Tyler climbed the marble stairs, passed a row of cannons from Napoleon's wars, and emerged on the balcony above the tomb.

The monument below was shaped like a mammoth scroll set atop a huge pedestal. Marble statues circled the tomb and faced the place where the emperor's ashes now resided. From above, the gold design embedded in the floor appeared like rays of the sun.

He glanced left, right, and across the space to the opposite side. "She's not here yet."

"Over there!" Brett pointed to where Margueritte emerged from behind a column.

He waved, but she raised both hands, opened them flat, and gave a sign meaning, "Don't." She shot a glance to the right then began walking left.

"What's she doing?" asked Brett. "Is she leaving?"

"I don't know."

Tyler started walking around the circle, intending to meet her on the opposite side when two men in suits—undercover CSA?—began closing in on her.

She broke into a run and headed for the stairs. Tyler and Brett raced around the balustrade in time to see the men descending the steps after her.

He and Brett followed, exiting the building onto the field before the entrance. A hundred meters beyond, Margueritte was running toward the parking lot, but two more men appeared on the far side. They wore the green uniforms and black armbands of the Truth Squads.

The men beyond would cut her off. The men behind her would be upon her in seconds.

"Plainclothes CSA and squaddies?" Tyler stopped on the grass. "They must have been watching this spot, waiting for another Friends' rendezvous."

"If we had arrived any earlier," said Brett, "they would have caught us too."

On the field's far end, the men tackled her and brought her down. They cuffed her and led her to a black van in the parking lot.

"Now what?" asked Brett. "She was supposed to tell us what they discovered from the Geneva meeting."

"I don't know. Let's return to the hotel."

On the way back, both were silent, and Tyler wondered if all their efforts to learn Aurora's whereabouts in Geneva had been for naught. How could they get in touch with the Friends of Light if their only contact had been captured?

Back in Brett and Tyler's room, the guys told the women the bad news.

"So all our efforts at finding Aurora have come to nothing?" asked Lisette.

"Aye," added Maeve. "It seems we're afloat without a compass. Again."

"What about the notebook?" Tyler turned to Brett. "Have you checked it lately?"

"Not since before we left Geneva. I'll look now." He brought it out from his pack and opened it to the last recorded page. "Nothing."

"Brett, we need to pray," said Tyler. "That's what Eli would have told us, and we haven't done much of that lately."

"Yes. We'll ask the Big Guy to give us a sign."

"I–I will help."

It was Maeve who spoke, and Tyler's eyes widened. "Did I hear you right?"

"I've seen the miracles from your notebook, the prophecies coming true, and I have to admit—your God is real, and so is your Jesus."

"Are you ready to confess your faith and become a Christian?" asked a startled Brett.

"Well . . . maybe not just yet. But I'll help you pray."

"Good enough." Tyler beamed. "One step at a time."

"You three go ahead," said Lisette. "I'll just watch."

They prayed. They asked God to show them the way to where Aurora was being held prisoner. They asked Jesus to smooth their journey and remove all obstacles. They also prayed that Margueritte could somehow escape being sent to the German internment camp.

After they finished, Brett checked the book again. Still, there was nothing.

"We can't expect an immediate answer," said Tyler. "Maybe something will appear later."

* * *

THAT AFTERNOON, THEY TOOK NAPS, had coffee downstairs, and went for walks. By nightfall, no message had appeared, and Tyler went to bed, praying silently for an answer.

The next morning, when they met again in the downstairs restaurant for expensive coffee, rolls, butter, and jam, Brett reported there was still no message. He'd brought the book, and as they finished their repast, he opened it once more.

"Yes!" he cried. "Something's here."

Tyler leaned over his shoulder and read.

The key to finding your missing companion lies in Edinburgh, Scotland, with Hamish Stewart in the Black Swan Pub. Proverbs 4:25–27.

"Do you have your Bible with you?" asked Tyler.

"No, it's back in Geneva."

Tyler pulled out his phone where he had a Bible app and looked up the verses. He read them out loud, "'Look straight ahead, and fix your eyes on what lies before you. Mark out a straight path for your feet; stay on the safe path. Don't get sidetracked; keep your feet from following evil.'"

"Seems straightforward enough." Lisette glanced up.

"So our prayers worked." Maeve's eyes lit up, and she faced Lisette. "You'll have to admit that, won't you?"

"I–I guess they did."

"Thanks to Bonifacio, we've got IDs and travel passes that should get us there without trouble." Tyler searched the train schedules leaving Paris for Edinburgh. "There's a train leaving in an hour and a half, arriving in Edinburgh this evening. But the earthquakes have damaged the tracks, so there are delays. Otherwise, it should have taken half the time. I'll get tickets online. We should pack and take a taxi to the station."

"Finally, some good news." Lisette smiled.

"Finally," said Brett.

CHAPTER 20

BANISHED!

From Ullapool to Edinburgh, Scotland ~ February, Year 3

When Finn Foster got the call he was expecting, he was sitting across from Hugo in the Caledonian Hotel restaurant with a glass of ale and a plate of fried hake. Opposite him, the smoke from Bagby Creel's pipe drifted his way.

"Hello?" answered Finn.

"Is this Gamma 6?" The woman on the other end had an Italian accent. He sat up straighter. Cupping his hand over the phone, he whispered his call sign.

"Acknowledged," said the woman. "Please wait for the director."

He faced Creel and Hugo. "Find something to do at that empty table over there until I'm finished. This is confidential."

Nodding, Hugo grabbed his mug of ale, Creel his pipe and mug, and they moved to seats across the aisle.

"Lieutenant Colonel Foster?" came the voice he recognized as Adam Turner's.

"Yes, sir. I'm so glad you returned my call." Finally, he'd get the support he needed.

"Yes, well, I understand you want to take a woman by the name of Aurora Carter into custody and another group is refusing to give her up?"

"That's right, sir. She's a threat to the empire and a high-priority target. I've been pursuing her for months."

"The report in front of me says you've made no progress on this for some time. Explain what's going on."

"Well, my target is being held by a certain Fergus McDuff, who's running some kind of off-the-books operation in a place called Castle Danger up here in northwest Scotland. His facility is under the auspices of the Ministry of Virtue, and McDuff doesn't respect the authority of

88

the IDS. They refused to hand her over to me. Then they escorted me off their base and said I was never to return."

"Yes, Foster, I know all about it." That the director used his last name and not his title was not good. "Sebastien Rey himself informed me of your visit to his facility. This, apparently, is his private project, and he asked me not to interfere. Until the Prophet changes his mind, you are not to pursue this any further. Where are you now?"

"In Ullapool." He sucked in breath. "It's a village across the bay from the peninsula where they're keeping her."

"And what have you been doing there for the last week?"

"Well, I–I ... I'm just waiting for you to override McDuff's authority."

"That's not going to happen. At least not for now. I don't like this either, but there's nothing we can do about it. There's also another aspect to this we must discuss. Aurora Carter is the daughter of Nick Carter, a trusted member of my staff. A few of our agents have caught wind of this, and they suspect he is involved in her activities, but I'm not so sure."

"I had wondered about that, sir. What do you want me to do about it?"

"I may want you to interrogate him. But we can't have you sitting up there just twiddling your thumbs. So I want you to return to Edinburgh and wait for further instructions while I look into this matter of Carter and his daughter."

"B–but my target. I–I—"

"They've got her locked up. She's not a threat to anyone right now. Follow my orders, go to Edinburgh, and wait. If needed, you can easily catch a plane to Jerusalem from there."

"Yes, sir."

After he hung up, he just sat, trying to control a rising frustration. Finally, he waved to the others, and they rejoined him.

"We've been ordered to Edinburgh. The director can't override McDuff's orders. I'm to wait there until he decides what to do. There may be another subject for me to interrogate."

"She got away again, didn't she?" asked Hugo.

"We'll get her eventually." Finn turned to Creel. "Can you make reservations for the three of us in Edinburgh?"

As Finn poked at his fried hake, Creel made the reservations on his phone. Then he looked up. "We're staying at the Hilton Edinburgh Carlton. The other hotels in the city are either closed or full. But the Carlton, you'll remember, is a good place with a good bar."

Finn scowled. He'd wasted an entire week waiting for the authority that should have been his. Now he was heading to Edinburgh where he'd no doubt waste more time. The only positive in this was that, if Turner could make up his mind about Nick Carter, Finn might be able to bring at least one of the Carters to the justice they deserved.

CHAPTER 21

NEAR MISSES

Edinburgh, Scotland ~ February, Year 3

Matthew 24:3–4A, 12 (HCSB): *While He was sitting on the Mount of Olives, the disciples approached Him privately and said, "Tell us . . . what is the sign of Your coming and of the end of the age? Then Jesus replied to them: . . . Because lawlessness will multiply, the love of many will grow cold."*

As the Eurostar from Paris whooshed through the chunnel and raced northward at speeds of up to two hundred miles per hour, Tyler slept off and on. The car was nearly empty, so he and Brett spread out on seats facing each other while Lisette and Maeve occupied seats across the aisle. In several places where the earthquake had damaged the rails, they slowed to a crawl but soon sped up again. The train was direct to Edinburgh with only one change in London.

But as Tyler and the others left the first train and waited on the London platform to hand their IDs to the CSA agents for the second train, someone behind him screamed.

He whirled.

Three youths were accosting an elderly couple and two young women. The youths carried chains, knives, and a cricket bat. "Give us your cash," the tallest, gangly youth ordered a white-haired older man. "And be quick about it."

The man hesitated. The youth swung his bat, and the man tried to duck. Then came the cracking of wood on bone, and the man fell to the pavement. Blood streamed from his forehead.

A whistle blew, four uniformed Truth Squad agents appeared down the platform, and the CSA man taking IDs before Tyler pushed his way onto the platform to give pursuit.

The youths ran. The uniformed squaddies were close behind.

91

Two shots exploded. One youth crumpled to the concrete. The other two stopped and raised their hands.

The CSA man descended and began beating the gangsters with a truncheon. When they lay, bleeding, unmoving, and prostrate, he handcuffed them, frisked them, and returned what they had stolen to their victims.

"The lawlessness," said the middle-aged woman in the line ahead, "it's everywhere, isn't it?"

"They got what was coming to them," said one of the young women behind.

The CSA man returned to the train, checked their IDs, and they boarded. Moments later, the train pulled out of the station. Soon, telephone poles, trees, and houses were again whizzing past.

Somewhere near York, Brett leaned toward him and whispered. "I was going to ask Maeve to marry me, but at the last minute, I chickened out."

"What?" Tyler's jaw dropped. This was a total surprise.

"It was on the night we arrived at the Intercontinental." Brett shot a glance toward the women. "I had a speech all prepared. I took her on a walk. But I couldn't do it. The words just wouldn't come."

Tyler swallowed. It was unusual for Brett to open up like this. "I can see that you love her. Why didn't you just come out with it?"

"I'm not sure. Maybe it's everything that's going on around us—the risks we take every day, the uncertainty whether one of us is going to get caught or killed or forever be on the run to somewhere else. Or maybe . . . maybe I was just a coward."

"So much uncertainty everywhere. And marriage is a big step, isn't it?" Tyler sat back, and his gaze went out the window. "We've been on a roller coaster of a ride since we found the notebook. Or rather, since it found us."

"Anyway, I just needed to tell someone."

"Thanks, Brett. Someday, maybe we'll have a double wedding—you and Maeve, me and Lisette."

Brett grinned. "I'd like that."

The train slowed again where the quake had damaged the rails and alternate tracks had been laid, and Tyler picked up the novel he'd been reading.

That delay and others like it kept them from arriving in Edinburgh until nine that evening.

They took a taxi to the Hilton Edinburgh Carlton, the only hotel with available rooms. After unpacking, he called Brett and Maeve's room. "We haven't eaten yet, and there's still time to check out this Black Swan Pub. They're still serving. How about it?"

"Sounds good to me," answered Brett. "Let's meet downstairs."

The pub was less than a kilometer away, so they strolled down an empty street.

Inside the stone building, light from the faux lanterns was dim. Bricks lined the walls, and a shiny brass railing circled the bar. The place was half full, and the buzz of conversation filled the air. A glance around the room revealed men and women in work smocks and dungarees, some wearing company badges from the local Heineken manufacturing plant. But there were also five CSA agents at two different tables.

Tyler asked the host to seat them at a table far from the agents.

A twenty-year-old blonde woman with tattoos covering her arms and rings in her nose, ears, and lips arrived with menus. If it were not for the rings, she would have been attractive. Hoping she might know their contact, he engaged her in conversation. "Do you know some of the locals who frequent this pub?"

"A few. Why do you ask?"

"We're supposed to meet a friend of a friend here. He goes by the name of Hamish Stewart."

"Hamish, you say?" She dropped menus before each of them. "I know several Hamishes, but not their last names. What does he look like?"

"We're not sure. Supposedly, he comes here quite often."

"I'll ask the manager. What'll you have?"

The others ordered, and Tyler chose a pint of the local Heineken and the traditional Irish coddle—a stew with pork and leek sausages, potatoes, onions, and bacon.

After their drinks arrived, a man with a black handlebar mustache approached their table. "I am Robert, the manager. I understand you're asking for Hamish Stewart?"

"We are. Is he around?"

"He's new in town, and he's been here twice. He and I talked, and he asked a lot of questions in confidence. I'm guessing he'd be frequenting other pubs. The Wild Pony. World's End. Maybe Tempest in a Tankard. He's not here tonight. You might try them."

"What does he look like?" asked Tyler.

"Medium build. Curly red hair and mustache. Wears a black ski jacket."

"All right. Thanks."

The manager started to walk away then returned. "A word of advice." He sent a glance to the CSA table. "Others have been asking about him. Not people like you, but obvious government types. I wouldn't get too cozy with this Stewart if I were you. Last year, the Truth Squads hauled away four of my regular customers, and I expect they'll do it again. Best to keep clear of the man."

"Thanks for the warning. We'd still like to meet him though."

"Up to you, of course. If I see him, I'll tell him you're looking for him. Who should I say is doing the asking?"

"Just say we're a Friend. Say it just like that, word for word. Say, 'We are . . . a . . . Friend'."

He frowned and cocked his head. "If you say so."

After the manager left, their food arrived. They ate, and then, to wile away the time, they drank another pint, hoping their elusive contact would show up. At eleven thirty, the pub closed, and they walked back to the hotel.

They entered the lobby and headed for the elevators with the bar on their left. But as Tyler glanced inside, he yanked the others back into the lobby, his heart pumping fast.

"What's wrong?" asked Lisette.

"You won't believe who's inside that bar, drinking ale and whiskey."

"Who?" asked Maeve.

"Finn Foster and Hugo."

"What?" Brett's hands formed into fists. "How did *they* get here? Are they looking for us?"

"Who knows?" Tyler started for the back stairs. "But tomorrow, we'll have to find a different hotel."

CHAPTER 22

HAMISH STEWART

Edinburgh, Scotland ~ February, Year 3

The next morning, Tyler called Brett's room, and they talked. "I tried to get another hotel, but most of the hotels in this city have closed, and the few that are left are booked solid."

"Why is Finn staying here?" asked Brett. "Is he looking for us?"

"I don't know. It's troubling, isn't it? We need to find this Hamish person and leave."

"Obviously, we can't eat in the hotel restaurant, so what about breakfast? I'm starving."

"You're always starving." Tyler tried on a smile. "I suggest that we eat all our meals at the Black Swan. That's where Hamish is most likely to show up anyways."

"Good idea. Let's all meet outside."

"But the building has a back entrance. Use that to avoid the lobby."

"Okay."

They returned to the Black Swan for breakfast and again for lunch. That evening, Brett and Maeve waited there while Tyler and Lisette checked out other pubs where Hamish might show up.

At the Wild Pony, the bartender didn't know any Hamish.

At A Tempest in a Tankard, one of the waitresses thought she remembered him stopping there once but couldn't be certain.

And at World's End, the substitute bartender didn't know Hamish Stewart, but he said that government types had also asked about him. He advised them to come back the next night when the regular barman would return.

That night before closing, Tyler and Lisette returned empty-handed to the Black Swan where Brett and Maeve reported that neither had they seen Hamish.

"Are we to do this every night for the next month until we find him?" asked Maeve. "I fear that too much ale and beer might fatten this lassie's slim figure."

"Try switching to wine." Tyler smiled. "Less carbs."

"Okay, boyo."

* * *

WHEN THE ELUSIVE HAMISH DID not appear for the next three nights, Tyler wondered if Maeve had been given the gift of prophecy. And every time they left the building, he feared they'd run into Finn or Hugo. They didn't even know if Finn was looking for them, if he were still in the hotel, or if he had another mission.

Still, it was troubling that Finn had appeared here, of all places. It had to be more than a coincidence.

After hearing the reports from the other pubs, Tyler guessed that the Black Swan was their best opportunity to find the dodgy Hamish.

And so, on their fourth night in Edinburgh, after Tyler and Lisette returned from yet another fruitless quest at the Wild Pony and Tempest in a Tankard, they all sat together in the Black Swan, thirty minutes before closing.

They'd barely sat when the now-familiar pierced and tattooed young waitress appeared and asked if they wanted to order something. "The bar is closing in a few minutes," she said.

Brett and Maeve still had their drinks, and Tyler shook his head. He'd already had three that evening. Lisette also declined.

"Four nights wasted," said Tyler after the waitress left. "Four nights lost, and we still don't know where they're keeping Aurora."

"I've checked the notebook," said Brett. "And nothing."

"Why doesn't it just tell us where we should go?" asked Lisette. "Why do we have to go through this Hamish person?"

"Who knows?" said Tyler. "But I can't fault God for not leading us straight to our goal. Everything has worked out so far."

The young waitress returned. "That man you were looking for—that Hamish Stewart? He just paid by credit card. When I saw his name on the card, I pointed you out and said you wanted to speak with him. But then he up and skedaddled out the front door."

"Okay, thanks." Brett threw some bills on the table. They stood and hurried for the door.

Outside, the air was crisp, and Tyler could see his breath. He looked both ways. A man with Hamish's description was walking north, about seventy meters away. "Hamish Stewart? Wait!"

Hamish turned around, gave them one glance, then broke into a run.

All four raced after him.

"Stop, please," said Tyler. "We're with the Friends of Light."

Hamish slowed then stopped. One hand went to something under his jacket—a pistol? He turned to face them and waited until they caught up. When they did, he brandished the gun and waved them into an alley.

After they gave the correct pass phrases, he holstered his pistol and stood with arms crossed. "What's the matter with you? Are you the ones who've been broadcasting my name all over town? The CSA's been looking for me in this city, and I was certain you were part of them. I've been trying to keep a low profile here lately, and you're making it extremely difficult."

"Sorry. But we had to find you."

"Okay, okay." He ran a hand through his hair. "Now what's so important that you had to chase me all over town to find me?"

"It's about our sister. We think she's a prisoner here in Edinburgh, Scotland."

"And why do you think that?" His hands grabbed both hips.

After Tyler explained how Aurora was taken, Hamish widened his stance. "Now you begin to interest me. It is for just such a group I've begun scouring Scotland from one corner to the other—and without any luck, I may add. What else do you know about this?"

"We just returned from a failed mission for the Friends in Geneva, and—"

"You!" He slapped a hand on one thigh. "You were the ones involved in that operation?"

"That was us, laddie." Maeve grinned. "Too bad we were discovered, for it all came to naught."

"But nae, it didn't. Because of you, we now know that this rogue group you mentioned is here in Scotland. Somewhere. But we don't know where. That's why they sent me here a few days ago. But you didn't know that till just now, did you?" He frowned. "They said you disappeared and were on the run and no one had told you. So how did you come here to Edinburgh?"

Tyler's glance caught Brett's, and he raised his eyebrows. "Should we tell him?"

"Why not? We're all on the same side here."

Then Tyler told Hamish about the notebook, the prophecies, and their journey across the Atlantic. He told him about Eli, who turned out to be Elijah of the Bible and one of the Two Witnesses from the book of Revelation.

When he finished, Hamish crossed his arms. "Such a tale is so outlandishly far-fetched and impossible to believe that it must be true. So some kind of notebook led you here?"

"Yes," answered Brett. "But it was God speaking to us through the notebook."

Again, Hamish slapped his thigh. "Methinks, we're destined to close ranks, you and I. As I was saying, my mission here was to find the location where the Unitum Imperium goons have been taking the Christians they didn't send to the German camp. I've been checking every rumor of CSA activity in the country—far too many leads to get to them all. The next place on my list was up in the northwest corner, in a village called Ullapool. But only this evening, I received orders to return to London headquarters. Ullapool is a long shot, but if you can check it out for me, that might help."

"Anything to help find our sister," said Brett.

"Good. Those of us in the Friends network are few and far between. The forces of evil are many. They're powerful, and they're growing. Your help is just what's needed here."

Tyler beamed, stepped forward, and gave a short bow. "We are at your disposal. Like Brett said—anything to help find our sister."

Hamish offered his cell number and said to call if they found anything. They parted and began walking back to their hotel.

"Tomorrow, me lads and me lassies," said a cheerful Maeve, "it appears we'd be off to Ullapool."

"Finally," said Lisette. "Finally, we're doing something that might actually help find her."

Tyler faced her. "I think we have the answer to your earlier question, Lisette."

"What question was that?"

"The reason the notebook's message didn't send us straight to Aurora was that God wanted us to meet Hamish. He'll be invaluable in our quest."

CHAPTER 23

THE MYSTERY ACROSS THE LOCH

Ullapool, Scotland ~ February, Year 3

The following morning, Tyler rented a VW Golf with the Gavin Roberts credit card, and they drove northwest across Scotland. But ten kilometers before Ullapool, there was a checkpoint in the opposite lane, manned by armed officers.

"They're letting everyone through going north," said Brett from the back. "But they're checking every car going south. How odd."

Passing the checkpoint, they arrived in Ullapool after lunch. They checked into three rooms at the Caledonian Hotel then met in Tyler and Brett's room.

"Now what?" asked Lisette from her seat on the bed. "How do we go about this?"

"Good question." Tyler walked to the window looking out over the bay. "Maybe we should just go outside and take a walk? This village isn't big."

"Sounds good to me." Brett stood from his seat on the second bed. "I need some exercise."

They walked the streets, past one whitewashed house after another. Most had chimneys with two stovepipes. The village was only five or six blocks long, and after circling it, they ended up on Shore Street by the bay.

A helicopter flew overhead, heading west.

"What's a helicopter doing out here in the middle of nowhere?" asked Maeve.

"Good question," said Brett.

They passed The Edinburgh Woollen Mill, the Ceol-na-Mara (Music by the Sea), the Lochbroom Hardware, and the Seaforth Bar and Restaurant, and arrived at the Ullapool Ferry Company where passengers could book rides to Stornoway on the Isle of Lewis. Near the ferry, they found a fishing trawler beside the wharf. A black-bearded man and a young boy sat on the boat's deck, mending a net.

"Let's ask him." Tyler descended the steps to a landing beside the trawler.

The fisherman looked up and scowled before his fingers returned to the net where he was removing strands of seaweed.

"Sir, may I ask you some questions?" said Tyler.

"Depends on who's doin' the asking." The man glanced up once then returned to his net. "You government people?"

"No."

"You dinnae look like government people. What do you want to know?"

"We're looking for a place near here that might be run by the government. It might be a secret base of sorts."

Lisette, Brett, and Maeve descended the steps and joined Tyler.

The man's fingers extricated themselves from the nylon webbing, and he focused on Tyler. "A secret base, you say. And why might such a place be of interest to you?"

"Because," said Lisette, "we think they might be holding a good friend of ours." She waved to Tyler and Brett. "She's their sister."

The man wiped his hands on his shirt and, for some time, studied them. "There might be such a place. Aye, there might. Over yonder." He pointed across the bay.

"Across the bay?"

"Aye. We dinnae like to talk about it, but somethin's wrong over there. Folks complain about the copter comin' and goin', but nae a body tells us a thing. There was a secondary road, if you could call it a road, that used to head northwest off the A832, and now it's closed. And some farmers out that way were kicked off their land, though there weren't many there to speak of in the first place. Aye, there've been strange goings-on over there."

"What kind of strange goings-on?" asked Brett.

Then the boy beside him, probably no more than twelve, spoke up. "What happened to Ian Campbell, for one."

"Quiet, boy," said the older man. "Leave this to me."

"What about Ian Campbell?" asked Tyler.

"Well, you might as well hear it. He was lookin' to hunt on the moors over there. Elk and boar, you ken. Knew him well, I did, and he was careful with his boats, knew how to handle them, and would nae do anythin' foolish. Well, one day, he says to the men in the pub that he'd take his rifle across the bay, climb the monadh to the moors beyond, and bag himself an elk."

"Monadh?" asked Brett.

"For you Yanks, that'd be a mountain on the moors. Aye, there be elk over there, for sure. I've seen them on the banks. Campbell went over, but he never came back. After a time, we went over to make a search, and we found his skiff. Floatin' upside down, it was. Some said he fell into the bay and drowned. But I'm nae so sure. Like I said, he knew his seacraft, and he could swim. It dinnae make sense—him tipping the boat and drowning. But there it is."

"We saw a helicopter pass overhead," said Lisette. "Where does it go?"

"Good question, that, because there *is* a government facility up on the moors. But nae a body's seen it, and most dinnae want to talk about it. After what happened to Campbell, you ken. But sure and certain, the government's over there."

"How do you know that?" asked Brett.

"Used to be a good restaurant across the bay, in a place called Alltnaharrie. 'Twere good eatin', but pricey. Then the government bought it and kicked out the folks who ran the place. Now there's a sign sayin' it's some kind of outpost for the Ministry of Virtue with a warning for folks to stay away. But it's empty and abandoned."

"The Ministry of Virtue?" Tyler's eyes widened.

"That's what it says. Rather odd, dinnae you think?"

"Yeah, real odd. Can you take us there?"

The man squinted. "Some government fellow asked the same thing a while ago. About two weeks back, I took the fool over in the dark with his government goon. Nasty-looking fellow, that goon. But the next day, a copter left them both at the edge of town, so I'm supposin' they were kicked out. They stayed at the Caledonian till two days ago. Then they left. I dinnae like the looks of either one."

"What did they look like?" asked Tyler. "And why did you call one of them a goon?"

When the man described Finn Foster and Hugo, Tyler's jaw dropped. That might explain Finn's presence in Edinburgh. "We know them. We don't like them either. Still, can you take us over there?"

"Just a minute, sir." Brett pulled Tyler aside for a whispered conversation. "Should we go across now? Maybe we should wait for Hamish?"

Tyler scratched the back of his neck. "You're right. We should wait." He returned to the fisherman. "How about another time? But is there anything else you can tell us about the place?"

"Dinnae know for sure, but there's a woman in town who might know more. Fiona is her name, and she waitresses at the Arch Inn. Rumor has it she once worked over there. But 'tis only a rumor."

"Thank you, sir. You've been most helpful."

"Nae matter. If you've a mind to get to the bottom of what goes on over there, I'll take you for nothing. When I took those government types, I charged enough to make up for a week's worth of catch. And they paid it too." He grinned. "Ian was a friend of mine, and if that place had anythin' to do with his disappearance, well . . ."

"I understand. Thanks, again."

Back in the room, Tyler called Hamish and reported what they'd found. Hamish said he'd drop everything and be there the next day.

CHAPTER 24

THE RAID

Ullapool, Scotland ~ February, Year 3

The morning after their arrival in Ullapool, Tyler and Brett were getting ready to go down for breakfast when Maeve knocked on the door. Tyler opened it to find both Maeve and Lisette.

"Something's happening outside," said Maeve. "We'd better go look."

The women followed behind and out of the building. A fire engine, its siren blaring, raced down the street to the right.

They trailed a dozen others from the hotel and restaurant away from the loch down Quay Street. After a hundred meters or so, they stopped before flames rising from a bungalow on the left. Fire engulfed the house, the evergreens, and the magnolia bushes surrounding it.

Standing with pistols at their belts and guarding a circle around the conflagration were what appeared to be CSA officers. The firemen had parked their vehicle across the street and were arguing with the CSA men. Some had hoses at the ready, but none were pouring water on the blaze.

A crowd had gathered in the middle of the street to watch, and Tyler addressed one of the women there. "What's going on?"

"They started the fire, they did." She waved at the CSA. "The bloody CSA did it, and now they won't let the firemen or the butts near the blaze."

"The butts?"

She waved. "For you Yanks, that's what we call a fire engine."

"That's crazy. Not letting the firemen do their job, I mean."

"Aye." She grinned. "Who do these people think they are?"

The flames were so intense, Tyler and the others in the crowd backed up.

One of the CSA men brought out a bullhorn. "Let this be a lesson to you." His words blasted above the roaring blaze. "This is what happens to those who spy on the Unitum Imperium and break the law. If anyone has any information about the woman named Moyra Thompson, the one who used to live in this house, we are passing out flyers with a number to call. There's a reward of a hundred thousand euros for information leading to her arrest."

Two of the CSA began passing out leaflets displaying a picture of a woman with long blonde hair. She didn't wear glasses. Half the crowd turned their backs or refused to accept them, and some crumpled up the papers as soon as they got them.

Then a young woman, about twenty-five, approached the man with the bullhorn. "This is my place now, and you've burned it up," she shouted. "I never knew this Moyra person, and you've destroyed all my things."

"Can't be helped." He lifted his bullhorn again. "This is what happens to anyone who's had any association with Moyra Thompson, past, present, or future. Let this be a lesson to you. Come forward with her whereabouts, and nothing like this will ever happen again."

For another thirty minutes, Tyler and the others watched the blaze until Brett said it was time for breakfast, and they started back.

"Did you notice something different about their uniforms?" asked Tyler. "They wore the same uniforms as at the checkpoint yesterday."

"What?" Brett cocked his head.

"Something wasn't quite right. I'm wondering if they were regular CSA."

"Looked no different to me," said Lisette.

"Normally, one of their badges has a skull and lightning bolt. Instead, they had a skull, *a sword*, and a lightning bolt."

Brett waved away his objection. "So what?"

"I don't know. I'm just saying that it was different. Also, their trousers were blue black, not green."

"I noticed that, but what difference does it make?" asked Maeve. "Maybe they dress differently up here."

"Maybe. I don't know. I'll ask Hamish when he gets here tonight."

"Do it," said Brett. "But right now, I'm famished."

CHAPTER 25

DELILAH'S REVENGE

Jerusalem, Israel ~ February, Year 3

Psalm 10:1–2, 4, 7–9, 11–12 (HCSB): *Lord, why do You stand so far away? Why do You hide in times of trouble? In arrogance the wicked relentlessly pursue the afflicted; let them be caught in the schemes they have devised. . . . In all his scheming, the wicked arrogantly thinks: "There is no accountability, since God does not exist." . . . Cursing, deceit, and violence fill his mouth; trouble and malice are under his tongue. He waits in ambush near the villages; he kills the innocent in secret places. His eyes are on the lookout for the helpless; he lurks in secret like a lion in a thicket. He lurks in order to seize the afflicted; he seizes the afflicted and drags him in his net . . . He says to himself, "God has forgotten; He hides His face and will never see." Rise up, Lord God! Lift up Your hand. Do not forget the afflicted.*

Nick Carter was late for the meeting. He'd been in the apartment reading the Psalms, pondering the nature of good and evil and the trap he'd gotten himself into. Because of it, he hadn't read today's agenda.

So when he entered the conference room on the tenth floor of the Clal Center, not only did he not know the meeting's subject, he was surprised at the number of high-profile attendees.

Already seated were: Dino Castiglione, head of the CSA under Turner; Pierre Girard, head of Undercover Operations; Renzo Trentino, recently appointed head of the Department of Public Joy; and François DesRoches, vice president of the Unitum Imperium.

Nick found a seat.

Moments later, Adam Turner entered and took the front. "For some of you, this will be the first you hear of this operation, something we're calling Delilah's Revenge. I will begin by expressing what the Imperator has been saying in private for some time—the Jews are a problem and must be brought to heel."

A few gasps came from behind, and Nick turned in his seat to find a frowning Pierre Girard.

"But he's given them the Temple," said Girard. "He's publicly proclaimed a treaty of peace. He's said he stands behind the Jewish people. Why this sudden change of heart?"

Turner waved a hand. "The Imperator has always believed that the Jews have been in league with the Enemy. What he did by giving them their Temple was only a pretext to lull them into complacency before finally bringing them to the end they deserve."

"I, too, can attest that there's been no change of heart." DesRoches's voice rose from across the table. "It has always been our intention to wipe them out. But first, we must create the proper environment. The public must not see us acting arbitrarily. That's what this meeting is about: setting the stage so we can carry out a program of extermination."

"I can't believe what I'm hearing," said Girard. "If what you say is true, this is a betrayal of trust on a massive scale."

Nick agreed with what Girard was saying, and he marveled at the man's bravery. But to voice such objections out loud, before the director, the vice president, and so many other high-ranking officials? Risky, indeed.

Turner scowled. "We will talk later, Girard. For now, just accept that this is the plan."

"We are with you," said DesRoches. "Please go on."

"Right." Turner stood to his full height, moved to the side, and nodded to a nonbinary in back who turned on a projector.

Three bullet points appeared on the screen, and Turner continued. "To begin discrediting the Jews, we will create a number of incidents to blame on them. As you see on the screen, the first involves some of you. We want as few people to know about this as possible. And besides"—he smiled—"it will be good for you to leave your offices and get a taste of how it is in the field."

Nick focused on the list for the first affair and gasped, for his name was on it.

Turner pointed to the first bullet. "Nick, you will lead this one, along with Girard and one of his operatives. It will happen a few days from now."

"But I'm not a field person," said Nick.

"I understand, but it will be good for you. Are you saying you won't do it?"

"No, of course I'll do it." But the heat was rising to his forehead. Was this some kind of test? Was he under suspicion?

"Those involved will wear Jewish disguises. Fake beards. Skullcaps. And those disgusting side curls—payots, I believe they're called. No one will recognize you. You will take Molotov cocktails to a local Truth Squad headquarters here in Jerusalem. You will break the windows and firebomb the place. You will throw Jewish leaflets outside on the street, blaspheming the Imperator and the Unitum Imperium. Cameras will catch it all. The next day, the news will spread across the world about this heinous act committed by the Jews."

"What if people are inside?" asked Nick.

"At that time of day, it will be empty. As will the buildings beside it. We'll make sure of it."

"This is outrageous." Girard was shaking his head. "Who thought up this plan?"

"I did." Turner crossed his arms and glared. "And you will carry it out as ordered."

For a moment, the head of Undercover Operations held Turner's stare before he melted and nodded.

"But that's just the beginning. One week after that, you, Girard, will again dress yourself in Jewish garb. In full view of the street cameras, you will plant a bomb in the center of a crowded market in Düsseldorf, Germany. Unfortunately, the explosion will kill a number of civilians. Shortly thereafter, our investigation will find the criminal—the head of a local synagogue. We will arrest him and hold him for trial. Once he's imprisoned, he will be unable to communicate with the outside world."

"You can't be serious!" protested Girard.

"Ah, but we are," responded Turner.

"Brilliant!" said Dino Castiglione. "But I don't understand your third operation up there."

"Ah, yes." Turner's smile widened. "A month later, another of Girard's operatives, also dressed in Jewish garb, will kidnap the son and daughter of the London mayor while he and his wife are attending a ball we have arranged. This act, too, will be caught on camera. The perpetrator will kill the servant of the house. Later, he will demand a ransom of two million euros and the release of the man who bombed the German market."

"Then what?" asked Castiglione.

"We will follow the kidnapper's directions, giving him what he wants. He will tell us how to find the mayor's children in underground caskets equipped with air holes. But when we go to rescue them, they will have suffocated. The outrage that will generate will turn the populace against these Jewish monsters."

"Brilliant, indeed!" added DesRoches. "What will happen to the kidnapper? Will we catch him?"

"We will modify the camera footage so it identifies a certain Jew in a London synagogue known for rabble-rousing. We will send police to arrest him, and, unfortunately, he will be shot and killed while attempting to escape."

"You have thought of everything." DesRoches beamed.

Nick raised a hand, and Turner called on him. "What will happen with the man being held for the German bombing?"

"He will be tried and executed within days of the last event."

Nick nodded, appearing to play along. But inwardly, he was sickened. He must think of some way to extricate himself from this insanity.

They were willing to sacrifice innocent German civilians and the children of London's mayor, all to create a false narrative and lay the groundwork for the eventual extermination of an entire race.

When the meeting adjourned, he left the building for a long walk in the fresh air.

To clear his head.

To fight the nausea building within him.

And to plan how he and Brooke could escape the grip of Turner, the Imperator, and the madness taking over his world.

CHAPTER 26

AN EXPEDITION

TO THE MOORS

Ullapool, Scotland ~ February, Year 3

It was an all-day drive from London to Ullapool, and Hamish and his rented Jeep didn't arrive until seven that evening. He was famished, so they met at the Arch Inn for supper.

When the waiter came for their orders, Tyler asked the man if a Fiona Duncan worked there.

"Aye, she does," said the waiter. "But this is her night off. What'll you have?"

Everyone ordered fish and chips and mugs of ale brewed locally by the Highland Liquor Company. While they waited for their food, Hamish turned to Tyler. "Tell me what you have learned about this secret base on the moors."

Tyler then related what the fisherman knew about the missing Ian Campbell and about the sign on an abandoned restaurant across the bay.

"The Ministry of Virtue?" Hamish rubbed his chin. "How odd. What could they possibly want with a base way out here in the middle of nowhere?"

"And why would they be stealing prisoners from the CSA? We should check it out."

"Aye, but I'm beat. Let's plan on going over tomorrow night. After dark."

"There's something else the fisherman mentioned—that a certain Fiona once worked for the base. That's why I asked the waiter about her."

"Interesting." He studied his mug. "After we go on our scouting mission, we'll interview her."

Their food and drinks arrived, and they ate. Then they made plans for tomorrow night.

* * *

THE NEXT DAY, AN HOUR after sunset, the fisherman motored Tyler, Hamish, Brett, and Maeve across the loch in a fog. Lisette decided to stay behind.

When they stepped from the trawler onto a rickety wooden dock, their pilot spat a wad of chewing tobacco into the water. "You have my number. When you're done with your spy work, give me a call, and I'll come for you. Haste ye back, now, hear?"

"We can't thank you enough," said Tyler.

"If you can get to the bottom of what goes on over there, it'll be thanks enough." The man pushed off from the dock and turned the ship, and as the fog swallowed it, the puttering of his engine faded into the night.

They wore sweatshirts and hiking shoes, and they carried walking sticks and flashlights. Hamish patted the pistol in its holster. "Let's hope we don't need this, but one can never be too careful."

Hamish led, and when they reached the abandoned restaurant, they found the sign announcing it was an outpost for the Ministry of Virtue with its warning that trespassers would be shot. The glass on the door was broken, and someone had blocked the window by nailing wooden slats on the inside. They followed the deck around the house's perimeter, but there were no lights on inside.

"Like the fisherman said, it's abandoned," said Brett.

"This isn't what we're looking for." Hamish headed back. "What we want is up on the moors. Let's go."

Beyond the house was a path leading to a foggy trail, and they began climbing.

"This fog is unusual," said Tyler. "There's no trace of moisture on the heather."

"And look how it stops a few feet above the ground," added Hamish.

"Could this be part of Eli's curse?" asked Maeve. "That there will be no rain, snow, or moisture falling on earth for six months?"

"Eli?" asked Hamish.

"Elijah," answered Tyler. "The man we escorted from Minnesota across the sea to Jerusalem. I think Maeve's right. What we have here is a fog that doesn't wet anything. Weird, indeed."

"Aye," said Hamish. "You told me about Elijah."

They climbed for forty minutes up a rock-strewn path. When they reached a plateau, they left the fog behind. Mountains rose on both sides of the valley. Forests of dry Scots pine covered the slopes on the right and left. A half-moon shed a yellow light upon a field dotted with heather. A dim glow came from the distant horizon. "That light must be coming from the base." Hamish waved them on.

There was no trail, so they traversed a field littered with dry, moss-covered rocks and heather. Lightning flashed from a single dark cloud on the horizon. Moments later, thunder rumbled past them.

"Can't be a storm," said Maeve. "The curse won't allow it."

Another forty minutes brought them to the edge of a slope. They dropped to their stomachs and peered at the scene below. Floodlights lit a black-stone castle, low outbuildings, and a helicopter on its pad. Surrounding the compound was a high chain-link fence topped with razor wire. Five towers rose from the castle's battlements.

"We found it," Tyler whispered. "A Ministry of Virtue base, hidden in the Lochbroom Highlands. That's where they must be keeping Aurora."

For some moments, he stared at the towers, the wire, the helicopter pad. Down there, somewhere beneath that black stone, Aurora was a prisoner. How long had it been now? Over two weeks? What were they doing to her? Was she in good health?

The prison was well defended. How could they ever free her from such a place?

Far below, two uniformed men patrolled the grounds. They carried machine guns and led Doberman pinschers on leashes.

"It's heavily guarded." Hamish shook his head. "This will be difficult."

"So now what do we do?" asked Maeve.

"Let's speak with the waitress at the restaurant," said Hamish. "Maybe she's got information that can help us. Without her—"

But the chattering of helicopter blades broke the valley's stillness as the copter rose from its pad. It was headed their way.

Hamish glanced to both sides. "Over there!" He pointed right. "Under those pines."

They pulled back from the edge and ran over the rocks toward a grove of Scots pines.

The pulsing whoop-whoop-whoop of the blades came closer.

Just as Tyler dove into the shadows of the pines, he glanced back to see the machine rising over the plateau behind.

When they were sheltered inside the grove, he slowed his breathing and peered at the aircraft as it headed east.

"Laddies, that was close," said Maeve. "Me heart is pumping crazy wild."

"Aye, lass," added Hamish. "As soon as it's gone, let's get back to Ullapool. I could use a mug of something right now."

"I'll go along with that," said Brett.

CHAPTER 27

FIONA DUNCAN

Ullapool, Scotland ~ February, Year 3

By the time they returned to Ullapool, they had an hour and a half before the Arch Inn closed. They cleaned up, Lisette joined them, and they walked the short distance to the restaurant and pub. The man greeting customers at the door was short and stocky with a full red beard and a mop of reddish hair. Hamish asked him if Fiona was serving tonight.

"And who might be doing the asking?" He looked askance at them.

"Friends," said Hamish. "We don't work for the government."

"You don't look like government types. In that case, then aye, she's over there." The man pointed to a woman across the room, about twenty-five, with short, black hair, wearing black-rimmed glasses.

"Could you seat us at one of her tables, sir?"

"I can do that. Please follow me."

He led them to a table, but before Hamish sat, he faced the manager. "If it's all right with you, we'd like to talk with Fiona for a bit on a matter of urgent personal business." He pulled a fifty-euro note from his pocket and held it up. "We would greatly appreciate a moment of her time."

The manager looked at the bill, at Hamish, then pocketed the bill. "It's slow tonight. I'll send her over."

Moments later, she appeared beside them. "Oliver says you want to chat me up." Her glance shifted to the door and back. "You don't work for . . . the government . . . do you?"

They all laughed. "No," said Tyler.

"Okay, then." She breathed out, but Tyler sensed she was uneasy. "I guess it's all right. Could I get you something first?"

With everyone's permission, Tyler ordered two shrimp appetizers and mugs of Tennent's Lager for all.

Nodding, she went to the bar.

Moments later, she returned with a tray of mugs. She set one before each of them. "Now, what is this about?"

"Would you sit for a bit?" asked Hamish.

"I suppose. Oliver said it was okay." She sat. "But why chat with me?"

Hamish cleared his throat and wrapped big hands around his mug. "We understand you once worked at a government facility across the peninsula."

Her eyebrows scrunched together, and her glance again shot to the door as though she were ready to bolt. "There's nae a thing across that loch over there but elk, boar, and heather."

"We know differently, miss," said Tyler. "We were there tonight and saw the compound you say doesn't exist."

She gasped, and her eyes widened. "Nae, nae, you must nae go there. If they found you, they . . ."

"They would—what?" asked Hamish.

"They would kill you. And if I said anything about what goes on over there, they'd find me and kill me too."

"So you *did* work over there?" continued Hamish. "And you are Moyra Thompson, the one whose former house the government goons recently burned down."

Tyler shot him a surprised look.

She started to rise from the chair, but Hamish raised a hand. "We're on your side, lass. We'll keep your secret."

Startled doe eyes scanned the group and settled on Maeve.

"Aye, lass," said Maeve. "We'll keep your secret. It will be all right."

Fiona slumped into the chair and closed her eyes. "You guessed it. They dinnae know I'm here. I escaped—and aye, I had to escape to get out. I changed my name, my hair, and I wear these glasses now. I should've gone to Inverness. Anywhere but here. But then they put up that checkpoint."

"We won't tell anyone." Hamish lowered his voice. "But we were hoping you could give us some information. Maybe we can help you get away."

She cocked her head. "Who are you people anyway? And why are you poking your noses into something that could get us all killed?"

As Lisette listened, she had been leaning forward, and now she spoke up. "Because we think they've got a good friend of ours over there."

"She's my sister." Tyler gripped Brett's shoulder. "And his."

"Oh, I see." Fiona closed her eyes and covered her mouth with both hands. "I'm sorry."

"Why sorry?" asked Brett. "Because they've imprisoned Christians over there?"

"Aye. In the dungeon." She glanced up. "But they would nae let me down there. I was only allowed in the kitchen."

"They have a dungeon?" asked Maeve.

"That's what I'd call it. They paid me well—more than thrice the wages I get here. But it were an evil place." Fiona clasped both hands together, her fingers intertwining, releasing, then gripping themselves again. "I could sense it in the air, in the looks the people gave when I took the food cart to the top of the steps—stone steps leading down into the dark. I cooked their food, but others, nae me, brought it down to whoever they've got locked up down there."

"What kind of looks?" As the girl turned her gaze, Maeve's eyes caught hers.

"The kind you get after you see a thing that no one on earth should ever see."

The manager interrupted, bringing two bowls of shrimp with cocktail sauce, and he set it before them. "Everything okay here, Fiona?"

She nodded, and he left. Then she began to push away from the table. "Okay. I've told you what you wanted. That's enough."

"Wait." Hamish laid a hand on her arm. "Could you tell us a bit more about what goes on over there? Your information could help us. You see—" He released her arm, scowled, and took a deep breath. "We want to mount an escape."

"We're going to free my sister," added Tyler.

"What?" She gasped. "But that's impossible. You'd have nae a ghost of a chance. You'll get yourselves killed."

"Not if we get the information we need." Hamish plopped a shrimp in his mouth.

She swept her gaze along the table, landing on each of them. "You're serious. You're bloody, crazy serious."

"We are, lass." Maeve eyed the bottom of her glass. "And you wouldn't believe what we've been through and done so far."

"All right. All right. I'll tell you what I know. I dinnae know if any of it will help, but if it might, then I'll tell you."

"Good." Then Hamish asked how they brought in new prisoners.

She began by saying she was never allowed to see who they brought in, but she told them how she first entered the compound. "They drove me in a Jeep from Edinburgh. On the other side of the peninsula, they took the A832 going north. A secondary road comes off it, one of many. You have to go over a hill until you see a high fence. There's a gate across the road, but it's locked. And there's a warning sign. Some kilometers later, another dirt track heads off across the moors. It's little more than a cow path and easy to miss. And it's bumpy."

"How did you get that job in the first place?" asked Lisette.

"I answered an ad in the paper. They interviewed me, but I'd call it more of an interrogation. It were intense. And when they told me I'd have to live at a top-secret government compound and nae be allowed to leave for a year, and when they said that if I spilled any of their secrets the consequences would be severe, I almost dinnae take the job. But the pay was too good to pass up—three times any wage I ever received."

"We've seen helicopters pass overhead," said Brett. "What do they do with them?"

"Security owns the copters." Fiona crossed her arms. "They're nae for bringing in the 'patients' as they call them."

"Patients?" Maeve squinted.

"Aye." Fiona swallowed. "They do experiments on the prisoners. I know because I took meals to Dr. Creig in one of the towers. I've been inside his laboratory to deliver his tray, and it's creepy in there. Once, I brought his food too early, and he shouted through the door that I should leave the tray outside. The food were going to get cold, but I obeyed. But then, before I went down the spiral staircase, I heard screams from inside the room."

"Screams?" Tyler clattered his glass on the table and shot a worried glance to Brett.

"Aye. Like I said, the place were evil, and that doctor were part of it."

"We saw a sign at Alltnaharrie saying it was part of the Ministry of Virtue. Can you tell us who runs the compound?"

"Alltnaharrie?" Again, her gaze scanned the group. "You should nae have gone there. The director who runs Castle Danger is Fergus McDuff, but I hardly ever saw him. Wallace Sloan is his right-hand man. Calls himself a special agent."

"Castle Danger? That's what it's called?" asked Brett. "Like the beer."

"I dinnae know anything about a beer, but that's the name."

Hamish quizzed her for a few more minutes, gathering up more tidbits of information before thanking her. Then he laid a hundred-euro bill on the table. "For all your help."

"Thank you! 'Tis appreciated." She pocketed the money then headed for the kitchen.

When they were alone again, Hamish turned to the others. "Tomorrow, I'm going to call our people in Inverness. It may take them some time to gather what we need. If they can get what I want, then with Fiona's information, I have a plan."

CHAPTER 28

WARNINGS

Jerusalem, Israel ~ February, Year 3

Following Turner's explicit directions, Nick arrived early in the first-floor lobby to wait for Pierre Girard. Footsteps echoed across the vast space as the ground-floor restaurant leaked the smells of lamb cooking on a rotisserie. But that eatery was not their destination. He and Girard were heading for Machneyuda, a nearby restaurant where Adam Turner awaited.

But Nick still puzzled over Turner's orders. He was to meet Girard here, in the lobby, then walk with him, leading him on a certain route, and only that route, to Machneyuda.

Those arrangements weren't the only thing weighing on him this afternoon.

Ever since the meeting yesterday, Nick had prodded and poked at every idea he could think of, searching for a way he and Brooke could flee the country. If only he could return to the States—but showing up at an airport for an overseas destination was out of the question. Security going out of the country was now over-the-top.

Brooke had to know what was happening, so yesterday he'd taken her to a nearby park to discuss it. And that conversation still reverberated through his head.

* * *

It had been late afternoon when they sat on a bench, shivering in the wind. A cold front had moved in, and he was glad he'd worn a jacket.

"You're telling me they want to start killing the Jews, but first they want to make it look like they're terrorists?"

"That's about the size of it."

The wind rolled a pile of crinkled, dried-up leaves toward their feet. Ever since the Two Witnesses had declared the drought, everything was drying up and dying. Not just the trees, but his prospects for a safe and peaceful life.

"And they want to involve you in this, this—what would you call it?"

"A false flag operation. If I don't do what they tell me to, well—" He closed his eyes. "I have no choice. Either I do it, or we'll both end up in prison."

"Can we leave?" She gripped his right hand.

He opened his eyes and caught her glance. "Yes. But that's not as easy as it sounds. I'd like to go back to Minnesota, but . . . but no. I'd never get a travel pass for the US. They're restricting all overseas travel now. And without that pass, they'd pick us up on the other end the moment we stepped off the plane. If we stay in Jerusalem, they'll find us for sure. We have to leave the country."

"So where do we go?" She squeezed his hand tighter. Her forehead wrinkled, and worry lines appeared. He loved her. And after seeing that kind of fear and uncertainty grip her, the desire to protect her welled up, but mixed with anger at how he'd let this happen.

"I'm not sure. Maybe Italy. We both speak Italian—well, you do somewhat, and I'll begin lessons to make you fluent. We could blend in with the people there. And it was my home country." He stared across the park. "Once. A long time ago."

A long time ago. Back before Davato, the Unitum Imperium, the Truth Squads, the Central Security Agency, and the Sixth-Day Celebrations. Back before evil had taken over the planet.

"I'm scared, Nick. What are we going to do?"

He grasped her arms. "It will be all right." He leaned over and kissed her forehead. "I'll think of something."

But as they walked back to the Clal Center, he had no idea what that something might be.

* * *

"HEY, NICK, AM I LATE?"

Startled, he turned to find Pierre Girard beside him. "No, I guess I'm early. Let's go."

They pushed through the revolving doors onto the sidewalk and waited with others to cross the street. When the light changed, they crossed.

"I'm not happy with the plan we heard yesterday." Girard was still dwelling on their roles in it, and Nick couldn't blame him.

"Neither am I, but you can't be saying the things you're saying, Pierre. It's not safe."

"Someone has to say something."

"Maybe, but it's risky. You know what's happened to dissenters." Nick stepped aside as an old woman with a cane approached. What was with all the people out today?

"I do know, but I'm disgusted. If Davato plans to kill the Jews, I want nothing to do with it."

Nick shot him a glance. "I'm with you, but what can we do? How can we refuse to do what they order? You know what will happen to us."

They came to a busy intersection where the trams were speeding by, and they stopped.

"I know." Girard wiped his brow and stared straight ahead. "I know."

A man wearing sunglasses, a floppy hat, and a floor-length trench coat appeared behind Girard. Nick thought he recognized the man. He was about to say something when the man put a finger to his lips, shook his head, and mouthed, "No."

Was that a warning? Puzzled, Nick faced the street again. Another odd thing in a sequence of odd events. Who was this man, and why was he following them?

The squealing and clicking of tram wheels rushed toward them. Apparently, this wasn't one of its stops. It was going too fast.

What happened next was a dream, a hallucination, a nightmare.

Girard leaped from the sidewalk onto the tram's path.

Metal slammed into flesh and flung the body onto the tracks ahead.

The tram's brakes squealed, but too late—heavy metal sliced into flesh and bone.

There was blood and gore, and people screamed.

Nick glanced aside in time to see the man in the trench coat fleeing into the crowd.

A nearby policeman blew a whistle as the tram slowed. The crowd beside him erupted in horrified exclamations. Some pointed to where the mystery man had fled, but he was gone.

Girard was dead, and nausea swirled in Nick's stomach.

He'd been an unwitting patsy, hadn't he? He'd led Girard straight to this busy intersection, straight to an assassin.

He whirled and hurried back the way he'd come.

That Turner had used him in this way was troubling. Was this, too, some kind of warning? First, there were the interrogations. Then the orders to firebomb a Truth Squad headquarters.

Now this!

Somehow, he had to find a way to leave the country.

CHAPTER 29

THE FRIENDS OF INVERNESS

Near Inverness, Scotland ~ March, Year 3

1 Thessalonians 5:1–11 (HCSB):

About the times and the seasons: Brothers, you do not need anything to be written to you. For you yourselves know very well that the Day of the Lord will come just like a thief in the night. When they say, "Peace and security," then sudden destruction comes on them, like labor pains come on a pregnant woman, and they will not escape. But you, brothers, are not in the dark, for this day to overtake you like a thief. For you are all sons of light and sons of the day. We do not belong to the night or the darkness. So then, we must not sleep, like the rest, but we must stay awake and be serious. For those who sleep, sleep at night, and those who get drunk are drunk at night. But since we belong to the day, we must be serious and put the armor of faith and love on our chests and put on a helmet of the hope of salvation. For God did not appoint us to wrath, but to obtain salvation through our Lord Jesus Christ, who died for us, so that whether we are awake or asleep, we will live together with Him. Therefore encourage one another and build each other up as you are already doing.

On the first day of March, Tyler drove the VW with Hamish sitting in front. Because of the checkpoint outside of Ullapool, it seemed safer if the others stayed behind.

"They waved us through," said Hamish. "But in the car ahead of us, they asked for the women's IDs. Apparently, this checkpoint is only for Moyra Thompson."

"Our waitress at the Arch Inn. Let's hope no one recognizes her."

"Some of the townsfolk must know. But 'Sympathy for the Devil' doesn't play well around here. I'm glad most of them are on the right side of this."

"Let's hope they all are."

Beyond the checkpoint, it was good to be moving again, to hear the hum of tires over asphalt, and to see deer and elk foraging in the dry fields. The trip to Inverness took a little over an hour.

In the center of town, they turned left on the A82 and drove for another twenty minutes. Low, forested mountains rose on both sides, and traffic was sparse.

Hamish looked up from the GPS on his phone. "Turn right at the next road and go up the mountain."

Tyler took the turn up a winding road of crumbling asphalt between groves of birch and oak that bore a few crumpled, dried-up leaves. It was winter, but the drought was taking a heavy toll on the forests.

Ten minutes later, Hamish directed him onto a bumpy dirt road. Less than a kilometer after the turn, the drive ended at a low brick building. Ten cars were parked under the trees alongside the drive.

"I thought we were going to pick up supplies." Tyler's hands slid from the steering wheel. "What's with all the cars?"

Smiling, Hamish left the vehicle, and Tyler followed. "I have a surprise waiting for you. Trust me."

Hamish knocked.

A gray-haired woman opened the door. "What stands against the darkness?"

"Friends," answered Hamish.

"And where does the light come from?" she asked.

"The eternal Son. I'm Hamish, and you must be Senga."

She smiled. "Aye, Rory is expecting you. Follow me. We're about to start."

Hamish led them down a hallway into a large open room occupied by eight men and five women.

What was going on?

A tall man with wavy red hair, brown-framed glasses, and a twinkle in his eyes rushed forward, reaching a hand in greeting. "Hamish, my friend! It's been too long."

A smiling Hamish took the hand. They shook. Then they hugged. When they parted, Hamish introduced Tyler. "He will accompany me on this mission to Castle Danger."

Everyone in the room thanked Tyler for his part in the mission, and Rory's left hand grasped Tyler's. A bandage wrapped the fingers of his right hand.

"They have my sister." Tyler's glance swept the room. "My brother and I and two of our friends will do what we must to get her back."

Rory placed his bandaged hand on Tyler's shoulder. "If at all possible, we hope to free her and more besides."

Would they help free the entire compound? Was it possible? Tyler's heart surged.

Grabbing a notebook, Rory went to the front, took a guitar from its stand in the corner, frowned, and set it back down.

As one woman passed out song sheets, Rory waved his bandaged fingers. "Sorry about this. If my hand hadn't slipped on that wrench, I could have played today. I guess, we'll have to sing a cappella."

Tyler whispered in Hamish's ear. "This is a church service, isn't it?"

"You guessed it, laddie."

He glanced at the two songs on the sheets. He knew the chords printed there, and he raised a hand. "Maybe I can help."

"Can you play?" Rory's eyes lit up.

"Been a while, but yes."

His host beckoned him forward and handed over the guitar. Tyler found the pick, tuned the strings, and placed the song sheet on the music stand. As Rory hummed the melody, Tyler ran through the chords of the first bar. When he was ready, he nodded.

"With the help of our guest"—Rory sent Tyler a grin—"we'll start with the oldest known hymn in existence. It's Irish, possibly from St. Patrick's day, but I think we can forgive where it came from."

Laughter spread through the group.

Rory nodded to Tyler. While he played, the group sang.

"Be thou my vision, O Lord of my heart. Naught be all else to me, save that Thou art . . ."

On the next song, "May the God of Peace Go with Us", Tyler needed Rory to hum a few bars before discovering the tune. It had been years since he'd picked up a guitar, and it felt good to press his fingers on the chords and draw a pick across the strings. By the end of the song, he even hammered a few of the notes.

The song ended and Tyler sat.

Then Rory placed his notebook on the music stand.

"My message today is from First Thessalonians five, verses one through eleven." He read the verses before facing his audience again.

"We all missed the Day of the Lord. And, aye, we were fools back then, but we've since repented and found our way to the light, out of the dark. Because of the gospel, we are new creations. Instead of being fools, we have become wise. Instead of a future in death and darkness, we have joined the land of the living and the light. Indeed, we call ourselves the Friends of Light.

"The passage says we must put on faith and love as a breastplate. What's a breastplate? It's a hard, defensive barrier worn on the chest to stave off the blows of the Adversary, the one called the Dragon, the one we call Satan. And he's got plenty of minions to do his bidding—the Antichrist, and the false prophet who rules the Ministry of Virtue, a misnomer if ever there was."

He paused for a deep breath before continuing. "Our helmet, another defense against the darkness, is our hope of salvation. For no matter what happens to us in this world, we are assured of a blessed eternity in the next."

He went on and on. Because they'd missed the Day of the Lord, he reminded them they were living through a wrath meant only for unbelievers. But now, even though it was too late, they had given their hearts, minds, and souls to the Lord of lords and King of kings. They had become God's light in a world of darkness.

"So let us do what we can to support and pray for Hamish, for Tyler and his brother, sister, and their friends. Our hope is that this plan to infiltrate the castle on the Lochbroom peninsula will succeed. We will swing a sword of light against that place of darkness and evil, against those who would persecute our brothers and sisters in the faith and hold them prisoner."

Then, one after another, the circle of Friends prayed for the mission's success. And when they were done, Tyler was comforted and buoyed by their faith and the knowledge that their prayers had risen to God and that the Lord was behind them.

Rory dismissed the others then turned to the newcomers. "And now, Tyler Carter, let us see what kind of equipment we have for you."

While the others were leaving, Tyler and Hamish followed their host to a back room where cartons of supplies lined the shelves. Rory led them to a large box the contents of which, according to him, were collected by accomplices in London after various interceptions. Inside were Ministry of Virtue uniforms, high-peaked hats, a box full of C-4, detonators, timers, and sidearms—Glock 17s with 9mm ammunition. Rory also gave them backpacks.

"We lost our Bible in Geneva," said Tyler. "Do you have another for us?"

"Certainly." Rory lifted a Bible from the shelf and added it to the box.

"Do you know how to use this?" Tyler squeezed a wad of C-4.

"I do, and I'll teach you when we get back."

He tried on several uniforms until he found one that fit. He strapped on a pistol belt and shoved the Glock into its holster.

Rory held up two smart cards and shiny badges. "We were able to borrow the badges and IDs of several Ministry of Virtue officials after they disrobed to visit a certain London brothel." He grinned. "After Hamish sent us your pictures, we created new IDs and badges for both of you."

Tyler pinned on his badge and stepped to a mirror. "I look like a Nazi SS officer."

"It becomes you." Hamish grinned.

"It doesn't become me." Tyler frowned.

"That's good, my friend," added Rory. "Not that it will go to your head, but that the enemy might accept you as one of their own. But do you know what kind of uniforms and IDs we have procured for you?"

Both Hamish and Tyler shook their heads.

"These are uniforms of the Ministry of Virtue and badges for the Office of Internal Affairs. It seems every one of Davato's ministries has something like this, some kind of extra-official unit to monitor and spread fear into the hearts of his minions. You report directly to the Prophet himself, and when he sends internal affairs agents on a mission, the object of their inquiries never knows when or how or why they are targeted." He winked. "To come across these is a stroke of luck. Or should I say divine providence? It's absolutely perfect."

"Since they're only checking female travelers leaving Ullapool," said Hamish, "we should be fine with this stuff in the trunk."

"When do you plan on going in?" Rory asked Hamish.

"Soon. Our first venture will be to plant a cache with some of this stuff on the moors near the castle. We can't carry it on our first encounter. We'll have to sneak out and bring it back in when we're ready."

"Everyone here will be praying for you." Rory slapped Hamish's shoulder.

"We'll need all the prayers we can get."

They packed everything into the box, took it to the car, said their goodbyes, and started the trip back to Ullapool.

"We should be back in time for supper," said Hamish.

CHAPTER 30

THE INTERROGATION

Jerusalem, Israel ~ March, Year 3

As he watched his target through the one-way glass of the Clal Center's interrogation room number 6, Finn sucked on his third cigarette. Today, he had high expectations that he could finally implicate one of the Carters in crimes against the Unitum Imperium.

His subject had now been waiting for thirty minutes, enough time for anxiety to creep in, possibly even alarm. A long wait was always good to instill fear in a subject.

"At last! We've got one, haven't we?" Standing beside him, Hugo grinned. "Will I be able to have a go at him?"

"Not this time. The man in there is a high-level employee of Adam Turner. We have to tread carefully today."

"Of course. Just kidding."

"I know what you'd like to do, and so would I. But not this time." Finn dropped the last cigarette to the floor and stubbed it out with his shoe. "Time to go in."

He left the observation room, turned the corner, and entered the interrogation chamber. One wall held one-way glass. The other walls were barren. Above, fluorescents hummed and shed a harsh light.

Finn sat across the table from Nick Carter, pulled another cigarette from its pack, and lit it.

"Who are you?" asked Carter. "And why has the IDS brought me to an interrogation room?"

"My name is Finn Foster, and I have been authorized by the Ministry of Truth to ask you some questions about certain questionable activities you have been involved in."

He had no intention of revealing who he really was, and Carter didn't seem to recognize him. Finn was wearing the uniform of the feared IDS. He wore his hair shorter now. And after he examined his face in the mirror last week, he was shocked by how much he'd aged. His skin appeared weathered, even though he rarely went out in the sun. Was it from the smoking? Or the whiskey? In any event, his uncle didn't realize his nephew now stood before him.

Carter narrowed his eyes and placed both hands on the table. "Do you not know who I am, Finn Foster? I work directly under your boss, and both of us are many, many levels higher than you."

Finn had expected this, but not so early. "I'm aware of your position. So is the director. In fact, it was he who asked me, personally, to meet you here in Jerusalem and take over this interview. I came from Ullapool, Scotland, waiting for permission to take your daughter, Aurora Carter, prisoner. For some time, we have been searching for her. She was arrested by another department and is being held on charges of conspiracy against the Unitum Imperium. But this interview concerns you, Nick Carter, not her. And the director deemed it important enough to bring me back here to do it."

That brought the reaction he'd been hoping for—a tightening of the jaws, a widening of the eyes, a quickening of the breath.

"What does that have to do with me? My daughter's affairs are not mine."

"Possibly, but we have evidence pointing at you, not your children. A Bible, for instance."

Carter's eyes widened further, and he sat back. "What Bible?"

"Don't play dumb with me, Carter. You know very well what I'm talking about. When you and your lover were out, we found a Bible in your apartment. That alone is enough to send an ordinary man to the camp. But you, of course, are not an ordinary man."

At first, Carter didn't answer, perhaps stunned that they'd searched his apartment.

Finn sucked on his cigarette and blew smoke across the table.

"I bought the Bible so I could understand who we're up against. It was research."

His answer came too late, surely an excuse, but Finn had more cards to play. "That's not the only thing we've got on you."

Was that sweat forming on Carter's forehead now? Good. The day was going well.

"Whatever you think you have," said Carter, "I'd like to hear it. I've been nothing but a loyal supporter of Davato, the director, and the Ministry of Truth. If you're trying to frame me, you'd better tread carefully, or it's you who might get the worst from this affair."

Finn smiled. "What I have is a recording of a conversation you had with Pierre Girard right before his unfortunate accident."

That got another reaction. Was that fear in Carter's eyes now? He had no idea that the man they'd sent to take out Girard had followed close behind the two men from the moment they left the Clal Center. And he was wearing a highly sensitive mic. From a pocket, Finn brought out a pocket player and pressed a button.

Carter's conversation with Girard played, ending with this incriminating statement from Carter: "I'm with you, but what can we do? How can we refuse to do what they order? You know what will happen to us."

Finn shut off the recording, sat back, and started another cigarette. For a time, he stared at his subject, trying to keep glee from crossing his lips. "It's enough to send you away, I think."

"I don't think so."

"Maybe. Maybe not." He blew smoke across the table. "Adam Turner has heard this, and he wants to wait. He still has faith in you, but it's hanging by a thread. Tomorrow, you are scheduled to participate in the first of several operations discrediting the Jews and turning the population against them. As if that was necessary." He laughed. "The director wants to see your loyalty in action, not in words. But I would like to see a bit more from you. Because I know you're a traitor, Nick Carter. You and your entire family have been working against the Unitum Imperium, and every last one of you should be in prison."

"That's enough!" Carter pounded the table with two fists and leaned forward. "This interview is over. Your tape proves nothing. You'd better be careful, Foster, because, no matter what you think you've got, you've just overstepped your bounds."

Now it was Finn's turn to fear. Maybe he had gone too far. Turner wasn't completely sold on Carter's guilt. He wondered if Carter was just playing along with Girard in that conversation. Turner had been upset over the tape, surely, but he wasn't ready to put the man away.

Carter shot out of his seat, headed for the door, then whirled to face him. "People in my position, Foster, have levers and tools at their disposal to do what they want with people like you. For your own good, I would stop this inquiry at once."

Then he left the room.

Finn stepped out and watched Carter stride to the elevator. No interrogation had ever ended like this. Surely, Carter was bluffing. The evidence Finn had was more than enough to put an ordinary man away.

But then doubt crept in. He was playing a dangerous game with someone in such a high position as Carter's. Would the man really be able to strike back against his accuser?

* * *

AFTER NICK LEFT THE INTERROGATION, he didn't return to work. Instead, he called Brooke and said to meet him in the park at the same bench where they'd talked before. Before she arrived, he paced, slammed a fist into a palm, and wiped his brow. He'd been bluffing with his interrogator, of course. He didn't know how to stop what looked like a solid case against him.

"Nick, what's wrong?"

When he faced Brooke, he closed his eyes and shook his head. "We have to get out, and fast. I was just interrogated by someone from the IDS, and it didn't go well. They found the Bible in the apartment, and they have a recording that incriminates me."

She slapped both hands over her mouth. "Oh no!"

"What's worse is that I'm scheduled to participate in their false flag operation tomorrow, and I can't get out of it."

"You're going to do it?"

"I don't want to. But I don't know how to avoid it." He whirled, took a few steps, then returned. "We've got to leave. But not tomorrow. First, I need a plan for how to get away without getting caught."

She ran to him, and he wrapped his arms around her. "What will become of us, Nick? I'm scared."

He kissed her neck and pulled her closer. "It will be all right. I'll find a way."

But as they walked back to the Clal Center, he didn't yet have a plan.

CHAPTER 31

THE CAVE

Lochbroom, Scotland ~ March, Year 3

It was a night without fog, and Tyler and Hamish motored across the loch in the fisherman's trawler. Above, geese honked as their silhouettes passed a sliver of moon hanging over the bay.

When they left the boat for the creaking wooden dock, the man faced them. "For whatever mischief you're about to inflict on the bampots up there, I wish you all the luck. Haste ye back, lads."

Hamish thanked him. Then they switched on their flashlights and headed for the trail. On his back was a knapsack holding the gear for the cache. In their hands, they carried hiking poles. Once again, they climbed a dry and rocky path between crumbling heather and boulders until they reached the plateau. Tonight, the moon was a mere sliver, and as they made their way across the rock-strewn plain, the footing was treacherous in the dim light.

As before, the horizon glowed with floodlights from the compound. When they reached the edge of the slope, they again dropped to their chests and peered into the valley below.

But from somewhere on their left came the sound of barking dogs.

"Somebody's patrolling outside the base." Hamish waved to the left. "We'd better find a place for our cache and get back."

"Right."

Hamish led them into the grove of Scots pines clinging to the slope on their right. But the needles were yellow, and everything was dry. Within the thicket, the ground was rocky, interspersed with trees, boulders, and brittle heather. About fifty meters up a gentle slope, Tyler spotted an opening between the rocks. He approached and peered inside a dark hole. "It's a cave, I think."

"Aye, perfect for our supplies."

The entrance was barely big enough for one person to enter. Hamish crawled in first, and Tyler followed. Inside, the passage broadened, and the pungent smell of some wild animal accosted Tyler's nostrils.

"Badger? Or fox?" Hamish held his nose. "Doesn't matter. They shouldn't bother our gear."

They placed the backpack with the explosives, timer, ammunition, and pistols in a corner behind a stalagmite. Before they left, Tyler squinted into the darkness beyond. The cavern continued into the hill, and he saw no end to it.

They backtracked to the plateau, but as they were about to leave the pine grove, men's voices echoed from across the ledge, and Hamish brought them to a halt. Moments later, two figures appeared about a hundred meters away.

"A patrol," whispered Hamish. "And they've got dogs. We'd better hide in the cave."

"What if the dogs catch our scent?"

Hamish shot him a worried look. "Let's hope they don't."

But as they hurried back over the rocks, Tyler tripped and fell. When he stood again, pain shot up from his ankle. "I think I've sprained it."

"Tyler, we've got to get to the cave, or they'll find us!"

"Right. Keep going. I'll be okay." The walking sticks helped, but even with those, each step was more painful than the one before. How was he going to make the long trek back down the mountain to the boat?

The sound of dogs barking rose behind him, and he hobbled after Hamish, who was now far ahead.

"The dogs've got a scent!" came a voice from far back in the pines. "Could be someone's out here."

"If true, the dogs'll find them," responded a deeper voice.

"And if you dinnae keep them under control, they'll make a mess of whoever it is, and we'll nae discover what they're doing out here."

The barking rose in pitch. They had Dobermans, dogs bred for fighting with teeth powerful enough to rip through clothes and muscle.

He was leaning heavily on the poles now. Grimacing, he hurried toward the cave mouth where Hamish was pacing and wringing his hands.

Before Tyler arrived, Hamish crawled in first.

On his knees, Tyler crawled in after him.

"I've got the pack." Hamish's voice echoed, and his light shone into a wider passage beyond. "Let's go in as far as we can."

Nodding, Tyler followed into a rock room where dry stalactites dropped from above but failed to reach the stalagmites rising from the cave floor.

Two paths led off from the cavern, and they took the left turn. But ten meters later, the passage ended.

Hamish sat and switched off his light. Tyler did the same, plunging them into darkness.

Moments later, barking echoed down from the opening, and the dim beam of a flashlight played in the cave room beyond their tunnel.

After his race from the plain, Tyler was breathing heavily, but he doubted anyone could hear him back here.

"It's only a badger hole," echoed a man's voice from the cavern. "The dogs're chasin' a bloody badger."

"Aye, stinks like a badger in here," said a deeper voice.

Someone whistled, and the dogs stopped barking. There was faint scuffling by the cave entrance. And then . . . silence.

Minutes passed in the dark before Hamish again switched on his light. "We'll give them time to be gone then try to get you back. Can you walk?"

Tyler rubbed his ankle and nodded. "I'll be all right. I can walk."

They waited half an hour before Hamish scouted past the entrance and returned with news that the patrol had gone. Then they made the trek back across the moor.

The fisherman was waiting, and he brought them back across the loch. And after Hamish placed a hundred-euro note in his hands, the man thanked them.

At the hotel, Tyler showered, and Lisette bandaged his ankle.

The group then met at the Arch Inn a half hour before closing and ordered a round of ale.

"Now, we'll have to wait for your ankle to heal," said Hamish.

"Sorry about this." Tyler sipped from his mug. "That's the second time we were nearly caught out there."

"Aye." Hamish drank his ale. "They're keeping a close eye on things beyond the compound. 'Tis risky business we're about."

"Whatever we have to do to get Aurora out of there," said Lisette, "we have to do."

CHAPTER 32

THE FALSE FLAG OPERATION

Jerusalem, Israel ~ March, Year 3

Nick stood before the mirror in the staging house and examined his disguise. Glasses were perched on his nose. A curly black beard covered his face. False payots—those long corkscrew strings of hair worn by orthodox Jews—fell beside both ears. A white shirt, dark pants, and a skullcap completed his outfit.

Beside him, Amato, his Italian companion from Undercover Operations, was similarly dressed. After Girard's death, Turner decreed that only two were needed for tonight's operation.

"No one will recognize you, sir," said the shorter man.

"No." He left the mirror and picked up the backpack they'd filled for him. "I look like an orthodox Jew. So do you. But is it too obvious?"

"That's the point, isn't it?"

"I suppose." He checked his watch. It was nearly midnight, and everyone at the Truth Squad headquarters, their target tonight, should have left for the day.

He swallowed and wiped his brow. They were watching him, and he had to go through with this. His plan to leave the country was not quite ready. But now, it was time to go.

They left the building for the street, empty but for a few passing cars. At this hour, even the trams weren't running. The quakes had shattered half the city's streetlights, but tonight, a fragment of moon cast a dim silver beam over the dark alleyways, barely lighting their way.

They turned down a side street still cluttered with bricks. Except for some less-traveled lanes like this one, workers had cleaned the rubble from the center of most major thoroughfares.

At the end of the block, they turned a corner. The Truth Squad building would be just ahead on the right, one of many in the city.

His heart sped up. He needed to get this over with and get home.

Their target was the ground floor of a three-story stone structure. Once holding a tobacconist, now it was headquarters for a Truth Squad.

Posters filled its plate-glass front. One declared the greatness of the Imperator. A second showed the Dragon in the center, Davato on the right, and the Prophet on the left. A third implored passersby to report suspected Christians to the authorities with the promise of reward.

Beside the Truth Squad building was a bakery on the right, closed for the day, with Hebrew, English, and the word *ma'afiah* written on a sign above. On the left was an abandoned apartment building.

His companion opened his backpack, and Nick helped drop propaganda leaflets everywhere on the street. He read a few of the messages:

"Resist the Occupiers!"

"Fight the Goyim!"

"Death to the Unitum Imperium!"

When they'd scattered all the flyers, he opened his pack and removed two bricks. Nodding to Amato, he counted to three. Then they threw them, smashing the glass plate.

An alarm began clanging.

Nick pulled out two Molotov cocktails and a lighter. He flicked the striker, but nothing happened. The alarm continued to clang its warning. He flicked it again.

Still nothing.

On the third try, a flame appeared, and he held it to the Molotov's wick.

He handed the first firebomb to Amato and lit the wick for the second. Amato threw his bomb through the opening, and Nick followed. The glass bottles smashed on the floor and under a table, spilling gasoline everywhere. Flames exploded in a whoosh. Within seconds, the interior was aflame.

"Let's get out of here!" he said.

"What's that?" Amato pointed to a third-floor window in the supposedly abandoned apartment building.

Nick glanced up. There was a light on. Was someone living up there?

From their right came a sharp whistle. Four men in CSA uniforms were racing toward them. No one was supposed to be patrolling this sector tonight. What was going on?

He turned left and broke into a run. Amato was already ahead of him.

"Stop, or we'll shoot!" came a cry from behind.

His blood pumping fast, Nick broke into a sprint.

Amato stopped, knelt, and—what was this? He had a gun! The fool had brought a pistol!

"What are you doing?"

Nick didn't wait for an answer but kept running, only glancing back in time to see Amato fire two shots.

"I'm not aiming to hit them," cried Amato. "Just to slow them down."

But the CSA didn't know that, and they returned fire. Bullets rammed into the building ahead of Nick. Stone chipped off the sidewalk beside him, and something stung his right calf.

He glanced back.

Amato had been hit. He was lying on the ground. Blood was pooling around his unmoving body.

"Stop, or you'll be next!" shouted an agent.

He couldn't escape. Nick slowed to a stop and raised his hands.

Within seconds, the men surrounded him, frisked him, and ordered him to lie flat on the ground. This wasn't supposed to happen. This was a disaster.

They jerked him roughly to his feet, and the tallest among them slammed a fist into his jaw so hard that his beard fell off. "What's this?" The man stepped back. "Why are you in disguise?"

"Let me explain." Nick began to reach for the ID he'd brought, just in case, but the leader waved a pistol, stopping him.

"What's to explain?" said the man. "You are in deep trouble, Jew."

"I'm not a Jew, and your presence here is a mistake." He ripped off the skullcap and the false payots. "If you will let me show you my ID and my orders, you will discover you have interrupted an undercover operation ordered by Adam Turner, the director who rules over you. This is a false flag operation designed to discredit the Jews."

The four men exchanged confused glances, and the tall leader lowered his pistol. "Show me what you've got."

Nick dug inside his shirt and presented his ID and orders. He'd brought them along for a contingency like this, never imagining they'd be necessary.

Leaving one man to guard him, the other three retreated several meters. After examining his documents and discussing it among themselves, the leader returned and handed Nick's credentials back. "This is crazy, Nick Carter, but we believe you." He shook his head. "But this means we just killed an undercover operative."

"He's dead?" asked Nick.

"Afraid so."

"He shouldn't have fired." Rubbing his temples, Nick closed his eyes. "This is a disaster. Also, there was a light on in the third story of the apartment building beside the Truth Squad building. It was supposed to be empty."

"We already called the Fire and Rescue Service," said a brown-bearded companion. "But the first floor of the apartment building is now a raging inferno. If anyone's up there, it may be too late for them. You've done your work well, sir."

"Yes." He wiped sweat from his forehead. "Unfortunately, we did."

"What should we do now?" asked the tall leader.

"Allow this to play out," said Nick. "The minister wants this operation to succeed. I'm sure they'll give another identity to the man you killed. I will tell the director you acted as only you could."

The leader gave his thanks, and they parted.

In the next alley, he removed the Jewish garb he wore over his civilian clothes, stuffed it in a garbage bin, and returned to the Clal Center where he sat in silence until two.

* * *

After a fitful sleep, Nick woke the next morning and turned on the television to hear the reports of the night's work:

> Last evening, Jewish radicals attacked the headquarters of the
> Third District Truth Squad, setting it on fire. They left

pamphlets on the street inciting the populace to rebel against the Imperator and the Unitum Imperium. The Fire and Rescue Service arrived but was unable to stop the blaze from consuming three buildings. In the apartment beside the headquarters, a woman and two children perished in the blaze. A CSA patrol spotted the two terrorists as they left the scene, killing one. The second man escaped. Davato himself has condemned this affront by the Jewish people against the Imperium. "If it continues," said the Imperator, "there will be consequences."

"That's what happened with your false flag operation?" Brooke turned off the television and faced Nick.

"It was a disaster." He stood, approached her, and whispered in her ear. "But I have a plan. We'll be out of the country within the week."

CHAPTER 33

WALLACE SLOAN

Castle Danger, Scotland ~ March, Year 3

Wallace Sloan's footsteps echoed off the stone passage as he rounded the corner. He stopped before the new woman's cell, out of sight.

Ewan, the guard who accompanied him, shot him a quizzical look, but Wallace ignored it.

What was it about this woman that made him want to let her go? She was attractive, yes, but there was more to it than that. He'd felt the same thing about some of the others he'd led to Dr. Creig's chamber of horrors. Only with Aurora Carter, the feeling was stronger.

"Sloan?" Ewan was getting impatient. Bald, with a black goatee and devil tattoos on both arms, he was in charge of the dungeon guards. It was rumored the man could bench press over a hundred kilograms. In the gym inside outbuilding number 3, Wallace could manage only forty-five.

Nodding, he continued to the woman's cell, punched the button on his device, and heard the opening click.

"What now?" She stood from the bed and entered the light.

"I'm to take you to Dr. Creig today." He motioned toward the hall.

She hesitated, glanced toward the bed, but nodded.

With Ewan following, he led her down the corridor, past the demon beastie, up the stone steps, and into the yard. They began crossing the cobblestones under the cold light of a sun struggling to shine through a leaden-gray ceiling.

His phone beeped, and he read the text. "Dr. Creig's not ready. It may be a while, so we'll wait here." He turned to the man beside him. "I don't need you, Ewan. She won't be a problem."

Ewan scowled. "That's not what the regulations say. I—"

"I don't care. Find something to do. I'll take it from here."

"If you say so." Then Ewan left.

Alone with her now, Wallace led her to a bench beside a cluster of dwarf pines. Their scent, despite the drought, filled the clearing. He waved, she sat, and he took the seat beside her.

"What is he going to do to me today?" She swiveled to face him. The worry lines on her face crinkled.

"I don't know. They just tell me who I'm to bring to him and when. I only follow orders."

"The guards at the Nazi concentration camps gave the same excuse."

That stung, and he was surprised she knew the history. So many people nowadays, young and old, didn't know the history of the world wars. "I suppose you're right. But what can I do? If I disobey, I'll end up like you."

"You don't like what you're doing, do you?" A hint of a smile flicked the corners of her lips.

"Good guess." He stared into her deep hazel eyes. "Can I ask you a personal question?"

"Depends on what it is."

"Why did you become a Christian?"

Her eyes widened. "Are you asking because you want to help Dr. Creig with his theory? Because you believe there's some flaw in anyone who follows Jesus?"

"No, no." To emphasize the point, he shook his head. "I'm asking because I'm curious. And for your information—though I'm not supposed to say this—Creig is giving up on that theory and is focusing on a cure." He uttered a laugh. "Do you know what I think about all this?"

"No, what?"

"Just as he could never find a cause, he'll never find a cure. You and the others became Christians because you *chose* to become Christians. Creig might as well seek a cure for why I like chocolate and someone else likes vanilla. So that's why I'm asking you, Aurora, if I may call you that. You weren't taken in the Great Catastrophe. You became a Christian later. So why did you?"

Now the smile that was trying to break through lifted the corners of her mouth. "Do you believe the nonsense they're peddling that aliens took the missing people?"

"Of course not."

"Then there's hope for you, Wallace Sloan." She reached across and laid a hand on his left shoulder.

He shouldn't have let her do that, but her touch was strangely comforting. And was that a tingling he felt beneath her fingers?

She removed her hold and faced the trio of dwarf pines that circled the patio. "On V-Day, I saw a good friend of mine disappear before my eyes. Later, I listened to the confession of a priest who was left behind. He knew the Bible, but he hadn't given his heart to Jesus. Then he told anyone who was listening to his broadcast what was going to happen. According to the Bible, he said that a mesmerizing leader would appear and make a treaty with Israel, and that when such a man appeared, we would know him as the Antichrist. He's also called the beast and the man of lawlessness."

"Davato?"

"Exactly. But that's not all." She frowned and focused on the cobbles as if something in the stones bothered her. "I don't know why I'm telling you this, but for some reason, I trust you."

Then she lifted her gaze. "Believe it or not, Wallace Sloan, my family has received a book of prophecies that have been directing us to do the will of God. They tell us what is going to happen in the future. And before you ask, I left it behind in Tel Aviv when you took me. That notebook has predicted events that eventually came to pass. But you don't have to believe in the notebook. All you have to do is read the Bible. If you understand it and study it, you'll see that what's happening to the world right now was predicted long ago. Only an all-powerful, all-seeing, all-knowing God can predict the future, and if those predictions came true—and they did!—then Jesus is who he says he is. And do you know what is the single most important attribute that Jesus possesses?"

He offered no response.

"It's love, Wallace. Love."

What she was saying was so far-fetched, so far beyond his understanding of the world, he was left speechless. Was she delusional? But no, before him now, he didn't sense insanity. He recognized deep personal belief.

But if what she said was true, then he must question everything he'd been doing here at the castle in the service of the Ministry of Virtue.

He closed his eyes and dropped his head into his hands.

"Jesus is love, Wallace. And he wants to love you, if only you would believe in him and accept him. He offers an eternity of love, peace, and happiness to anyone who believes in him." Her voice was soft, comforting. "All you have to do is give your heart to him. But if you refuse, if you reject his offer, what awaits you is an eternity in the lake of fire."

He'd heard it all before, but here, now, coming from this woman, the message was different. And it seemed true, real, and important.

His phone beeped. Glad for the interruption, he read the text. "They're ready."

Her smile vanished, and she lowered her gaze.

All business now, he led her to the tower, and they climbed the spiral stone steps to the fourth level. A towheaded guard opened the door and brought out another of Dr. Creig's victims—a black man about thirty, and he was shaking all over. Sweat covered his forehead. His eyes darted this way and that. And his lips kept uttering the same thing, over and over: "Dear Jesus, protect me and save me. Dear Jesus, protect me and save me."

Wallace stepped aside to let the guard escort the man to the tower staircase.

"You may bring in the next subject," said Creig from inside.

Wallace waved, and they entered Creig's chamber.

"Sit in the chair, miss." Creig pointed to the metal chair with its opened claws waiting to clamp down upon wrists and legs.

Fright in her eyes, she backed up.

"Please," said Creig, "let's not do this. Sit, or I'll order our friend Wallace to force you."

She sat. Creig touched something behind the chair, and the metal jaws snapped shut.

Wallace whirled and returned to the hall.

He sat on the bench, and time passed. Like flotsam circling a whirlpool, her words swirled through his head. They connected with something he'd been struggling with for some time. What he'd been doing here every day had been fighting against something deep within his soul on some unconscious level. Then here came this woman, presenting a worldview that was the exact opposite of everything McDuff, the Prophet, and Davato believed in.

He'd heard her spiel before, of course, from others. But hearing it from her, today, connected with him in a new, more powerful manner.

He stood now on a narrow ridge, and below him on either side were opposing worlds. Down the left slope was Davato, the Unitum Imperium, and, if Aurora Carter was right, an eternity in the lake of fire.

But down the right slope was—what? Rebellion? A trip to the German internment camp? But also a pleasant eternal destiny.

He was trapped with no way out.

Creig kept her inside for three hours, far longer than normal, and when he opened the door to say he was finished, Wallace went in to get her.

Sweat drenched her forehead, her eyes were dilated, and her hands were trembling. She looked up into his eyes and shook her head as if to say, "This is wrong, Wallace, terribly, terribly wrong."

He winced, took her arm, and escorted her into the hall.

After Creig closed the door, he whispered, "I am so, so sorry, Aurora."

"So am I."

He helped her down the stairs, across the yard, and back to her cell.

Then he hurried to his quarters, a three-by-five-meter stone room on the second level of the second tower. Under the window was a small wooden desk. To soften the stone, he'd filled one wall with a replica of a tapestry depicting the Battle of Bannockburn where Robert the Bruce had defeated the English army—a small act of rebellion, that tapestry. Against the opposite wall was a bed with a nightstand and a bookshelf loaded with books approved by the UI. Now he reached behind the volumes on the bottom shelf and pulled out the one book no one was allowed to own, something that, if found, could send him to the German camp—a pocket Bible.

It was barely bigger than his palm, and he'd stolen it last week from another patient who'd somehow slipped it through a pat down. The introduction said it contained the Psalms and New Testament, whatever those might be.

He opened it now for the first time and flipped through it, landing on
Psalm 5:

O Lord, hear me as I pray;
pay attention to my groaning.
Listen to my cry for help, my King and my God,
for I pray to no one but you.
Listen to my voice in the morning, Lord.
Each morning, I bring my requests to you and wait expectantly.

O God, you take no pleasure in wickedness;
you cannot tolerate the sins of the wicked.
Therefore, the proud may not stand in your presence,
for you hate all who do evil.
You will destroy those who tell lies.
The Lord detests murderers and deceivers.

Because of your unfailing love, I can enter your house;
I will worship at your Temple with deepest awe.
Lead me in the right path, O Lord,
or my enemies will conquer me.
Make your way plain for me to follow.

My enemies cannot speak a truthful word.
Their deepest desire is to destroy others.
Their talk is foul, like the stench from an open grave.
Their tongues are filled with flattery.
O God, declare them guilty.
Let them be caught in their own traps.
Drive them away because of their many sins,
for they have rebelled against you.

But let all who take refuge in you rejoice;
let them sing joyful praises forever.

Spread your protection over them,
that all who love your name may be filled with joy.
For you bless the godly, O Lord;
you surround them with your shield of love.

He closed the book. It was as if whoever wrote this prayer had written it for him. He was surrounded by wickedness, liars, and people plotting endless evil.

It was as if Aurora's God was calling to him.

Still, he was trapped on a ledge between two worlds. And he didn't know which way to go.

PART IV
A DEMON

Matthew 12:22–28 (HCSB):

Then a demon-possessed man who was blind and unable to speak was brought to Him. He healed him, so that the man could both speak and see. And all the crowds were astounded and said, "Perhaps this is the Son of David!"
When the Pharisees heard this, they said, "The man drives out demons only by Beelzebul, the ruler of the demons."
Knowing their thoughts, He told them: "Every kingdom divided against itself is headed for destruction, and no city or house divided against itself will stand. If Satan drives out Satan, he is divided against himself. How then will his kingdom stand? And if I drive out demons by Beelzebul, who is it your sons drive them out by? For this reason, they will be your judges. If I drive out demons by the Spirit of God, then the kingdom of God has come to you."

CHAPTER 34

THE DEMON BEASTIE

Castle Danger, Scotland ~ March, Year 3

For the last ten minutes, Wallace had been waiting in the courtyard, wondering why he'd been summoned. Then came the clicking of a cane on cobbles, and he turned to find his summoner. "What's this about, Director?"

"I need your help today." Fergus McDuff stopped to catch his breath. Lately, even a short walk seemed to tire him out.

"Why? Where are we going?"

"To visit the beast."

No other words coming from McDuff's mouth could have sent a deeper chill down Wallace's spine than those. A shudder began in his shoulders and rippled down his back.

McDuff laughed. "Why so glum? You've been there before."

"Aye, b–but why me? I've no desire to see the demon beastie again."

He waved across the yard. "We go there because communing with it is a source of inspiration."

"For you, maybe." Wallace ripped his gaze away.

McDuff's cane rapped on stone. "Let's go."

Wallace followed the director, who hobbled across the yard, through the door, into a hallway, and down the stairwell.

Down they went, their feet echoing off stone. The drought had dried up the usual dripping of water, and the steps were unnaturally dry. He'd heard the rumor of a curse that the Two Witnesses had placed upon the earth, and now, who could deny it? Everything was drying up.

Past the rows of cells they went, under the shafts of light, dim today because of the cloud cover.

At cell number 20, McDuff opened the door.

A young woman, not more than nineteen, looked up from where she sat on her bed.

"You will come with us." McDuff waved his cane. "Joline, isn't it?"

The woman nodded, stood, and gave him a puzzled expression.

"We have a special job for you today." McDuff motioned to Wallace, and he grasped the woman's arm.

This was the part he hated the most—this enlisting of blameless passersby. Every time McDuff did this, he would choose a patient from the control group, some innocent they'd plucked off the street. Creig had tried Christian patients, but for some reason, it didn't work with them.

Joline stepped into the light, revealing red hair, freckles, and a slim figure. He could imagine she might have been someone's sweetheart, perhaps engaged, though he hadn't read her file. That Creig had the authority to steal guiltless bystanders away from their lives was bothersome.

They left the cell and continued down the hall.

"Where are you taking me?" she asked, and he cringed. Her voice was sweet and innocent. She was a lamb being led to the lion's den.

"Drink this first." McDuff screwed the top off a glass vial and held it out to her. "Don't spill it, or you'll be beaten."

She glanced at the green liquid inside the glass then back at McDuff. "What's in it?"

"Something to make you happy."

By the way she stared at it, she might not have believed him.

Yet she downed it in one gulp and returned the vial.

They walked, and Wallace let go of her arm. Just ahead, the cells would end, and the stone would level off. Down below the horizontal bars was the demon beastie.

But here they stopped. Beside him was the outline of a doorway cut into stone. McDuff pulled a key from his pocket, inserted it, and the mechanism clicked. He pointed to the metal handhold attached to the stone, and Wallace grabbed it. McDuff, of course, had not the strength to open such a massive door. That was one reason he'd brought Wallace.

He tugged, and stone ground over stone. The metal hinges squealed, and the door opened, revealing a dark, open maw.

Inside, torches poked from a holder, and McDuff took one. He lit it with a lighter.

"I'm not going down there," she said.

"You are, my dear." McDuff rapped his cane on stone. "You will follow me."

She looked to Wallace.

He held her forearm and squeezed. "You don't have a choice." He gave her a push, and she followed the director down the steps.

Wallace brought up the rear.

The farther they descended, the stronger came the all-too-familiar sense that some great evil lay below. It was like an icy chill seeping into his soul, a cancerous cold that sucked and prodded and grew, a chill that would not be satisfied until it had permeated every cell in his body. And every time he came down here, he wished he were somewhere else, far, far away.

Ahead of him, the unwitting Joline must have felt the same thing as she slowed, glanced back at him, then stopped. "I can't go on. The monster is down there. I feel it. I want to go back."

"We can't. Please. It will be all right. When it's all over, you will be all right." He motioned, and she kept going. He hoped that what he'd just said wasn't a lie.

At the bottom of the steps, the way opened into a stone chamber, and Joline lurched back, crashing into Wallace.

Gripping her arms, he twisted her around to face what had frightened her.

"The plexiglass is at least twenty centimeters thick. The demon beastie can't get past it. We're safe here."

Beyond the translucent barrier, the demon whirled to face them, and now, even Wallace stepped back. No matter how often he'd been down here, his reaction was always the same.

What was this thing they'd captured? A demon from below? Half animal, surely. But surely half spirit or half devil? Had the gates of Hell opened long enough for it to escape? Or was it some earthly aberration infused with the spirit of the Dragon? What had ever possessed McDuff to bring it down here? What was wrong with the age they lived in that such a thing could escape and exist in the world above?

Green eyes as big as saucers stared out at them. The light behind those orbs was dim, cold, and soulless. Its mouth was a grinning, lipless receptacle for incisors befitting a lion or wolf. Its nose was two long slits, and as it breathed, they opened, closed, opened, closed. Hair as thick and sharp as porcupine needles covered its torso, and its arms were simian appendages, hanging stupidly at its sides. Five claws as long as a man's hand extended from each arm. And its feet were like an elephant's, stumpy and wide.

Everywhere across the den's floor were the bones, antlers, rib cages, and skulls of cattle, deer, elk, pigs, and, yes—even humans.

Inside the den to the right was a wide metal door, and the first time McDuff brought him here, Wallace had asked where it led. "To a hidden passage that leads to the courtyard," came McDuff's answer. "In the yard, you will find a set of rusted metal doors lying over the entrance. Electronic locks in the control room open and close the upper and lower doors to the passage."

"How," Wallace had asked, "did you ever carry it down here?"

"We drugged it, bound it, and tied it to a stretcher. It took six men to carry it."

Wallace still marveled at the answer. And he never ceased to wonder why McDuff would ever want such a creature locked up down here in the first place.

Now, McDuff slipped the torch into a holder on the wall behind them, and the light it shed wavered and sent flickering shadows over the walls and against the glass. Dim light filtered down from the opening in the bars above onto the creature beyond.

"Sit, woman." McDuff rapped his cane on the sole piece of furniture in the room—a steel chair without arms.

Her glance went to the chair, to Wallace, then back to McDuff. "What are you going to do to me? I feel lightheaded."

"Nothing physical." McDuff leaned on his cane. "Please sit."

The drug must be working now, and she sat.

McDuff went to a hook embedded in the wall behind them and uncoiled a length of rope. He passed this to Wallace, who fixed the rope to the chairback and tied the woman's hands behind her.

When he looked into her eyes, her pupils were dilated, and she smiled. "It won't hurt me, will it?" she asked, and her voice was slurred.

"No." It was a lie. Though the demon beastie couldn't get past the plexiglass, sometimes McDuff's victims were never quite the same afterward.

McDuff ignored her and approached the glass. "Akanji, beast from the underworld, speak to us now. You are a creature of the Dragon, so now I implore you to speak for him through this woman. It has been a month since last I heard from the one we worship, and you, Akanji, are the vessel I have chosen as my pathway for communion."

The thing that called itself Akanji stepped closer to the glass. Again, Wallace crept back.

Despite the drug, Joline struggled in the chair.

The demon beastie's eyes focused on Joline, on McDuff, and on Wallace.

For the third time, Wallace stepped back until his spine hit the stone wall behind him.

The light from the torch and from the opening in the bars above dimmed. A shadow surrounded the demon beastie and grew. A chill breeze passed over his skin, and he shivered.

The woman's head snapped back, and an impossibly deep groan escaped her mouth.

Then she turned her head to face McDuff, and the words that came out of her sounded nothing like the sweet, innocent tones of Joline, the woman McDuff had stolen off the street.

"You are starving me, McDuff. More meat."

With every word uttered through the woman's mouth, Wallace shuddered. What kind of power allowed it to invade the woman's mind and use her like this? And why did it not work on those who called themselves Christians?

"More food, or I will break free and feast upon whom I wish. I may do that anyway."

"I–I'm doing what I can. I send out hunting parties every day. But game is getting scarcer, and I—"

"More meat, McDuff!"

"I will try." McDuff wiped his forehead. "But now I want to hear from the Dragon, not from his servant. Now let the Dragon speak through you and through this woman."

The room darkened even further, and new shadows appeared, dark smudges of light that swirled and hovered and flitted this way and that beyond the plexiglass.

The veins on the woman's neck pulsed, and Wallace slid to the side so he could see what was happening.

The muscles of her jaw tightened, and her eyes bulged. Then her mouth opened, and a new voice, grating and even deeper, spoke.

"THE WORLD IS RIPE FOR THE PLUCKING. EVERYWHERE, THE ENEMY IS RETREATING, AND VICTORY IS ASSURED. DO WHAT YOU CAN, FERGUS MCDUFF, TO WORK FOR ME, FOR I ASSURE YOU"—but the laugh that next came out of the woman was anything but reassuring—"YES, I ASSURE YOU THAT YOUR REWARD WILL BE GREAT."

Even before McDuff voiced his next question, Wallace sensed deceit behind that laugh.

"What must I do"—McDuff's tone was groveling—"to increase my reward in the Underworld, my lord? You have promised to put me in charge of an entire city, and I am grateful for that. But I want more. I want some assurance. Will you also give me women to use at my pleasure? As many as I like? And when I get there, will you take away this infernal limp? I know you've promised this before, so I'm merely asking for some solid assurance that what you say will actually—"

Sudden darkness swept the room, accompanied by a dark and evil shadow rushing past him. Was it a pique of anger, solidified and given physicality, that had just blown past him?

"DO NOT QUESTION ME, MCDUFF! MY WORDS ARE TRUE. YOU WILL GET EVERYTHING THAT'S COMING TO YOU AND MORE. WORK FOR MY KINGDOM AND AGAINST THE ENEMY, AND EVERYTHING YOU ASKED FOR WILL SURELY BE GIVEN TO YOU. BUT DO NOT EVER AGAIN QUESTION MY PROMISES!"

Now it was McDuff who cowered and shrank back from the glass.

The torchlight brightened, the light from above increased, and the woman's chin dropped to her chest. Then the demon beastie stepped away from the glass and turned its back on them.

"Wh–what happened?" The sweet voice that was Joline's had returned.

Wallace rushed forward and untied her bonds.

Shaking all over, she looked into his eyes and cringed. "What did he do to me? Why am I shaking all over? Why do I feel so, so violated?"

"It will be all right." Wallace helped her out of the chair. "You will be all right. Let's get you back to your cell."

Without waiting for McDuff, he grabbed the torch and led her up the steps and out of this deepest part of the dungeon. McDuff's footsteps echoed up from behind.

After McDuff followed them into the hall, Wallace shut the heavy stone door. Again, without waiting for the director, he led her back to her cell and helped her to her bed. When he pulled the blanket over her, she rolled away from him and faced the wall.

He hurried back to his room and shut the door.

What was he doing here? Why was he working for this man who used others in such a way?

Then he thought back to what Aurora Carter had said about her God. That the single most important attribute of this God was something that was sorely lacking in everything he'd witnessed here today.

And that was love.

CHAPTER 35

UNAUTHORIZED HYMNS

Castle Danger, Scotland ~ March, Year 3

Psalm 95:1–2 (NLT): *Come, let us sing to the Lord! Let us shout joyfully to the Rock of our salvation. Let us come to him with thanksgiving. Let us sing psalms of praise to him.*

Somewhere in the farthest recesses of the dungeon, something had happened. Aurora felt it, and so did Colette, the new woman in the cell beside her.

"Did you feel that?" asked Colette. "What was it?"

"Did you pass the demon beastie when you came in yesterday?"

"Was *that* it? The demon in the pit?"

"It has to be. Something is happening down there today, and it's not good."

"No. Not good at all," said Colette.

Only yesterday, Colette had moved into the cell beside her. Aurora had been startled but relieved to hear a voice coming from the empty cell. Colette and her husband had been arrested while attending a service in a secret house church. And like with Aurora, Ministry of Virtue goons had separated her from the others. But Aurora had barely begun to make her acquaintance when the guards dimmed the lights and ordered everyone to be silent. That was last night.

"What do you know about the demon?" asked Colette.

"Not much. But there's a rumor the director meets with the thing." Aurora shuddered. "Eventually, the director will meet with you."

"You've met him, then?"

"Yes." To hear better, she moved to the front of the cell and gripped the bars.

"How long have you been here?" Colette, too, sounded like she was just around the corner.

"Over a month. But it feels like a year. I'm already losing track of time."

"I assume you're a Christian?"

"Everybody in this block is."

"Where did they get you?"

"In Tel Aviv, but I'm from Minnesota. We crossed the Atlantic in a yacht to bring a holy man to Jerusalem."

"From America to Jerusalem by sea? That must have been some journey."

"You wouldn't believe it." Aurora shrugged. "It's a long story."

"I imagine it is."

"You said yesterday you belonged to a house church," said Aurora. "Like everyone else here, I came to faith late, and I've only been to a church a few times. I really liked the music."

"Yes, and the singing!" Colette's voice rose with excitement. "When everyone joins together in worship, giving praise to God in song, oh, how uplifting and joyous that can be!"

By the sound of her neighbor's voice, Aurora imagined she was smiling. "I bet you know a lot of Christian songs. I wish I knew some."

"Have you read about how the apostle Peter sang when he was in prison? At least I think it was Peter. Or maybe it was Paul?"

"Yes, I remember reading that." Aurora gripped the bars tighter.

"What if we did that now? Here in this awful place."

"But I don't know the words to anything."

"No problem. I'll teach you a simple, yet reverent hymn. It will sound good in this place." It was an easy refrain to learn, and at first, it was only the two of them. But soon, Christians from other cells joined in.

Holy, holy, holy.
Merciful and mighty.
God in three persons.
Blessed Trinity.

Over and over, they repeated the refrain. The rock walls echoed and magnified their voices so that their singing became what could only be described as a heavenly choir.

But they'd barely begun when a guard appeared outside Aurora's cell and banged his truncheon on the bars. "Stop this at once. That kind of thing is prohibited."

But she kept on singing. So did Colette. So did the unseen others.

"Again, I say stop." The guard slammed his club against the iron. "Or it's the pit and the demon for all of you."

She stopped singing. Reluctantly, she moved to the bed. As the guard advanced down the row, banging his weapon and repeating his threat, the others also stopped.

For a minute or so, there was silence.

But then, from three or four cells away, the singing started again. And it spread. New voices from far down the passage joined in. Again, Colette sang, and Aurora jumped off the bed, rushed to the bars, and she, too, sang.

The guard returned, rapped his truncheon against the bars, repeating his threats. But no one was listening now. Nothing, it seemed, could stop the union of their voices rising to God in praise, but also crying out in peaceful rebellion against their oppressors.

The music issued from earthly vessels of flesh and bone, but so heavenly was their collective effort, so deeply did it lift the willing ear to ethereal heights, it could well have originated from some celestial body of angels hovering above the planet.

Frustrated and seething, the guard sheathed his club and spat onto the stone walkway. For him, the music was probably blasphemous, heretical, and against the law. He slammed his palms against his ears and disappeared down the hall.

* * *

AFTER HIS EXPERIENCE WITH THE demon beastie, Wallace needed comfort—something, anything, to cleanse his mind and soul of the evil he'd witnessed this day. He brought out the pocket Bible and read again in the Psalms. There, among the verses, he found words to soothe a troubled soul. But he barely started reading when a knock came on the door.

He shoved the book inside the desk drawer and faced the door. "What is it?"

"There's a disturbance in the dungeon, sir. The Christians are in rebellion, and nothing we have done can stop it."

Was it possible? Would the Christians overthrow their jailers? "Have they broken out? Do we need to issue firearms?"

"No, no," came the muffled voice through the wood. "You must come and see for yourself."

"Okay. All right." He returned his Bible to its secret hiding place and opened the door. Then he followed one of McDuff's musclemen down the tower steps and across the yard. It was evening now, and the clouds had given way to the silvery light of a quarter moon hovering just above the ramparts.

As soon as he entered the stairwell, he heard it—dozens of heavenly voices raised in beautiful song. He laid a hand on the shoulder of the large companion ahead of him. "This is what the ruckus is about?"

"Yes, sir. Listen to the words. They are worshiping the Enemy."

"I see." Wallace struggled to keep from smiling. "And you haven't been able to stop them?"

"Yes, sir. I mean, no, sir. They won't listen to us."

He gestured down the steps. "Keep going."

When he entered the main passage, he stopped and let the words and the music wash over him.

Holy, holy, holy.
Merciful and mighty.
God in three persons.
Blessed Trinity.

Over and over came the refrain, and it bounced and echoed and magnified off the rock. After he'd just read the praises in the Psalms, it was a salve, a healing ointment for a troubled mind.

"What should we do, sir?" Ewan appeared beside him from around the corner, his forehead twisted and blotchy red.

"You've warned them, I assume?"

"Of course. But they won't listen." Ewan waved his arms in frustration. "Should I begin taking them to the pit?"

"All of them?" Now he couldn't stop the smile that burst forth. "No, let it play out. They'll tire of this eventually."

The burly guard frowned, glanced up and down the aisle, then shrugged. "I suppose."

Wallace nodded and began walking, slowly, down the row of cells. All the Christians had joined in. Most of them, it seemed, were in glorious, ethereal rebellion. And there was nothing that he or the guards or even McDuff could do about it.

As if even thinking about the castle's overlord had summoned him, Fergus McDuff himself appeared beside him. "What's going on, Sloan? The guards tell me the prison is in full rebellion."

Wallace shot him a wry grin. "It appears they are, Director, if only in song. And there's nothing anyone can do to stop it."

"It doesn't go beyond E section, sir." This came from Ewan, appearing from around the corner.

"The control group." McDuff shook his head. "So it's only the Christians. And the words are a prayer, so to speak, to the Enemy." He faced Wallace. "What do you suggest? Can we stop it?"

"How? They've ignored the guards' threats. We can't send all of them into the pit, can we?"

"No, that would destroy our work here."

McDuff listened for a few minutes then shook his cane toward the cells, his whole body seeming to quake. "Eventually, they'll tire and stop. Let it play out. Tomorrow, withhold the morning meal. Lunch and dinner too. Ensure they know why we're doing it."

Then he whirled, and with his cane pounding the stone, he ascended the steps and was gone.

But Wallace remained. He found a bench, sat, and listened. For another hour, the singing went on. And when it concluded, he returned to his room, buoyed and comforted by the simple hymn and the faith behind it.

CHAPTER 36

FLIGHT FROM JERUSALEM

From Jerusalem to Rome ~ March, Year 3

All morning, Nick kept checking his watch. When it reached ten o'clock, it was time. That's when Davato and Adam Turner should be on a plane leaving for New Babylon. He locked his desk, left his office, and informed the aide in the main room that he'd be out doing a few errands and would be back later this afternoon. The aide smiled and nodded. Rank had its privileges, and today, like many others with the bosses gone, he would appear to abuse them.

At the apartment, Brooke was waiting impatiently with the two backpacks they'd prepared. It wasn't unusual for people to wear rucksacks in the city, especially if they were shopping. But theirs were crammed full of everything they'd need for the trip.

They took the elevator to the bottom and crossed the atrium.

But as they left the revolving glass doors, they met Colombo Nucci, the new manager for Undercover Operations, on the sidewalk. "Hello, Nick, rather early to be going out, isn't it?"

Surprised to encounter someone outside in midmorning, Nick stammered. "I–I, well, yes, but Brooke wanted me to accompany her to the people's market this morning. For safety." He wiped his forehead. "All the robberies and murders, you know?"

"Ah, yes. Very concerning." Colombo frowned. "I suppose that's the price one pays for too much freedom. But why the people's market? Our commissary is better stocked."

He was right, of course. The elites always treated themselves better than they did the common folk.

Brooke jumped in to save him. "That's true, but I think those of us in such high positions should show we aren't above shopping at the common stores. Besides, I'm up for an adventure. I'm sick of sitting inside the Clal Center. Who knows? Maybe I'll find something the UI employee store doesn't have?"

Now Colombo smiled. "I see your point. Well, happy shopping." He waved and entered the building.

Releasing his breath, Nick gave Brooke an appreciative wink, and they left the Clal Center behind. They made turn after turn, heading deep into the Old City until they came to a store selling every variety of drug imaginable—opium, heroin, fentanyl, marijuana, and hashish. He'd heard that a man named Avi ran a black-market operation on the side, and two days before, both he and Brooke had given Avi a payment of ten thousand euros and sat for photographs.

They were here now to pick up fake IDs, travel cards, and a UI credit card connected to a new bank account containing seven thousand Euros out of Nick's ten-thousand-euro payment.

But when they entered, a tattooed young man about twenty-five was manning the shop today. "Can I help you?" he asked.

"Uh, we were here a few days ago and talked with Avi. Is he around?"

The young man shrugged. "Avi is home with a bad cold. He asked me to mind the place for him today. What can I do for you?"

"He was preparing a special purchase for us." Nick shuffled his feet.

"I don't know anything about any special purchase."

"You say he's home? Can you call him? Maybe he can tell you where it is?"

"I–I suppose." The youth pulled out his phone and punched the numbers. Moments later, he looked up. "No answer."

"Please try again."

He did, and someone did answer. As the young man was speaking, he walked through an open doorway into a back room. Long seconds later, he reappeared, holding a package wrapped in brown paper. Looking askance at it, he passed it to Nick. "I don't know what this is, and I don't want to know. But Avi said you paid for it, and I should give it to you without question."

Nick took it, thanked the man, and hurried Brooke from the shop.

They turned a corner, and at a bench outside an abandoned bakery, they sat.

Nick ripped off the paper. Inside were two ID cards with their pictures and two travel passes, supposedly good for travel to Italy. Also inside was a UI-approved credit card.

"I don't like this, Nick. The man who sold us these wasn't here, and that young man back there was suspicious."

"I know, but this is the best we can do." With travel passes and IDs in hand, he searched for flights to Rome on his phone. He made a reservation for one leaving this afternoon. "We've got a little over two hours to catch a flight to freedom from Tel Aviv."

Brooke laid a hand on his shoulder. "Are we actually going to be free of these people and this threat hanging over us?"

Smiling, he leaned over and kissed her cheek. "Yes. But we've got to move if we're going to catch that flight. Let's go."

They left the bench and began walking. When he spied a taxi, he gave the driver directions.

Forty-five minutes later, they arrived at the Davato International Airport in Tel Aviv. Nick paid and overtipped the cabbie. He found a ticket kiosk for the newly formed Air Imperium airlines, entered his itinerary and credit card numbers, and received their tickets.

They went to the security checkpoint for their gate. But the line was long, and they waited nearly fifty minutes before they reached the Unitum Imperium border officer.

"We're barely going to make our flight," he whispered to Brook.

He handed the officer their IDs and tickets.

The man glanced at their faces, at their IDs, then back at their faces. Then he waved to a second officer who was manning one of the conveyor belts that scanned carry-on baggage. The woman came over, the man asked her to take his place, and he faced Nick and Brooke. "These IDs don't have the new classification code for UI affiliation. You will follow me."

Nick glanced again at his watch. They were running out of time.

The officer led them to a glass-enclosed booth beyond the conveyor belts. "You will wait here." Then he took their IDs and tickets, left the booth, and approached an older man outside.

The minute they were alone, Brooke gripped Nick's hand. "This isn't working, is it? There's something wrong with the IDs you paid for, and our flight is leaving. What are they going to do to us?"

He squeezed her hand and shook his head. "I don't know. Apparently, Avi wasn't keeping up with the latest directives. Try to stay calm."

The officer returned to his post, and now the older man, obviously his superior, entered the glass-enclosed booth. He sat across from Nick and Brooke.

"My name is Horst Braun, and I am the supervisor of this checkpoint. These IDs are out-of-date. When was the last time you used them for travel?"

"Oh, it must have been a year ago." Nick hoped there was no way to check that, but he had to come up with some excuse. "Why, officer? Is there something wrong with them?"

"They should have been updated with the new classification codes. All holders of these IDs were notified as to the procedure they should follow to correct them."

"Oh no." Nick checked his watch. "Our flight leaves in twenty minutes, and the gate is far away. I'm terribly sorry about this. Is there some way we can fix this?"

"I understand if you had trouble. So many of our websites are difficult to navigate. But now, if you tried to follow all the steps necessary to update these cards, you'd be here well after your flight was in the air." The man sat back and smiled. "Fortunately, I am intimately familiar with that procedure. And yet—it is such a shame you'll miss your flight. In situations like this, what can a person do? But, perhaps, just maybe, there might be an alternative . . ."

Nick released his breath. The man was giving them a way out. "There must be a fine or something we could pay to compensate someone like you for the time it would take you away from important duties so you could help us?"

The man frowned. "There is such a procedure. Rarely used, of course, but it's in the manual. If I remember, the fine is four hundred euros to correct each item that is out of compliance." He cocked his head. "Can you manage that, sir?"

"Of course." But as Nick counted bills amounting to eight hundred euros, he knew that no such procedure would exist anywhere in any manual. He pushed the bills across the table. If this were a legitimate transaction, it would have been handled via a credit card and forms.

The man took the cash, smiled, and stood. "I'll be right back."

When he left, Brooke turned to him again. "You bribed him?"

Nick smiled. "Whatever it takes."

Less than five minutes later, the man returned and handed them their IDs and tickets. "Now you will follow me. They were closing the doors, but I held the plane for you."

"Thank you, sir. Thank you very much."

He led them to a cart, and they sped through the airport crowds to their gate. Horst Braun himself ushered them to the gangway, and the moment they entered the plane, a stewardess closed and locked the door behind them.

As the plane left the ground, Brooke leaned over and whispered in Nick's ear. "It is going to happen, isn't it?"

"Yes, it's actually happening."

* * *

AFTER ALLOWING TIME FOR RUNWAY taxiing and waiting at the gate, the flight took four hours. They departed the plane with their backpacks and followed the Noleggio Auto signs for auto rentals. Nick rented a Fiat 500, and by late afternoon, they were driving up the E80 toward his villa at Lake Bracciano. By now, most of the abandoned vehicles from V-Day had been cleared from the highway.

As Nick drove, a smiling Brooke clapped her hands. "This is so good, Nick. To be going back to the villa. I never felt at home in the Clal Center. After all, it was the Antichrist's building. But at the lake, I can be happy again."

"Let's hope that Dante has kept everything in order. The bills are being paid automatically from an account I set up a while back under an alias."

171

"So much subterfuge," she said. "So many lies. All just to live a normal life."

"But I must warn you—we may not be able to stay long at the villa."

She frowned, whipped her gaze away, and fell silent.

He kept driving.

When they pulled into the villa's drive and knocked on the front door with their bags, his heart sped up. Would Dante be here? Or would the Unitum Imperium have discovered his flight to freedom? Would agents be here, waiting for him?

When no one answered, he knocked again.

Then old, solid, gray-haired Dante Marino opened the door. When he saw Nick, his mouth opened. "B–but it's you, Signore. How?"

Nick opened his arms and hugged the old man. Then, as was the custom, he kissed him on both cheeks. "I'll explain later. We've been traveling all day, we're famished, and a glass or two of wine would surely be welcome."

"Sì, sì, what's wrong with me? Come in, come in."

They entered and followed Dante to the kitchen. There, he prepared a meal of arugula salad, vermicelli with pomodoro sauce, meatballs, and garlic bread. As Dante busied himself with that, Nick and Brooke sipped glasses of red wine from Nick's vineyard, and he explained that he was in trouble with the Unitum Imperium.

Dante stopped stirring the tomato sauce and faced him. "It's bad business we live with today, Signore. I remember a quote from years ago, from one of those Communist leaders. He was a Marxist high up in the Kremlin hierarchy, and he said something like this: 'Show me the man, and I'll show you the crime.'"

"So true, Dante. They can do whatever they want with us, can't they?"

"For men without honor, sì, Signore. And now that you've confessed your government troubles with me, I'll mention a trouble or two I've had here."

"What?" Nick's heart sped up. "What kind of trouble?"

"Truth Squads, Signore." Dante returned to stirring the pot with a vengeance. "Every few days, they've been dropping in, asking questions, wondering if the owner is coming back." He began stirring again with too much force. "They know about you, Signore. It's not safe for you here."

"Just as I feared. We can't stay." Nick turned to Brooke. "We'll have to leave. But not for a few days."

CHAPTER 37

THE DIRECTOR'S REVENGE

Castle Danger, Scotland ~ March, Year 3

Psalm 37:12–13 (NLT): *The wicked plot against the godly; they snarl at them in defiance. But the Lord just laughs, for he sees their day of judgment coming.*

Wallace woke after a fitful sleep, troubled by his role with the woman Joline but not knowing what to do about it.

As he did every morning, he left his tower room and crossed the yard. It was cold this morning, and he could see his breath. Then he joined the UI staff and guards in the castle's banquet hall on the first floor for a breakfast of fried eggs, sausage, black pudding, and toast. He was just finishing his coffee when Ewan approached.

"The director wants to see us, sir."

"What about?"

"About a penalty he has in mind for the rebels." Ewan smiled.

"He was going to withhold today's meals. He wants more?"

"Apparently. As well he should." Then he frowned. "As you should too."

Wallace shot him a glance. Was that a rebuke? Was Ewan becoming suspicious of Wallace's motives? He gulped the last of his coffee, stood, and followed the man from the hall. Together, they made their way to McDuff's quarters, knocked, and entered.

This morning, McDuff was eating alone the breakfast they always delivered to his quarters. He asked them if they wanted tea or coffee.

Both declined.

As if insulted, McDuff sharpened his tone. "The rebellion in the dungeon yesterday is concerning. And after considering my first response—well, it's just not enough."

"What do you have in mind?" asked Wallace.

"In the lowest section of this tower are four iron cages from medieval times. They're called gibbets, and they were used to suspend prisoners from the crossbeam structure in the courtyard. The front of each cage opens on hinges, and after a prisoner is placed inside, the cage closes and locks so that whoever is inside cannot move."

As Wallace listened to McDuff's speech, the words seemed to ring and echo and come from far away. "A–and what . . . what about these cages? What do you want us to do with them?"

"Bring two of them out of storage along with some of the heavy chain we have down there. There are also ratchets to lift the cages to the top. Bring two of those also."

Wallace's heart was pounding in his ears. "And then what?"

McDuff brought out a bowl filled with slips of paper. "I have here the numbers of every cell containing a Christian. When the gibbets are ready for occupants, I want you, Wallace, to pick two numbers from the bowl at random. That is how we will decide which prisoners will pay the penalty for what happened down there yesterday."

For a moment, Wallace couldn't breathe. What was he supposed to do now? McDuff's plan was barbaric, inhuman.

He glanced aside at a grinning Ewan.

"Well, Wallace?" McDuff cocked his head. "What do you think?"

How could he voice his true opinion to this man? If he disagreed, he could become the next target of McDuff's wrath. It had happened before. Perhaps he should just go along and look for a way out later?

"I asked you a question, Wallace?" McDuff's tone darkened. "What do you think about hanging two of our rebels in the courtyard?"

"H–how long will you hang them there?"

"Until the sun and wind rot the flesh from their corpses, and I can see the white bones of their skulls. Until the birds peck the eyeballs from their sockets."

McDuff faced Ewan. "What do you think of my plan, Ewan?"

"Any right-thinking person dedicated to the Unitum Imperium should welcome such a penalty." Then he speared Wallace with a look of accusation.

A shivering started in Wallace's shoulders and crawled down his spine. "B–but don't you think this is overkill for what they did? After all, they were just singing."

"Just singing!" McDuff's voice rose. "It was a full-scale revolt. It was a direct challenge to my authority. No, Wallace, it's not overkill. It's entirely appropriate. And today, after you have our two prisoners suspended in the gibbets, you will then march all the Christians, five at a time, past the cages. You will do this once a week to drive home the penalty of what will happen if they ever again challenge my authority. Do you understand?"

Wallace swallowed.

"Do you understand?"

"Aye, sir."

"Good. Now, the both of you, go and do what I have commanded." He gave a dismissive wave.

"Yes, sir," said Ewan.

But Wallace didn't reply. He just turned on his heels and followed Ewan out the door.

In a remote corner of the tower's lowest level, past cobwebs, dirt, and dust, they found the four gibbets, the chains, and the iron ratchets. But they had to enlist two more guards to haul the heavy iron up the stairs to the yard.

Wallace attached one end of a chain to a gibbet. Then Ewan climbed a post to the beam and pushed the first chain through a ring. Wallace rattled that chain through the ratchet and hooked the chain end to the nearest rusted metal loop a few meters behind the gallows.

But the iron bars were coated with grime and rust. After they ratcheted the structures to make them upright, Wallace ordered two men to clean the bars.

When that was done, Ewan turned to him. "We should go to the dungeon now and pick the numbers."

"Right."

They entered the hallway and descended the steps to the cells. He stared at the bowl with its folded white papers and froze. If he went along with this, he would be just as bad as McDuff. But if he showed hesitation, Ewan would report him. What else could he do?

"Sir?" Ewan looked askance at him. "Are you going to pick a number?"

"Give me a minute." As Wallace stared at the bowl, his heart hammered in his throat. The weather had turned. How long would anyone last up there, exposed to the freezing wind, suspended inside cold metal bars?

"Sir?" Ewan pointed to the bowl. "Should I do it?"

"No." Wallace picked a slip of paper and handed it to Ewan.

Then it was Ewan who gave the orders. "Follow me."

They took the passage past the demon beastie and around the corner, but as they neared a familiar cell, Wallace's heart pounded wildly in his chest.

"It's this one, sir." Ewan stopped them at the cell belonging to Aurora Carter.

"Let me see that." Wallace reached out and snatched the paper from Ewan's hand. He read the number, and, aye, it was her cell.

Wallace faced his companion. "You've misread it." He grabbed the bars of the cell beside Aurora's. "It's this one."

"No, sir. I did not misread it. I'm sure of what I saw."

Wallace narrowed his eyes. "You are mistaken. The number on the slip points to this cell."

For some moments, he kept Ewan's stare.

"If you say so, sir." Ewan shrugged. "Then, aye, maybe I was mistaken."

Feeling as if he might be sick, Wallace motioned for Ewan to open the door. If he remembered right, the woman's name was Colette, and she had arrived only two days ago.

They escorted her to the courtyard where they shoved her into the iron cage, locked it, and ratcheted it to the top. But the wild-eyed look of fright and accusation she sent him was a rusty dagger ripping into his soul.

He returned to the dungeon with Ewan. He picked another slip of paper and brought out a middle-aged man, already thin from too many weeks as one of Dr. Creig's subjects.

Now two Christians were suspended inside the iron cages. The bars were far enough apart so as to admit wind, rain, and sun, but so confining as to leave little room to do anything but move an arm.

Feeling ill, Wallace was about to leave when Dr. Creig approached. "What is this? Why have you hung these subjects on that crossbeam?"

Wallace's heart surged. Perhaps Creig would intervene and stop this madness?

But from behind came the rapping of a cane on stone, followed by a familiar voice, and Wallace's hopes were crushed.

"I ordered it."

He whirled to find Fergus McDuff leaning on his staff.

"What's going to happen to them?" His face reddening, Creig turned to McDuff.

"They will hang there until they rot." The director was smiling. "Punishment for yesterday's rebellion."

Creig shook his head. "You cannot do this! Do you know how much time I have invested in these subjects? How am I supposed to run a proper experiment if you sabotage it?"

"Live with it, Doctor. I *will* maintain order. I *will* have obedience, or there will be anarchy. Those are my orders, and they will *not* be countermanded."

For some moments, Creig stared at the director. Then he spun on his heels and stalked away.

Wallace's hope to undo what he'd just done vanished.

CHAPTER 38

THE INCURSION

Lochbroom, Scotland ~ March, Year 3

They'd been searching for Aurora for a month now, and it was time to follow Hamish's plan. It was late afternoon when Hamish drove his Jeep south out of Ullapool with Tyler in front. Brett was behind them in the VW they'd rented in Edinburgh. They'd discussed it and decided that if this road was so well hidden, Brett should see the turn so he could lead the Inverness folks when the time came.

Several kilometers after the checkpoint, Hamish pulled over. Then they changed into the uniforms of special agents for the Ministry of Virtue.

Back on the road, Hamish faced his companion. "Who am I, again?"

"You are Agent Callum Reid, and I am Agent David Allan."

"Don't forget, David. One slipup, and we'll both be joining the prisoners."

"Right, Callum."

Tyler adjusted his high-peaked hat and patted the Glock 17 holstered on his belt. He looked in the sun visor's mirror and turned his head this way and that. Last night, they dyed his hair again. Hamish thought he should appear at the castle wearing his Gavin Roberts disguise, complete with tawny hair, fake mustache and goatee, and heavy plastic glasses.

Beside him, Agent Callum grinned. "Just like they said back in Inverness, you look like a Nazi."

"This is a dangerous ruse we're trying to pull off. I don't have a Scottish accent."

"The Ministry employs people from all over. They won't question your accent. Besides, we came from New Babylon, not Scotland."

"Right."

When the A832 branched off to the right, they took the turn around the loch as it led them north. Brett was in the car behind. Pines gave way to moorland and heather-covered mountains. Fifteen kilometers later, Hamish spotted a one-lane side road, and they veered off. But it ended in a field with no outlet.

Backtracking, they continued to the next dirt side road. But that, too, led nowhere.

After two more dead ends, they followed a fifth side road over a hill, down a valley to another hill.

And there, a chain-link fence dropped down from above, crossed the dirt, and continued to their right where a gate barred the way. Hamish parked. They left the vehicle and approached a sign affixed to the fence.

No admittance behind this point!
By order of the Ministry of Virtue.
Violators will be shot!

Brett stopped, and he walked up beside them. "Looks like the place. The waitress's description was a bit off, wasn't it?"

"Indeed." Hamish rattled the gate. "It's padlocked."

"How are we going to get inside?" asked Tyler.

"Wait." Hamish returned to the Jeep and brought over a bolt cutter. With a few snips, he released the lock, faced the others, and grinned.

"I'm saying goodbye, here." Brett shook their hands, got in the VW, and left.

Hamish opened the gate and drove onto a narrow dirt road. A few kilometers later, a weedy path branched off to the right, and Hamish stopped the Jeep. "Could this be what she was referring to? I don't know. This looks dicey."

"She said it was only a cow path."

Nodding, Hamish drove onto a dusty track overgrown with dry, brittle heather. He slowed the Jeep to a crawl as it bounced back and forth, up and down, and the tires rammed ruts and small boulders.

Fifteen minutes later, the sound of whirring, chattering propeller blades topped the rise, and a helicopter approached. It landed on the path ahead, and two men bearing automatic weapons stepped out. Black scarves covered their mouths and noses.

"Who are you, and what are you doing here?" asked a tall, thin man with a mop of black hair.

"We are here," said Hamish, "on a special mission for the Ministry of Virtue to see Director Fergus McDuff."

The second man, short, squat, and red-haired, shouldered his weapon, stepped forward, and whispered to the other one. After a few moments, the second man spoke. "May I see your IDs, please?"

Tyler and Hamish presented their cards, and the man perused them. "We were not informed of your arrival. This is highly unusual."

"Do you not know the ways of the Office of Internal Affairs? We never announce our arrivals." Hamish puffed out his chest. "It's also a means of testing your security."

The taller man nodded, took the IDs from his partner, and examined them. He returned them, and again the two held a whispered conversation.

Then both men removed their scarves. "Ewan will accompany you in the Jeep and guide you to the castle. The director will handle this."

"Of course," said Hamish.

As Tyler and Hamish took the front, the guard identified as Ewan sat in back and waved them on. "It's about twenty minutes ahead."

The helicopter took off and preceded them.

They bounced and jostled over the path. On the right, a field of brown heather reached toward a distant green mountain. On the left, heather dotted a field broken by a dry stream with a brown pine forest beyond. They topped a ridge, descended, and the castle with its five towers came into view. Tyler glanced back and to the right. The ridge behind him must be the one from which they'd looked down so many nights ago. Up there and to the left would be the cave with their cache of weapons and explosives.

When they reached the valley floor, Hamish parked the Jeep before a chain-link fence topped with razor wire. Ewan approached a keypad and punched the numbers. Something clicked, and the gate opened.

Ewan returned to his seat and ordered them to keep going.

Ewan directed Hamish to park near the helicopter, already on its landing pad.

When they exited the Jeep, a new man was waiting for them. "I am Special Agent Wallace Sloan, and I will take you to the director."

Tyler introduced himself as Agent David and Hamish as Agent Callum.

They followed Sloan past low outbuildings over bare trampled clay and dust. They crossed a drawbridge over a dry moat and under the spikes of a portcullis. But when they entered the courtyard and Tyler spotted a man and a woman suspended in iron cages about six feet above the ground, he stopped. A cold wind blew through the yard, rustling dried leaves at his feet. Up there, trapped inside close iron bars, the two prisoners were shivering.

"W–why are those prisoners up there?" he asked.

"There was a rebellion in the dungeon yesterday." Sloan's gaze found the cobbles at his feet. "This is the director's punishment."

"B–but—" Before Tyler could finish, Hamish kicked him in the shins and shot him a quick frown.

"Excellent, Agent Sloan," said Hamish. "A fitting response to rebellion."

Sloan stood before Hamish with a face devoid of emotion. "Apparently, that was also the director's belief."

Then Sloan led them to one of the towers where they climbed a spiral stone staircase to the third floor.

"You will wait here." He knocked, a voice commanded Sloan to enter, and he went inside.

"He's buying our cover story," whispered Hamish, and Tyler nodded.

"But what they're doing to those people in the yard back there . . ." Tyler couldn't finish.

"What did you expect?" said Hamish. "They belong to the Antichrist."

Moments later, the door opened again, and Sloan waved them in.

They entered a room warmed by blazing logs in a stone hearth. To Tyler's right, books filled a floor-to-ceiling bookshelf. Before the fire were three easy chairs, one of which was occupied by a gray-haired man who reached for a cane, stood, and turned toward them.

The director was middle-aged with a weathered face, and as he regarded the newcomers, he frowned. "For what possible purpose could the Prophet have sent two internal affairs investigators to my castle?"

"This is merely a routine inspection, Director McDuff." Hamish's tone was ingratiating. "The Prophet is doing this with every one of his important projects."

Hamish then introduced himself as Agent Callum and Tyler as Agent David. He extended his hand, expecting McDuff to take it.

At first, McDuff didn't. Then he switched the cane to his left hand and shook both Hamish's and Tyler's hands.

"Here at the castle, you will find everything in order." The director's frown deepened. "I still don't understand the reason for your visit. I sent a report to New Babylon only a few days ago and received no complaints."

"The Prophet has no issue with your operation, Director," said Hamish. "But he does want a firsthand report from every area by sending people like us into the field."

"I suppose. But it's late. Whatever you plan to do can wait until tomorrow. Have you eaten?"

"Aye," answered Hamish.

"Good." McDuff turned abruptly to Sloan. "Please escort our guests to suitable accommodations."

Sloan nodded then led them down the spiral steps, across the courtyard, past the shivering victims in the iron cages, and into another tower. On the fifth floor, he opened the door to a four-by-six-meter room with stone walls, two single beds, a water closet in the corner, a desk with a lamp, and replicas of ancient tapestries covering two walls. "There's water and a bottle of scotch on the desk with glasses. There's also a basket with bread and cheese. If you need anything, just press the buzzer next to the door."

Then he left.

But before his footsteps echoed away down the walkway, there came the click of a lock.

Tyler went to the door and tried to open it. "We're locked in," he whispered. "They've locked the door. Do they believe us?"

"One moment." Hamish removed a small pen-like instrument from his jacket and swept the room. "No bugs. We're free to talk. If they didn't believe us, you'd think they would have sent us straight to the dungeon."

"What's the difference? Right now, we're effectively prisoners, even if they've given us scotch and a snack of bread and cheese."

"Right. I think I'll try the scotch."

CHAPTER 39
THE DUNGEON TOUR

Castle Danger, Scotland ~ March, Year 3

Micah 2:1 (NLT): *What sorrow awaits you who lie awake at night, thinking up evil plans. You rise at dawn and hurry to carry them out, simply because you have the power to do so.*

The next day, Sloan opened the door and led them down to the main floor where they ate breakfast. Then they took a tour of the outbuildings. One Quonset-hut structure was devoted to physical fitness with weights, exercise machines, and a track on the perimeter. A second long building was reserved for the guards' quarters. They peeked inside to find it divided into individual rooms. Like the others, it had two exits—one in front, another in back. Other buildings contained a gun range, a machine shop, a garage, and equipment storage. A smaller structure beside the castle's dry moat was the power plant. Then Sloan brought them back to the castle and the yard.

But up in the gibbets, the two prisoners whom Tyler had seen yesterday were slumped and unmoving in their cages. "Are they dead?" he asked.

"Aye." Sloan spat to the side. "The night was cold. They probably died of hypothermia."

From behind came the clopping of a cane, and Tyler spun to find Director McDuff. "Agents Callum and David, I will now accompany you on a tour of the dungeon. I want you to see what we do with traitors."

"Certainly," said Hamish. "We will include it in our report."

Nodding, McDuff led them across the yard. They descended a flight of stone steps to the dungeon at the bottom. But as they turned left, Tyler's gaze fell on a large wooden board with a label announcing, "Tally of Prisoners". Whatever it contained was covered by two wooden panels on hinges opening in the center.

"What's this?" he asked.

"A list of every prisoner—or should I say patient?—with their cell numbers," answered Sloan.

Tyler stared at the board and what it might reveal. Would Aurora's name and cell be under those panels?

"To the right"—McDuff pointed his cane—"you'll find cells containing Dr. Creig's control group. Our purpose here, of course, is to support the doctor in his experiments for the Decency Inquiry Project."

"And how is the project going?" asked Hamish.

"He can tell you himself later, but he has abandoned his search for a cause and is now seeking a cure."

"A cure?" asked Tyler.

McDuff shot him a puzzled look. "A cure for why people become Christians, of course."

"Yes, of course." Tyler swallowed. Maybe it was best not to ask questions.

"And where did you get the individuals for your control group?" asked Hamish.

"They were snatched off the street," answered Sloan. "They are not Christians."

By his tone, Tyler had the impression he didn't approve.

"Right."

As they walked, ceiling shafts shed a dim light at intervals onto the walk ahead, so some parts of the dungeon were not under the castle. The cells themselves were cut from rock with little illumination except from the ceiling shafts.

"Have you bugged the cells, Director?" asked Hamish. "Do you have cameras on the prisoners?"

"Spoken like a true agent from internal affairs." McDuff shook his head. "No, we have neither. Our purpose here is to support Dr. Creig in his research, not to spy on the patients, as we like to call them. Besides, we don't have the manpower needed to monitor so many individuals. We don't need cameras because the guards are constantly patrolling the perimeter."

"Of course." Hamish nodded, and Tyler was glad he'd asked the question.

But as they strolled further, a growing feeling that something wasn't right rose up inside him. It was the same sensation he'd had at the Intercontinental Conference Center and Hotel back in Geneva after he entered the room with the bent statue of gold.

Ahead and to his right, heavy bars stretched horizontally over a deep pit. A sense of great evil suddenly gripped him, and the smell of some feral, unwashed creature, mixed with sulfur and offal, accosted his nostrils. "W–what is that ahead?" he asked.

"The demon beastie." Sloan's pace increased. "Do not look into the pit."

"A demon?" asked Hamish, his eyes widening.

"Yes," said McDuff. "And now we will watch as it delivers my judgment on a woman who violated our trust and jeopardized this project."

Wanting nothing to do with what was below, Tyler shivered.

McDuff stopped before the horizontal section at the outline of a door cut into the stone. He slipped a key into a lock then motioned, and Sloan opened the heavy door. Dark stairs beckoned. Sloan grabbed a torch from a holder at the entrance, lit it, and started down.

"After you." McDuff lit another torch then waved. All four headed down the stairwell.

The farther they descended, the stronger came the sense of evil. And when the stairs opened into a stone room and Tyler's gaze went past the plexiglass to the beast beyond, he jerked back and gasped.

Giant green eyes stared out at him. A wide mouth opened, revealing dagger teeth. Two long slits substituted for a nose. Covering its body, the hair, if you could call it that, was nothing but sharp needles. Muscled arms hung nearly to its knees. Its fingers were claws, each as long as a man's hand. And its feet were as stumpy and thick as an elephant's.

McDuff went to the wall, flicked a switch, and leaned close to a speaker. "Release her."

Tyler's gaze snapped back to the cage.

On the far side of the rock enclosure, what had been barely visible before now revealed itself. Another panel of plexiglass, smaller than the one separating his group from the beast, began rising. Behind that divide was a young woman.

A look of terror so twisted her face, he almost didn't recognize her. It was Moyra Thompson, the waitress masquerading as Fiona Duncan, and he gasped.

"For some time, we've been searching for this traitor." McDuff aimed his cane at her and faced his two guests. "When one of our agents visited the Arch Inn a few nights ago, we finally caught up with her. It's amazing what one can find with the right methods of interrogation."

A scream from beyond brought Tyler's gaze back to the monster in the pit. But what happened next was too horrible to watch, and he averted his eyes.

Only when Sloan headed for the stairs did Tyler cast a final glance back into the cage.

Blood and arms and legs were scattered everywhere. Its back to them, the monster held one of the woman's arms in its claws and was gnawing on her flesh.

His gorge rising, Tyler spun toward the exit. Hamish and Sloan were already ahead of him.

They ascended in a silence broken only by the clopping of McDuff's cane behind. When all were back in the main hall, McDuff faced them with a stony glare. "Under the doctor's ministrations, she became quite forthcoming with everything that has been happening in Ullapool. For some time, an agent has been working there on my behalf, and he discovered more than just the presence of this woman."

He addressed Sloan. "You may finish the tour without me." Then he turned on his heels and hobbled up the steps toward the courtyard.

When he was gone, Sloan faced them. "I–I must apologize for that— that disgusting display. It was entirely unnecessary. I shouldn't be telling you this, but I am concerned about the director and his thing with the demon."

"What do you mean?" Hamish raised his eyebrows.

"He communes with it. He comes down here, and, using an innocent bystander from the control group, he talks with it. We feed it live elk, deer, pigs, and even cattle, but the thing is insatiable. It begs constantly for food, and McDuff obliges. Even then, the demon beastie threatens to kill us all."

"That is . . . concerning," said Hamish.

"It holds him in its power, I think. None of this needs to go in your report. Unless, of course, you think that's what headquarters wants to hear."

"They don't need to hear about this." Then Hamish seemed to catch his breath before going on. "What did he mean when he said his agent in Ullapool discovered more than just the woman?"

That was the same thing whirling through Tyler's thoughts. Had she divulged her meeting with them? Did McDuff already know that the two visiting agents weren't who they said they were?

"I–I'm not sure. He let Dr. Creig interrogate her. Some of the doctor's methods are—how should I say this?—excessively brutal. I was not privy to what happened." Sloan pointed toward the cells beyond the horizontal section. "Let's finish the tour."

They continued around the corner, passing numerous cells containing prisoners sitting on beds in semidarkness, and Tyler wondered if Aurora was in one of them.

Sloan waved to the way ahead. "After we loop around the rest of the cells, we'll return you to your rooms in the tower. From here on, I see no need to keep your door locked."

"How many prisoners are down here?" asked Tyler.

"Thirty-five Christians." Then Sloan shook his head. "Correction. Minus the two who died in the gibbets last night."

Behind him, Tyler heard someone gasp, but he continued walking. He was still recovering from the death of Moyra Thompson, too startled to look back.

* * *

WHEN AURORA HEARD A VOICE like Tyler's, she gasped. She shot from her seat on the bed and rushed to the bars. Was it possible? Was it really Tyler, or had she imagined it?

Three men had passed her cell, and all she could see was their backsides. But they were wearing UI uniforms, so how could one of them be Tyler? And, one of the men's hair was tawny, not black like Tyler's.

Should she call out? But no. If it was Tyler, he was in disguise. That meant that he and the man with him were here to rescue her. And Wallace was with them, so if it was Tyler, whatever plan they had, she must not call attention to him.

If only she could have seen his face. If only he had kept speaking.

But no. They were gone. And if they followed the loop, they wouldn't be back.

She returned to the bed and began to doubt. How could Tyler have found her? Even if he had, how could he be in a UI uniform? She must be imagining things.

CHAPTER 40

THE TALLY OF PRISONERS

Castle Danger, Scotland ~ March, Year 3

That evening, Tyler and Hamish again ate dinner in the great hall with the castle's staff. But Director McDuff, it seemed, always ate in his room alone. Tonight, the menu was haggis, neeps, and tatties. When Tyler asked what he was eating, Sloan smiled.

"Haggis is sheep's heart, liver, and lungs mixed with oatmeal, onions, and spice. Neeps are turnips, and tatties, of course, are potatoes."

"Heart, liver, and lungs, hey?" Tyler stared at what he'd speared on his fork. "Actually, it's quite good."

"Glad you like it."

When they were nearly finished, Tyler caught Sloan's glance. "How did they capture the demon beastie, as you call it? And what, exactly, is it?"

"Good questions, Agent David." Sloan sipped from his mug of ale. "I was hired after the thing was already here and have never received a proper answer. As to what it is . . ." He waved one hand. "I can only guess. As to why the director wants the thing down there—it's beyond my ken. He's unduly obsessed with the creature."

For some reason, Tyler was beginning to trust this man. Too many times, Sloan betrayed a sense of doubt—or was it disapproval?—of what went on here. "But what is it, Sloan? A demon or an animal?"

"I've only my opinion. Perhaps it is a combination of both earthly beast and demon released from below. It hates us, and were it not caged, it would surely go after us and kill us all. That is why the director's fascination and communion with the thing so concerns me."

"Yes." Tyler rubbed his chin. "Who knows what might happen when one communes, as you say, with a demon."

"Exactly." Sloan's phone beeped, and he pulled it from his pocket. After reading a text, he turned to them. "It's Ewan in the dungeon. He's on the night shift, and he wants a bottle of scotch sent down. You will please excuse me."

But he'd barely risen when his phone beeped again. Again, he answered and read the message. "The director wants to see me in his quarters at once. My delivery to Ewan must wait."

"If you want," said Tyler, "I can take the scotch to your man Ewan."

Sloan cocked his head, appearing to consider the suggestion. "No, I shouldn't." He began to walk away then stopped and returned. "What's the harm? Certainly, you can take a bottle to the men below. You know the way. Wait here."

He went into the kitchen, returned with the scotch, and handed it to Tyler. "When you're finished, one of the men is giving a bagpipe concert in tower number 2. If you wait here, I'll take you there when I'm done with the director."

After Sloan left, Hamish grinned. "Quick thinking, Tyler. Get her cell number. But be quick about it. And be careful."

"I will." With bottle in hand, he followed the hall until it intersected with the dark stairway leading down into the dungeon. LED lights instead of the ceiling shafts now lit the way.

At the bottom, a tall, thin man with a mustache met him and rushed over. "What business have you here without an escort?"

"I'm doing a favor for Agent Sloan." He waved the bottle of scotch. "I'm to give this to Ewan. Is he around?"

When the man saw the bottle, a smile lifted the corners of his lips. "Aye, he is. Wait here, and I'll get him."

Tyler waited until the man's footsteps rounded the corner and he was alone. Then he hurried to the board marked "Tally of Prisoners". With one hand, he opened both panels. He scanned the rows of names, searching for Aurora's.

"What are you doing?" came a voice from behind.

His heart sped up, but he kept reading. "I'm looking at the list of your prisoners."

"You are not authorized to do that."

Then he found it—Aurora Carter. Cell 52. And the sight of that name and her location so filled him with joy, he could almost shout. Always, there had been some doubt as to whether she was even here. But now, they knew.

A hand reached from behind and slammed the panels shut.

Tyler whirled to face the man who'd escorted them into the compound. "Agent Sloan sent me here to give this to you." He lifted the bottle of scotch.

Frowning, Ewan took the bottle. "Thank you. But you should not be poking your—"

"Do you not know who I am and why we are here?" It was time to exert some authority and put this guard in his place. And hadn't others described him as a Nazi SS officer? Tyler brought himself to his full height and stared into the man's eyes. "I am a special agent from the Office of Internal Affairs for the Ministry of Virtue with the power to investigate anything I wish. If I want to examine how you keep track of your prisoners, I have every right to do so."

Apparently, his bluster worked, for Ewan averted his eyes and nodded. "Of course, Agent David. Forgive me."

But as Tyler headed back for the staircase, Ewan added, "And tell Sloan I do thank him for the scotch."

"I will."

Tyler returned to the great hall where Hamish was nursing a second mug of ale.

"Did you get it?" asked Hamish.

"Yes." Tyler grinned. "She's here!"

Hamish slapped him on the shoulder. "Then our plan can proceed!"

CHAPTER 41

THE HUNTING TRIP

Castle Danger, Scotland ~ March, Year 3

The next day, as Tyler and Hamish were finishing lunch with Sloan in the great hall, Ewan approached them. "The director invites you to join him this afternoon on a hunt for red stag up on the moors. You do hunt, I presume?"

"Aye," said Hamish. "We would be happy to hunt with Director McDuff."

"It's overcast and cold today. As such, someone is bringing warm jackets to your room now. Meet us in the courtyard at sixteen hundred hours." Then he left.

"Odd, indeed." Sloan's gaze followed Ewan to the exit. "McDuff always hunts alone. This is the first time he has ever invited visitors to accompany him. He only takes Ewan, who holds his gun. Or sometimes, he goes with Brodie."

"Who is Brodie?" asked Tyler.

Cradling his mug of coffee, Sloan frowned. "One of McDuff's goons. I don't like the man."

Both Tyler and Hamish gave him questioning looks. Sloan obviously had issues with the director and some of his ways.

"Well!" Hamish pressed both hands on the table and stood. "The idea of hunting on the moors this fine afternoon is pure dead brilliant."

Tyler stood and faced Sloan. "Will you be joining us?"

"I have never been invited." He, too, stood. "If you return in time for supper, I'll meet you here."

They said goodbye and returned to their room where mottled red, yellow, and green hats and jackets awaited them both.

"With all this red, won't the deer see us in these?" Tyler lifted the heavy coat.

"If I remember, they can't distinguish red from green. The red is for safety." Hamish shot Tyler a wry grin. "Keeps us from shooting each other."

"Right."

* * *

UPON THEIR ARRIVAL IN THE courtyard, Ewan and another man were waiting with Director McDuff. Above them, the bodies of the two prisoners still hung in the gibbets. But birds were pecking at the eyeballs and the flesh of their faces, and Tyler tore his gaze away.

When they approached McDuff, the director waved to Ewan. "Give them their pieces."

Ewan handed each a .308 Winchester with a box of shells. "The .308 model holds five rounds in the chamber."

Tyler hefted the gun and peered down the sight.

"We use a lower quality scope," came the gravelly voice of the new man. "Gives the stags a better chance. Better sport, you ken."

Tyler nodded.

McDuff rapped his cane on the cobbles. "Our peninsula is rife with stag, some with big racks. I believe you'll find this outing quite adventurous."

"Thank you, sir, for inviting us," said Hamish.

"For two Ministry of Virtue agents with your credentials, you deserve no less than what awaits you." McDuff opened his hands then faced the Neanderthal who had spoken earlier. The man was muscled, with a bulbous nose, a permanent frown, and a mop of red hair falling over a sloping forehead. "This is Brodie, and he will be your guide. We will hunt in two parties today. As usual, Ewan will accompany me. Once on the plateau, we will separate. Too many of us in one place will scare the game. But now I must give you a warning."

"About hunting safety, I presume?" Hamish smiled.

McDuff shook his head. "Recently, there have been intruders, unauthorized personnel, up on the heath. If you see anyone other than us on the hunt, you are authorized to shoot them without warning."

"Without warning?" asked Tyler.

"Yes, and if such trespassers cross your path"—McDuff grinned—"then the hunt will change, and these violators, not the red stag, will become your quarry."

Tyler shuddered. The man was serious. He wondered if he could get out of this, but—no! To back out now would cause suspicion.

"Let's go!" came Brodie's gravelly order.

They left the castle, the outbuildings, and passed through the perimeter fence. McDuff led with his cane while Ewan carried McDuff's rifle behind him. The rest followed the director's halting, clopping gait, but no one wished to outpace him. Though he limped, the man pressed on, even as they climbed the ridge to the plateau.

Then they were near the spot where Tyler and Hamish had looked down upon the compound so many nights ago.

"Here, we will separate." McDuff pointed his cane to the right. "Ewan and I will go that way, and you will take the rocks and pines on the left. That is where you will most likely find a stag."

Brodie raised his rifle in acknowledgment and started off to the left.

"Good hunting!" said Ewan as he and McDuff headed for the forested slope on the right.

Brodie led, but he was already fifty meters ahead of them. The man shot a look back. "Keep up. Don't fall behind."

Hamish glanced at Tyler with a frown and increased his pace.

A pine forest covered sloping, rocky ground, and the footing was often treacherous. Brodie never slowed, and now he was nearly a hundred meters ahead.

"What's he doing?" asked Tyler. "We're going to lose him."

"Aye, but watch your step. The footing here is tricky."

Nodding, Tyler continued.

But a few minutes later, he heard a cry and looked back.

Hamish was on the ground, clutching his foot. "I think I sprained an ankle."

Tyler returned to him. This was the second time one of them had slipped on these rocks.

"I'm going back." Hamish stood again and tried some weight on his injured foot. "Sprained or not, I can't keep up with that jackrabbit up there."

Tyler glanced toward where he'd last seen their guide. But the man was gone.

"This is odd, Hamish." Tyler's gaze searched the pines where Brodie had disappeared. "What kind of guide leaves his party like this?"

"I don't know." Using his rifle butt as a crutch, Hamish began hobbling back the way they'd come. After a few meters, he looked back. "But you'd better continue the hunt and play along. Just be careful."

"Right." Then Tyler headed off in the direction of his missing guide. They were already well past the area containing the cave with their cache.

For maybe thirty minutes, he walked the rock-covered slope beneath towering Scots pines. The drought had yellowed most of the needles. Even so, the scent of pine still hung in the air.

Something whizzed close to his ear, followed by the echo of a gunshot. Someone had shot at him!

He dropped to the ground before a small clump of boulders. Removing his hat, he found a slice missing from the material.

Who was shooting at him and why? Was it one of the intruders McDuff had mentioned? But no, he and Hamish had been the intruders, and somehow the castle had found evidence of their presence on the moors that night.

Here, he was too much of a target. He glanced behind him toward a larger rock outcropping. That would make better cover. He shot to his feet and began sprinting toward it.

A bullet slammed into a tree trunk beside him.

Tyler whirled and raced back to the safety of the boulders. Again, he dropped down. But just before he did, he caught a glimpse of someone about a hundred yards away, a man wearing a jacket like his—mottled red, yellow, and green. Was it Brodie?

"Brodie!" he called from the shelter of the rocks. "It's me. Stop shooting."

He poked his head up and waved. "It's me, Brodie."

Another bullet whizzed close by Tyler's head, followed closely by a second shot that sparked off the rocks beside him, sending a piece of rock against his forehead. He fell to the ground and felt where something had stung him. His hand came back red. But the wound was superficial.

Brodie was trying to murder him!

Was this the plan all along? To lure them out on the moors and kill them both? Then Brodie could claim he thought they were the so-called intruders, and without witnesses, who could object?

In the distance, the overcast sky lit up with lightning. Seconds later, thunder rumbled through the valley.

What should he do? Brodie meant to kill him, and if Tyler just sat here, doing nothing, his attacker would eventually get a clear shot. He was left with only one option—he must shoot back.

Another lightning strike lit up the sky. More thunder boomed in the distance, and wind rippled the needles at his feet.

He chambered a round in the .308 then grabbed a branch from the ground at his feet and placed his hat upon it. Taking a deep breath, he stuck the hat above the rocks.

A bullet—Brodie's fifth—hit the hat, throwing it off the stick. That would be the last round in his chamber, and Brodie would have to reload. Now was the time to act.

Tyler peered over the top of the rocks.

There! A coat of mottled colors hiding behind a tree only fifty meters away. So close! Brodie had moved far from his original position, and while he was reloading, he didn't see Tyler.

He snapped his rifle up, rested it against the rocks, and oh, so carefully, aimed. Just as Brodie looked up, Tyler squeezed the trigger. The rifle kicked back, and the man who was trying to kill him fell behind a rock pile.

Tyler fell back behind his cover, breathing heavily. Had he shot his target? Or had Brodie just ducked? For long minutes, he lay there on his back, wondering what to do. Retrieving his hat, he raised it again. But all that resulted was silence.

He called out.

But he received no response, only a flash of lightning and distant thunder.

Slowly, he stood. But no one fired at him.

A fierce wind tore through the branches above, felling needles all around him.

He walked the distance to where his opponent lay sprawled, unmoving, on the ground. He nudged the body with his foot. But there was no response. A pool of blood on the pine needles was all the testimony he needed—Brodie was dead.

For the first time in his life, Tyler'd killed a man. But what else could he have done? Brodie was trying to kill him. Tyler stared at the corpse.

One moment, Brodie was alive, with blood pumping through his veins, with feelings and aspirations and desires. The next instant, he was a lifeless pile of flesh.

Where was Brodie now? Was he regretting what he'd done with his life? If the Bible was correct, Brodie was writhing in the flames of Hell.

Still focused on the corpse, Tyler whispered, "Dear Lord, forgive what I have done. But what else could I do?"

Thunder shook the ground as a bolt of electricity lashed the valley. He raised his glance to the overcast sky. The light was already dimming, and some kind of storm was brewing—one with wind, lightning, and thunder. But without rain.

It was a forty-minute trek back to the compound.

He started out.

CHAPTER 42

TIME TO ACT

Castle Danger, Scotland ~ March, Year 3

As lightning played along the ridgetops and thunderclaps rumbled through the valley, Tyler arrived at the gate after dusk where a guard let him in. He passed through the portcullis and entered the courtyard where Director McDuff was waiting to meet him. Ewan stood not far away.

"What happened?" McDuff leaned against his cane and glanced through the open gap toward the moors beyond. "Where is Brodie?"

"He began shooting at me, and he wouldn't stop. He must have thought I was a–an intruder."

"He was shooting at you." But McDuff said this more as a statement than a question.

"Yes. He pinned me down. And he wouldn't stop. So I shot back. I had to."

"You shot back?" McDuff's glance searched the yard beyond the gate. "Where is he?"

"He's dead."

"You shot him?" The director's eyes widened. "You killed Brodie?"

"I had no choice."

The director stared at Tyler for long seconds before speaking. "He must have thought you were one of the intruders we've seen on the moors. I apologize for what he did. I expect you had no choice."

Then he turned and hobbled away.

Tyler hurried into the yard, and Ewan approached. "I heard everything. Where did you leave Brodie?"

Tyler tried to describe the location.

"And you're certain he is dead?"

"Yes."

"Lamentable." Ewan frowned. "Brodie was a good man. Truly lamentable."

"Yes."

"It's too dark, too late, to bring him back now. And there's a lightning storm." Ewan's tone was like some chill wind blowing off an icebound lake. "Tomorrow, you will lead us to where you shot him, and we will retrieve the body." Then he left.

Tyler climbed the stairwell to his tower and entered the room where Hamish was waiting. "What happened? You're late."

After Tyler described how Brodie tried to murder him and how Tyler had killed his opponent, Hamish went to the barred window and looked out at the lightning. "They know. This was planned. If we're going to free Aurora, we have to act fast."

"Do you think they contacted Jerusalem or New Babylon about us?"

"Possibly."

"Then why don't they just arrest us now?"

"Good question." Hamish turned back into the room. "Maybe they're hoping to discover if others are in league with us here? I wonder if they know about Lisette and Brett in Ullapool."

"So what do we do now?" Tyler went to the desk and poured a shot of scotch.

"Tomorrow night or the night after. That's when we'll do it. They've said we could stroll beyond the compound. If they don't stop us, then after supper, one of us will go to the cache and bring back what we need. With the C-4, we can create a diversion to keep everyone busy long enough so we can free Aurora."

Tyler pulled out the desk chair and plopped into it. "I don't know, Hamish. This plan sounded great when we were outside. But now, here, inside, knowing what we know, how can it possibly work? Even if we free her, how are we going to get both her and us out?"

Hamish nodded. "I know. But what else can we do? Can you think of another plan?"

Tyler shook his head. "No."

"If we're going ahead with this, I need to let our Friends in Inverness know. But I'll tell them not to enter the peninsula until we give them the signal. You should also contact Brett. He should go to Inverness tonight. The Friends insisted that someone lead them to the hidden road, and given how difficult it is to find, they have a point. Give Brett their number so they can direct him to their place. Tomorrow night, either Lisette or Maeve can take the boat to Alltnaharrie. That's our escape route."

While Hamish called the Friends of Inverness, Tyler called Brett and told him the plan.

After both had delivered their messages, Hamish sat on the bed. "It's done. If the time is right, tomorrow or the night after, we'll free Aurora. And maybe a few others."

But moments later, a fist pounded on the door.

Tyler left the desk and opened it to a frowning Ewan. Behind him, one of McDuff's muscled goons held a semiautomatic rifle. "We just detected cell phone traffic from somewhere inside the castle." Ewan pointed to the phone lying on the bed beside Hamish. "You have cell phones, do you not?"

"We do." Hamish rose from the bed. "As is our right as agents of the Office of—"

"It is our policy to allow no unauthorized outgoing calls from the castle. We neglected to collect your phones before. Now, you must turn them in."

"We need them for our work here so that—"

"I'm sorry, but this is not negotiable." Ewan waved to the guard behind him who entered the room, shouldered his gun, and extended his hand.

First, Hamish, then Tyler relinquished their phones.

Ewan's frown morphed into a smile, and he nodded. "Thank you. They will be returned to you when you leave."

After they were gone, Tyler went to the door and tried the knob. He faced Hamish. "He didn't lock it. Do they suspect us or not?"

"Brodie tried to kill you, didn't he? So McDuff knows. But why didn't Ewan lock the door?" Hamish rubbed his chin and turned a questioning look to Tyler. "Like I said before, they must be waiting for us to implicate others in the castle."

"Which means the sooner we act, the better. So tomorrow night, it is. We're doing the right thing."
"Aye."

CHAPTER 43

THE NEXT MESSAGE

Ullapool, Scotland ~ March, Year 3

Lisette, Brett, and Maeve were on the street, returning from dinner at the Arch Inn when Brett received a call on his phone. It was from Tyler, and Brett relayed new orders to Lisette and Maeve. "Looks like I'm driving to Inverness tonight," he said.

"Why tonight?" asked Lisette.

"Because if they're going to free Aurora and as many prisoners as they can—and that's a big if—then the Friends at Inverness must be there on the moors with transportation. But they won't go until we get the signal from Tyler."

"Right," she replied.

Moments later, Maeve spoke to Brett. "I want to go with you."

"And leave me behind?" Scowling, Lisette crossed her arms. They always assumed she wanted the safest job.

"Someone's got to take the boat to Alltnaharrie," said Brett.

"All right. You two go. If you must."

Up in the room, she watched Maeve pack a bag. Then they met Brett in the hall where Lisette said goodbye to them. "I guess I won't see you until this is all over. After you've led the Inverness Friends to the turn, when will we meet again?"

"We'll return back here." Then Maeve hugged her. "It will be all right."

"Okay."

Brett passed her the key to his room. "If Tyler gets back before me, he'll want to get into the room and change."

"Then I'll keep the key for you." She took it, and they left her.

A half hour later, Brett sent her a text from the road, saying he forgot to check the notebook today. He'd secured both it and their new Bible in the room's safe. He also gave her the combination.

Now she was glad he'd left his key. In his room, she opened the safe and pulled out the notebook. She flipped through the pages, and—there was a new message! She read:

> *If Tyler attempts to bring his cache of destruction back into the castle of evil, he will face discovery. He must leave the cache where it is. Ecclesiastes 3:1–3.*

She took Brett's Bible and found the passage.

> *For everything there is a season, a time for every activity under heaven. A time to be born and a time to die. A time to plant and a time to harvest. A time to kill and a time to heal. A time to tear down and a time to build up.*

"What does that mean?" she said to herself. She gripped the top of her head with both hands and circled the room. The plan was for Tyler to take the C-4 into the compound and create a diversion. Without the explosives, there was no plan!

She read the message again. It was clear. If Tyler tried to bring the cache into the castle, he'd be captured.

She took the notebook and Bible back to her room and put them in her safe. Then she called Tyler.

But there was no answer.

She tried again, and a strange voice answered, "Who is this?"

"Who are *you*?" she asked. "Where is Tyler?"

"Tyler?" came the answer. "Who is Tyler?"

"Sorry, I must have dialed the wrong number." Then she hung up.

Somebody else had answered, and like an idiot, she'd asked for Tyler. Did she just blow his cover?

Then she called Brett and told him everything that had happened.

"We're almost there," he said. "It's too late to turn back."

"It's all falling apart, isn't it?" she asked.

"Maybe not. We should continue to Inverness. You'll have to go to the moors tomorrow night yourself and stop him. Don't let him bring that cache back into the castle."

"But I don't know the way."

"Hold on. Maeve will give you directions."

After Maeve described the route she should take and Lisette hung up, she sat on the bed.

It was all falling apart, wasn't it?

CHAPTER 44

SQUADDIES!

Lake Bracciano, Italy ~ March, Year 3

Nick and Brooke sat under the porch eaves, overlooking the lake. A brisk wind whipped his sweatshirt and tousled her hair. Out on the water, gulls circled and cried.

A hundred meters to the right, a group of teenagers was playing a game of soccer on the beach, what they called football here. Their shouts and encouragements gave the afternoon a sense of normalcy.

"Does it have to be tomorrow, Nick?" Brooke drew her jacket tighter about her waist and zipped it up.

"Yes, as soon as Carlita Marino returns." He reached over, clasped her hand, and squeezed.

He'd planned to leave the lake sooner, but arrangements had to be made.

Dante Marino was a good man, an old friend who had faithfully watched the villa in Nick's absence, and it was his suggestion they were following. "Go to my cousin Carlita's in Venice," he'd said. "She has a nice place in the Old City, and she doesn't care for what's been happening in the world today. You two will get along famously." Dante then winked and gave him a wry grin. "She's involved in the black market. Anything to thwart the Unitum Imperium."

Nick had accepted the offer, but when Dante had called her to make arrangements, she was in Bolzano, in the foothills of the Alps, on business. But she was returning tomorrow. So, using their fake IDs, Nick had bought train tickets, and their bags were packed.

Brooke lifted his hand to her lips and kissed it. Her eyes peered into his. "Let's get married."

His head jerked back, and his mouth opened, closed, opened again. Then he smiled. "Is that a proposal?"

"Sounds like it, doesn't it?" She swiveled so her whole body faced him. "I think it's time, don't you?"

The smile that parted his lips grew into a grin. "Yes, yes, it is. But maybe after things settle down. Everything right now is so . . . so unsettled."

She let go of his hand and turned away. "It always is, isn't it? Things *never* settle down." She faced him again. "But maybe if we find a quiet place in Venice—at this Carlita's—maybe we can finally relax without the Unitum Imperium breathing down our necks. Then—yes!—let's get married!"

"Yes, let's. I'm sure things will settle down. And then—"

But before he could finish, Dante rushed through the first-floor door onto the porch. His eyes were wide, and one hand was waving furiously. "They're here, Signore! Men in black vans. They're circling the house."

Nick caught Brooke's hand, shot out of his seat, and hurried her inside.

Dante gestured toward the stairs. "Go to the attic! And take your bags!"

They grabbed their bags from the hall and ascended the stairs two at a time, ending at the second level and its three rarely-used guest rooms. At the hall's far end, he tugged on the chain that let down the panel holding the folding ladder. Grasping the board, he pulled, and the steps unfolded until they touched the floor. Then he motioned to Brooke.

But she couldn't climb holding the bag, and she dropped it.

"Go without it." From the floor below came brusque voices of command and heavy footsteps.

She climbed to the top. Then he pitched both bags to her, and she caught them. He clambered up next, holding onto the cord attached to the bottom of the folding ladder. Once in the attic, he yanked, folding the ladder and shutting the panel behind him. From below, all anyone would now see was the outline of a ceiling panel.

The attic was dark and musty, but they'd planned for this. He fumbled for the flashlight they'd secreted beside the two-by-six, or whatever they called the studs here, and switched it on.

"Back there." He pointed the light into the far corner. "But walk only on the studs."

"Okay."

He carried both bags, stepping carefully, slowly, across the attic as footsteps and voices leaked up from below. The squaddies were on the second level!

At the attic's far corner, the sloping roof met the floor, leaving a gap of only one meter. Now he crawled on hands and knees over the plywood he'd placed there earlier. He shone the light on a hidden door in the roof, something he'd installed when they'd last lived here. Dropping the bags in the shadows, he pushed, the hinges creaked, and he cringed.

It opened a hole wide enough for a person to crawl through. He motioned to Brooke, and she climbed onto the tegole tiles covering the roof. No sooner had she done this than a light appeared from behind. He glanced back.

The attic door was opening from below. The squaddies would be up here in moments.

He climbed out the escape hatch. Kneeling on the terra-cotta tiles surrounding the hatch's flat surface, he lowered the door until it shut. Again, it complained, and again, he cringed.

He sat on the tiles, breathing fast. On the yard far below, a man wearing a green-and-white CSA uniform walked into view, peered toward the beach, then disappeared into the house. Fortunately, he never looked up at the roof.

Up here, the wind chilled, and Nick huddled close to Brooke. Time passed as they waited for Dante's signal. Brooke shivered in his arms, but she said nothing.

Finally, Dante appeared on the grounds beyond the house and waved to them. The squaddies were gone.

They retraced their escape route, and Dante met them in the upstairs hallway.

"That was close, Signore." The man wiped sweat from his brow. "They searched longer this time."

"But they didn't find us."

"Sì." Dante grinned. "Your hiding place worked."

But beside him, Brooke was shaking.

"They almost caught us, Nick." Again, she fell into his arms. "What if the same thing happens in Venice? What if there's no place that's safe? If this Carlita is in the black market, won't that attract the attention of these squaddies?"

"No, Signora." Dante shook his head. "She is very careful. She is clever. They will never catch Carlita. You will be safe there."

Nick nodded. "We'll be okay, Brooke."

"I hope so. We need to leave here. Tomorrow can't come soon enough."

CHAPTER 45

A MEETING ON THE HEATH

Lochbroom, Scotland ~ March, Year 3

As gulls cried and circled overhead, Lisette stood on the dock at Alltnaharrie and watched the fishing boat putter back across the loch toward Ullapool. Wisps of red, orange, and yellow clouds surrounded the western sun, still an hour or more from setting.

For tonight's trek, she wore Maeve's hiking boots and a heavy jacket. Each hand clutched a walking stick.

She wasn't supposed to be here. None of them were. But Brett and Maeve were doing their part, and now this was hers. Someone had to warn Tyler he was walking into danger.

Maeve had explained the route to follow. Lisette just hoped she wouldn't get lost.

No hiker was she, but she'd do whatever was necessary to save Tyler.

She climbed to the plateau by flashlight. But too many times, she had to stop and catch her breath.

A nearly full moon illuminated the way, but Maeve's boots were loose on her feet. Up on the flat, the going was easier, but the footing was treacherous. Too many rocks. And too much heather, all of it brittle from the drought.

By the time she reached the ridge overlooking the castle, she was tired, ready to quit.

She peered down on the compound surrounded by razor wire, illuminated by floodlights, and patrolled by guard dogs, and she shuddered. What kind of madness caused Tyler and Hamish to pretend they were UI agents and enter that place? What kind of madness drove the UI to imprison innocents like Aurora?

At the last minute, she'd discussed with Maeve how best to meet Tyler, and they decided she should wait for him at the edge of the pine forest, not at the cave. The cave would be harder to find. In any event, Tyler had to cross the ridgetop first.

The trek took longer than she wanted. She'd hiked as fast as she could, but her progress had been slow. What if Tyler had come and gone?

For half an hour, she lay on the heather, watching the castle below and waiting.

A helicopter rose from the pad inside the compound, heading her way. She glanced toward the pine forest on her right. Should she hide there? Or would the copter veer off?

No, it was heading straight for her.

She stood and raced across the heath. The whirring, chattering blades topped the ridge just moments after she entered the forest for the safety of a pine trunk.

Had they seen her? She peered between the yellowed boughs.

The machine didn't stop but kept going, following the route she'd taken to get here.

After it passed, she returned to the ridge and dropped back into her watching position.

Moments later, a man crossed the compound and stopped at the gate. A guard opened it, and the man passed through.

He was heading her way! Was it Tyler?

She squinted to get a better look, but he was too far away.

Her heart was beating fast now, and the minutes seemed like hours. But he was climbing the ridge. For a few moments, he disappeared from sight. Then he reappeared on the plateau to her right and headed toward her. But he hadn't seen her yet.

She backed away from the edge far enough so that those below couldn't see her. Then she began running toward him.

He stopped, possibly confused. She wasn't supposed to be here, was she?

But when she could see his face, he could see hers, and now he began running to meet her. When they met, he hugged her and kissed her on the cheek. "Why are you here?" He held her at arm's length. "What's going on?"

"We couldn't reach you, and we received an urgent message from the notebook."

"What kind of message?"

"A warning, Tyler. It said that if you attempt to bring the explosives and weapons with you into the compound, they'll catch you."

He released her and stepped back. "B–but that was our plan. Without the explosives, we have no diversion, no plan. It doesn't make sense."

"I know." She winced. That was exactly what she was thinking.

He rubbed his chin and stared at the ground. "But every other message has been right. I can't ignore it, can I?"

"No."

He peered into her eyes. "Where are the others?"

"Brett and Maeve went to Inverness to meet the Friends and guide them to the hidden turnoff."

He turned away and slammed a fist into a palm. "Our whole plan—ruined! This is bad, really bad."

"I don't know what to say. But the notebook has always been right."

"You mean God. It's not the notebook speaking to us; it's God."

"Right." She had to admit it. God had been speaking through the notebook.

The chattering of helicopter blades approached from the south. Lisette shot a glance toward the forest. "I'd better hide."

"Go!" He waved toward the pines. "It's coming fast!"

She whirled and again raced toward the pine forest. The safety of the trees was only fifty meters away when she slipped on a rock and fell. She stood, but she'd hurt her knee, and now she was hobbling.

When the helicopter crossed the ridgeline, she was still in view. She entered the forest again and looked back. But it continued, descending below the ridge. Tyler was also gone. He'd be making his way to the castle, but without the means to create their diversion.

She waited a few minutes, and when nothing happened, she began the long trek back.

Her progress was slow. The hiking sticks helped, but each step was painful. After twenty minutes, she was in the middle of the plateau when the whirring blades again appeared from behind.

She cast a glance to either side. There was no cover here, no place to hide. The pine forest was too far away up the nearest slope. She'd never make it. She did the only thing she could—she fell to the ground and rolled into a ball.

Maybe they'd think she was a rock.

But her ruse didn't work. The copter landed thirty meters ahead, and she stood.

Two men bearing automatic weapons got out. The tallest of them barked an order. "Drop what you're holding and raise your hands!"

She released her hiking sticks and raised her hands.

"You are under arrest for trespassing on Unitum Imperium property."

Then they handcuffed her, brought her into the helicopter, and took off for the castle.

CHAPTER 46

LISETTE

Castle Danger, Scotland ~ March, Year 3

The bald man with a goatee and devil tattoos on both arms led Lisette under the portcullis and into the courtyard. They stopped before a wooden pillar where waited a handsome man with a strong jaw and a weathered face.

"What should I do with her, Sloan?" asked the guard.

Taking a pistol from his belt, Sloan rapped it twice on the pillar. From above came the fluttering of wings and the cawing of crows. Only then did she look up.

Two bodies were hanging up there in two iron cages, two corpses upon which the crows had been feeding. One look at what remained of their faces started a shivering in her shoulders that wouldn't quit.

"Take her to a cell, Ewan," said the man identified as Sloan. "Creig will want to interrogate her later."

Ewan nodded, grabbed a shoulder, and pushed her across the yard. They entered a hall and descended a dark stone staircase. At the bottom, they passed cell after cell of prisoners in stone cubicles, and Lisette's shivering continued.

But where the cells ended and they approached a wide horizontal section covered with thick iron bars, panic rose up inside her like frightened bats fleeing a cave.

She gagged at the smell of something feral and unwashed, an odor of sulfur mixed with offal.

Then came a sense of some great evil, as if she were standing at the gates of Hell itself.

"'Tis McDuff's demon." Ewan waved at the bars. "Don't look at it."

He led her quickly past. They rounded a corner, and he took her to cell number 51. Taking a device from his pocket, he punched a button, and the door clicked open. He pushed her inside then left.

As his feet echoed away, she stared at the stone walls, the iron bars, the bed with a blanket covering a thin mattress, and her shivering wouldn't stop. She plopped onto the bed, dropped her head in her hands, and sobbed.

"Hello?" came a voice from the front. "Is someone there?"

Lisette drew a deep breath. "Yes."

"It's okay," came the voice again, and it was familiar. "Don't cry. You'll be all right."

Yes, the voice was familiar. Could it possibly be? "Aurora? Aurora, is that you?"

"Lisette! Yes, it's me. It's Aurora."

Lisette rushed to the front and gripped the bars. "I've made a terrible mess of things. I went to the moors to warn Tyler, and—"

"Tyler! What do you mean? Where is Tyler?"

Then she explained their plans, how Tyler and Hamish had infiltrated the castle in the guise of UI agents, how they'd planned to create a diversion with explosives, and how the notebook's message had warned Tyler not to bring anything into the compound or he'd be caught. She finished with, "All our plans have fallen apart."

"I see."

There followed a gloomy silence, broken only by the footsteps of an approaching guard. Lisette withdrew into her cell until he passed.

"We must hold onto hope, Lisette." Aurora had returned to the front.

"This place is evil, Aurora." Lisette met her at the bars and gripped them. "There were corpses hanging in the courtyard and a demon in a pit. And a man named Sloan told my guard that a Dr. Creig would interrogate me later."

Again, there was silence until Aurora spoke. "I wish you had become a Christian, Lisette. Then no matter what happens, you'd have God to pray to, someone to comfort you, someone to give you hope."

"I–I wish I could believe as you do." She closed her eyes. "Maybe someday."

"I'm glad to hear that."

They talked a while longer until the guards turned down the lights and ordered everyone to be quiet. Then she found her bed.

But before she went to sleep, she did something she'd never done before.

"Lord God, I have never prayed before, but hear me now. Please get me out of this place. No, not just me. Get me and Aurora and Tyler and this Hamish person—get us all out. Please accept my stupid prayer. Thank you."

After she prayed, she felt better, and sleep came quickly.

CHAPTER 47

A RISKY PROPOSITION

Venice, Italy ~ March, Year 3

As the train wheels screeched, Nick helped Brooke step onto the platform. Behind him, a troop of squaddies departed. All through their seven-hour ride, Brooke kept glancing at the uniformed agents across the aisle, fidgeting with a book she never read.

The journey took longer than expected. Part of the trip was via bus to bypass track damaged by the quakes.

The platform was outside, and already it was dark. Inside the Venice Santa Lucia Station, Nick found a sign for Informazioni Turistiche. This late in the evening, only a handful of passengers were departing from the station's sixteen tracks.

The tourist information booth was closed, but standing next to it was a middle-aged, black-haired woman wearing a suede leather jacket, and he approached. "Sometimes, the sun shines on cloudy days."

"Only the Son can banish the darkness." She extended a hand, and he took it.

"You must be Carlita," said Nick.

"And you are Nick and Brooke." She smiled. "Welcome to Venice. I was beginning to wonder what happened to your train."

"They bused us part of the way." He waved his free hand. "The earthquake, you know."

"Ah, sì, the hand of God falls heavy on our planet, does it not? My place is only a short walk from here. Follow me."

The station was on the Grand Canal, and they followed their host over a bridge into the Old City. She pointed to a barge puttering over the waterway beside them carrying boxes of produce. Lights illuminated the bow and stern. "Do you see the logo on the side of that ship?"

Squinting, Nick made out the hexagram with the globe, the map of Europe, and Davato's initials painted on the hull.

"That's for the Unitum Imperium elite," she said. "The rest of us have to scrounge for scraps."

They entered a warren of streets, crossed a half dozen canal bridges, and stopped at the door of a narrow, three-story house, painted red. She ushered them inside then led them to a room on the third floor where they dropped their backpacks. "You must be tired after your trip. Have you eaten?"

"Not since this morning," answered Nick. "There was nothing on the train, and when we switched cars, the price for two sandwiches was so outrageous, I couldn't bring myself to pay."

"The famine continues, does it not? Would you like supper?"

"That would be appreciated," said Brooke. "Can I help?"

"You can cook?" Carlita's eyes lit up.

"I can."

"Well, thanks for the offer, but I can manage." She showed them a small WC. "If you'd like to freshen up, I'll call you downstairs when supper is ready."

"Thank you," said Nick.

* * *

It was past nine when Carlita served them linguine in olive oil, followed by a course of sausages. The local red wine accompanied the meal, and he drank several glasses.

When they'd finished, Carlita brought them coffee and flan she'd made earlier that day. "I don't know how long I can get the ingredients for this kind of meal. Everything is harder to get nowadays. And so expensive!"

As they ate, she caught Nick's glance. "I understand from Dante that you used to work for the Unitum Imperium?"

"It wasn't by choice." He frowned. "A company called Veritas Systems hired me after Turner Enterprises went broke. I'm sure you've heard of both. I was working with Adam Tuner when Veritas was folded into the Ministry of Truth. Suddenly, I was trapped with no way out. But it finally became clear I had to leave. The things they wanted me to do to prove my loyalty . . ." Remembering how he had thrown the Molotov cocktail into a supposedly empty building and the deaths that resulted sent a shiver down his back.

"Davato lived and worked in the Clal Center where we had our apartment." Brooke's forehead scrunched. "I never felt safe there. I couldn't wait to leave."

"The Clal Center was his headquarters in the city?"

"It is." Nick cradled his mug of coffee. "The next thing they wanted me to do . . . well . . . I had to get out. They were also becoming suspicious."

"Are you both Christians?" Carlita cocked her head.

"No," said Brooke. "But I think, for me, the time is right."

"What about you, Nick?" Carlita's eyes brightened.

"Yes, now that we're out, now that Davato isn't watching my every move, then—yes!"

"Good." Carlita clapped. "If you want, I can take you to a house church where we can baptize you. But before we do that, I have a proposition for you both."

"What?" He tensed. Were strings attached if they wanted to stay here?

"I am in the process of leaving Venice and moving my black-market operation to Bolzano. That's fast becoming our distribution point for all of northern Italy. Right now, we're dealing mostly in IDs, travel documents, bank cards, and travel tickets." She raised her eyebrows. "Did Dante tell you any of this?"

"He said you were in the black market, but that's all."

"Sì, well, maybe that was for the best." She finished the last bite of flan and pushed the plate away. "After the move, I'll be leaving behind an empty house and a new mission here that I've recently begun."

"What kind of mission?" Nick didn't know where this was going, but he steeled himself for what she might say next.

"There is an increasing need for a way station, a safe house, if you will, for Christians fleeing the Unitum Imperium and their persecutions. I have done this off and on in league with another man who is arriving tomorrow. He arranges travel for those in need—things like I just mentioned. Most of these folks want to go to the Portuguese island of Madeira. Officially, it's part of the Unitum Imperium. But unofficially, the majority of the populace is in rebellion against Davato. They are fiercely independent, and the Truth Squad the UI stationed on the island became so corrupted, they were recalled. The island is essentially free of UI interference."

"I hadn't heard this." Nick leaned forward. "What does your man have to do with this island?"

"He facilitates passage for fleeing Christians who want to go there. But to do his job, he travels so often, he can't stay here in Venice. Only two of us are doing this right now, and to make it work, we need a couple to live here, maintain the house, and host travelers as they pass through. A couple will attract less attention than a single man or woman. Regardless of the nonsense spouted by our so-called Prophet, we here in Italy are still family oriented."

"Are you asking if *we* want to do this?" Brooke's eyes were wide.

"Sì." Carlita sat back and gave them questioning looks. "You are the perfect couple. So what do you think?"

Nick glanced at Brooke, but he couldn't read her. "Maybe we should talk it over."

"Fair enough." Carlita checked her watch. "I'm sure you're tired after traveling all day. We can talk in the morning."

When Nick and Brooke were alone in their room, he asked her what she thought.

"I'm not sure, Nick. It sounds risky. What if the squaddies find us? They'd send us to the camp."

"But Carlita and others like her helped *us* get away. Think of how many other people need to escape from the Antichrist and the squaddies. Shouldn't we do what we can to help them?"

She smiled and laid a hand on his. "You are a good person, Nick Carter. I would like to do it, but I need time to think about it. Right now, it's just too soon."

"All right." He kissed her cheek. "Take as much time as you need."

CHAPTER 48

CREIG'S CHAMBER OF HORRORS

Castle Danger, Scotland ~ March, Year 3

Romans 2:6–8 (NLT): *He will judge everyone according to what they have done. He will give eternal life to those who keep on doing good, seeking after the glory and honor and immortality that God offers. But he will pour out his anger and wrath on those who live for themselves, who refuse to obey the truth and instead live lives of wickedness.*

It was midmorning when, once again, Wallace knocked on the door to Dr. Creig's laboratory. Beside him was the new woman whom he had just brought up from the dungeon. Her name was Lisette, she was Italian, and they'd caught her on the moors only last night. What she was doing there was anybody's guess, and now she was in deep trouble.

The door opened, and Creig beckoned them inside.

Creig hadn't even begun, and already, the woman was shaking. This did not bode well for her.

"Put her in the chair." Creig nodded, Wallace motioned for her to obey, but she backed up.

"No, woman! Do not do this!" Creig sighed and waved to Wallace.

He grabbed Lisette's shoulders and eased her toward the metal seat with its open claws waiting to clamp down upon arms and legs.

She sat, the clamps engaged, and the woman was secure.

As Creig filled a syringe and fear filled the woman's eyes, Wallace hurried into the hall. He had no desire to witness Creig at work.

For the next two hours, he sat and examined the stonework patterns on the walls, the ceiling, the floor. From behind the laboratory door came Creig's muffled voice, and, occasionally, frightened screams from the woman. Then came silence.

The door opened, and Creig called out. "I need your help in here."

Wallace entered.

The woman's eyes were dilated, and even though there was a strap around her forehead, she was rocking her head from side to side. A silly grin parted her lips.

Creig whispered in Wallace's ear. "I've tried two different drugs to no effect. It's quite interesting that she hasn't broken yet. I've just given her a hallucinogen, and it's beginning to work. This will certainly get her to open up."

The doctor produced a metal headpiece with two tiny arms. "Hold her head still."

Frowning, Wallace stood behind the woman and gripped her head on both sides. As he did so, she peered back into his eyes with a wide smile.

Creig wrapped the headpiece around her skull. As Wallace held her still, Creig moved clamps toward each eye. One by one, he fastened them on her eyelids so she couldn't blink or shut her eyes. Then he moved another two-pronged device close, and, slowly, it began dripping drops of saline into both eyes.

Wallace backed into the corner while Creig donned sunglasses. Then the doctor switched on a projector that showered the room and the woman with a kaleidoscope of ever-changing colors—red, green, yellow, bright white, magenta, and purple. But the lights were so bright and disorienting, Wallace blinked and squinted. How could anyone tolerate that?

Then Creig began bombarding her with questions. "Why were you up on the heath, Lisette?"

"The heath." She giggled. "The moors. I was up on the moors."

"Yes, you were, Lisette. But why?" He lit another cigarette.

"Why was I on the moors?" A ridiculous smile parted her lips.

"That's the question, yes. What you were doing up there?" Creig's cigarette dangled between two fingers.

"Where am I? Why am I here?" She rocked her head from side to side, and the drops splashed on her cheeks. "It's bright. So bright."

"You are in a hospital, and I'm trying to help you." But his smile was condescending, smarmy, and Wallace wanted to slap him. "The light will help you."

"A hospital?" She giggled again. "Are you a doctor?"

"Yes, Lisette, I'm a doctor. Now focus." He sucked in on the cigarette. "Why were you up on the moors?"

This line of questioning continued for long minutes until Creig asked a new question. "Were you trying to reach someone on the moors?"

"Tyler was on the moors. I went to meet Tyler."

"Tyler?" Creig gave a nod to Wallace. "Yes, Lisette, we know about Tyler. He's here with me now."

"Tyler?" Now her forehead strained against the strap. "Are you there, Tyler?"

"Yes, he's here beside me, Lisette. But he can't talk right now." Creig shot another smarmy smile at Wallace. "He wants to know why you were trying to reach him."

"You didn't take it back, did you?" Suddenly, her silly disposition turned to fear. "Don't take it back, Tyler, or they'll get you."

"Why shouldn't he bring it back, Lisette?"

"If he brings it into the castle, they'll find him. That's what the message said." Then she began crying. "Didn't you believe me, Tyler? I thought I told you."

"What was he bringing, Lisette?"

"The light is so pretty, but so bright. So bright." Tears flowed from her eyes down her cheeks. "Where am I?"

The kaleidoscope colors washed the room, and Wallace had to squint to watch her.

"You are in a hospital, Lisette, and we're trying to help you."

"Why am I here? What is happening to me?" Now her arms and legs thrashed against the clamps.

"We gave you a drug." Creig's words were calm and smooth. "It will help you remember what happened on the moors. Why was Tyler on the moors, Lisette?"

"He came for Aurora. We have to get Aurora out."

Creig glanced at Wallace with a knowing smile. She'd spilled the names they were looking for.

Trying to keep from retching, Wallace nodded to Creig and played along. So this woman, Lisette, knew Aurora Carter? When McDuff learned about this, Wallace feared what would happen to them. More than that, he wanted to send a fist into Creig's jaw.

Creig sucked on his cigarette and again faced his victim. "Is Tyler in the castle, Lisette?"

"So pretty. The lights are so pretty, but they're too bright."

"Focus, Lisette. Tell me about Tyler."

"Pretty, so pretty and so bright." Then she was silent.

"Tell me about Tyler and Aurora."

Then she stopped speaking. No matter what Creig said, she wouldn't respond.

It was as if her senses had become so overloaded, she could no longer speak. Her opened eyes just stared at the ever-changing, brightly flashing colors. Had the drugs taken her on a trip into some kaleidoscopic fantasyland?

Wallace didn't know what kind of drugs Creig had given the poor girl, but he couldn't imagine what a hallucinogen and the flashing lights would do on top of them.

After another ten minutes without a response, Creig turned off the kaleidoscope and removed the clamps from her eyes. Then he injected what he called an antidote into a vein and ordered Wallace to return her to her cell.

But she was so weak, she could barely walk, and Wallace texted Ewan to come and help him.

When they'd placed her in her bed, Ewan left, but Wallace remained.

Creig would now report to McDuff that the woman, Aurora, was in league with a man named Tyler. They knew that Agent David had left the compound, returning only moments before they captured Lisette. So David must be Tyler, and the two agents from the Office of Internal Affairs were, in actuality, frauds.

Wallace had caught hints that something about the two men didn't match what he expected of internal affairs agents. Now it made sense. They were too concerned for McDuff's prisoners. They were too . . . human.

The woman would wake with a severe headache. Creig had explained that the antidote would make her drowsy and ameliorate most of the effects of the drugs he'd given her. But there was always a risk that the episode would cause some kind of psychotic break.

For long minutes, he watched her. She was sleeping now and seemed okay.

Turning on his heels, he started for his room.

CHAPTER 49

FROM DARKNESS TO LIGHT

Castle Danger, Scotland ~ March, Year 3

John 10:27–30 (HCSB): *"My sheep hear My voice, I know them, and they follow Me. I give them eternal life, and they will never perish—ever! No one will snatch them out of My hand. My Father, who has given them to Me, is greater than all. No one is able to snatch them out of the Father's hand. The Father and I are one."*

That night, Wallace lay in bed, deeply troubled by his role in escorting the woman Joline to the pit, by McDuff's communion with the demon beastie, by helping Creig torture Lisette and countless others. When he finally fell asleep, it was a fitful affair, troubled by dark dreams.

Then one of them turned into something more than a dream. It opened a gateway, a path from this world to another. To a realm beyond the physical. To a place of spiritual darkness. But it wasn't a dream at all.

It was a vision.

* * *

YOU WILL COME WITH ME, said the creature of light.

Wallace rubbed his eyes, rose from his bed, and faced the apparition. It was a man, but a man clothed in shining light. This was no normal man. Was he an angel?

You will come with me, repeated the voice. The words came not through the air, but materialized inside his head. Wallace sensed that the angel meant him no harm, and he offered his hand.

The angel reached out and grabbed Wallace's hand, and both began rising from the floor.

Then they were passing through the stone ceiling, appearing in the storeroom above, a room filled with boxes of pistols, semiautomatic rifles, and ammunition. Next, they floated horizontally and traveled through the stone wall. Soon, he was looking down on the entire castle complex.

He was flying, in the grip of an angel and rising above the earth. He jabbed a finger into his side, and it hurt. How could this be happening? Was this real, or was it a dream?

High above the moors they flew until a dark hole in the earth appeared below.

Now he realized his senses were more acute than they had ever been. And he knew, instinctively, that the hole below them was invisible to mortal eyes, and except for his current state—whatever that was—he would have been unable to see it.

They dropped into the hole, a tunnel really, and descended, faster and faster. The tunnel walls were dark and swirling, and as they fell, a pinprick of light appeared at the far end. The light grew larger, and a horrible thought gripped him.

Was he dead? Had he died in his sleep? He'd read about near-death experiences, and this fit the bill. Was that why an angel was escorting him to whatever was below?

They burst through the light and left it behind. Below was a nightmare land clothed in black fire, heat, and darkness.

They landed on a flat rocky plain that seemed to have no end. Every few yards, tongues of black flame rose from thousands of crevices.

The first thing that hit him was the heat. It was like nothing he had ever experienced. The heat was so hot, it drilled into his skin and began cooking his organs. He opened his mouth to scream, but his first intake of breath seared his lungs. His feet were burning, and when he glanced down, he realized he was naked.

The skin on the soles of his bare feet sizzled on the hot rock.

And the odor! The air was thick with the smell of offal, burning flesh, and sulfur, and he gagged.

From his right came a scream, followed by another on his left, and he whirled to look.

A man was running from a horribly misshapen being, a creature appearing much like the demon beastie, only with scales instead of spiky fur. The man ran straight through flaming vents that must have scorched him horribly.

Behind the man, the demon pursued. It was grinning, and though it was obviously faster, it slowed, as if to prolong the chase. Then it caught up to its victim. Its claws grabbed an arm, yanked, and ripped it from its roots.

Wallace stared in horror. The thing had ripped off the man's arm!

The man fell, bleeding and screaming, onto the burning rock.

Then the demon ripped off his other arm, his right leg, and finally, his left leg. But he didn't die. No, as the demon creature retreated, the man lay there, writhing in agony while his missing appendages grew back.

Whole again, he stood. He shot a glance at the creature.

Again, he ran. And again, the demon pursued.

Then Wallace caught a glimpse of the victim's face. And it was Wallace himself!

Wallace was looking down at his future self!

He searched in all directions until he found the angel. "Help me! Get me out of here. Why am I here?"

The angel nodded, grasped Wallace's right hand, and—

* * *

HE WOKE, SHAKING AND DRENCHED with sweat. Glancing down, he discovered he was wearing the same pajamas he'd gone to bed with.

What had just happened to him? That was no dream. It was a vision, and it was so real, he remembered every detail. He could still feel the heat and how it had been cooking his insides.

He reached down and felt the soles of his feet. They weren't burned.

He'd been to Hell. An angel had taken him in a vision to Hell.

It was a warning from the God he'd avoided all his life. He couldn't deny it. It had come from Aurora's God, and now, he must make a decision.

Still shaking, he went to his desk, turned on the table light, and checked his watch. It was two in the morning.

He poured a triple portion of whiskey and took a long sip. Then he brought his pocket Bible to the desk. Opening it to the book of Matthew, he began to read.

Time passed as he read at a furious pace. When he'd finished the book, his watch revealed that three hours had passed.

He returned to the bed, sat, and dropped his head in his hands. It was all true. Everything he'd read. Jesus was real.

Everything and everyone he'd worked for all his life had been a lie. And it was leading him to the very place the angel had taken him only hours ago. Filled with tears, his vision blurred.

He sank to his knees. He didn't know what to say or how to say it, but he had to say something.

"Dear Jesus, I have been a terrible fool. Forgive me. I believe in you now. After what you've shown me—and I know now that it was you who must have sent me that angel—yes, after what I've seen, how could I not believe? I want to become a Christian, but I don't know what to say or how to go about it. I hope you understand. Anyways, that's all."

He raised his head from his hands, and suddenly, such a feeling of happiness, joy, and peace swept over him that he knew something had happened to him.

"Have you heard me, Jesus?" he asked.

Then, into the silence of the room, came a whisper. And the word that broke the stillness was, "Yes."

CHAPTER 50

UNDONE!

Castle Danger, Scotland ~ March, Year 3

As Tyler and Hamish followed Sloan into the formal banquet room on the fourth tower's second floor, their footsteps echoed off the high stone ceiling. Tyler shot a glance to the walls, draped periodically with posters proclaiming the greatness of the Dragon, the Imperator, and the Prophet, but incongruously interspersed with faded medieval tapestries.

"Ah, yes. Agents David and Callum. Take a seat if you please." A stone-faced McDuff pointed to chairs across from a thin, nearly bald man with wire-rim glasses and a black mustache. Sloan took a seat beside the man. "May I introduce you to Dr. Creig? He runs the experiments here."

They acknowledged the doctor then sat at a table that had room for at least a dozen others. But the five place settings at Tyler's end of the table had no silverware or plates—only glasses.

Ewan and another man entered the room and stood in the corner, as if awaiting orders. Next to him was a waiter in uniform.

Tyler didn't know what to expect at this dinner, if that's what it was. Sloan had explained that the director wanted to give them a proper feast before they left, but Tyler didn't believe the explanation. He wasn't sure Sloan believed it either. Sloan's obvious dislike of McDuff and the goings-on at the castle contributed to a feeling that Tyler might be able to trust the man. Except for one thing—that UI uniform.

"You're probably wondering why I invited you here tonight." The director reached for one of the empty wine glasses set before each place. Again, Tyler wondered why there were no other place settings.

"Aye," said Hamish. "Whatever the reason, we thank you for your hospitality."

"My hospitality, yes." McDuff examined the glass then beckoned the waiter from the corner. "Serve the wine."

The man bowed. Then he filled everyone's glasses from a large decanter of red wine.

When all had been served, McDuff lifted his glass. "To the Unitum Imperium and the Imperator, may the Empire last a thousand years."

"Hear, hear!" Hamish raised his glass and drank. He was better at playing this game than Tyler.

Still holding his glass, McDuff sat back and speared his guests with an icy stare. "So tell me about this report you plan to send to the Prophet. What will it contain?"

"Oh, just the usual thing." Hamish smiled. "You will be pleased to know we have found your operation here to be entirely satisfactory."

"Satisfactory? Of course, it's satisfactory." McDuff's lips twitched with the hint of a smile. "And when did you see Sebastien last? How is his foot?"

"His foot?" Hamish's eyes widened, perhaps in surprise, and Tyler tensed. "It's much better, though he doesn't like to talk about it."

"Better, hey?" McDuff narrowed his eyes at Hamish and set his glass down. "When did you last see him?"

"I believe it was a month ago, just before we came here. In Jerusalem."

"I see." Now McDuff's frown returned. "That's interesting, because he spent the entire last month in New Babylon. Or at least that's what he told me yesterday when I talked with him. And not once did he mention an injured foot."

"Yesterday?" The blood seemed to have drained from Hamish's face. "I could have been mistaken if it was in Jerusalem. We've been traveling a lot, and I—"

"Enough! No more lies!" McDuff slammed a fist on the table. Then he waved to Ewan, who left the room. "There's someone I'd like you to meet, David Allan and Callum Reid, or whatever your names are."

Tyler's heart was beating wildly when Ewan opened the door, followed by—

Aurora.

Lisette.

And three more guards, all carrying semiautomatic SA80s.

Tyler tried to suck in air, but the breath stopped in his throat.

Lisette was shaking, and Aurora's strained, downcast look said it all—they were undone.

Ewan and the guards forced the women into seats to the left of Tyler. When Aurora placed her hands on the table, the metal from her handcuffs clanked against the wood.

"Now, Tyler—for Lisette gave us your real name under the good doctor's ministrations—who is your friend Callum Reid?"

"My name?" Hamish smiled. "It's Dougal O'Brian." Even now, he wouldn't reveal who he really was.

"All right, Dougal O'Brian and Tyler whoever-you-are. Now, you are going to tell me why you came here in disguise. And if you don't give me the truth, the lovely ladies beside you will spend whatever is left of their hours on earth in the courtyard gibbets."

Heat rushed to Tyler's forehead, and the room seemed to recede. Beside him, Aurora's cuffed hands tried to reach him but couldn't. "Don't," she whispered.

"The last two to end up in the gibbets didn't last a single night." McDuff pulled out a pipe, stuffed it with tobacco, and lit a match to it. "You've seen their rotting flesh hanging in the courtyard. It's much warmer now, so death will be prolonged. Do you want to see them dying a slow death, Tyler? Rotting in the wind? Fending off the birds?"

One hand gripped the other until it hurt. What if he told McDuff the truth? What harm could come of it? They'd come here to rescue his sister, and that was all. "All right, all right. I'll tell you."

"No," whispered Aurora beside him.

"Let's hear it." McDuff sucked in on his pipe and sat back.

"Aurora is my sister. We came here to free her."

The director guffawed and blew out smoke. "Oh, come, come. You can do better than that."

"It's the truth," said Hamish. "We planned all of this to free her."

"And Lisette?" McDuff pointed to her. "Who is she to you?"

"She's my girlfriend." Tyler caught her frightened glance.

"So you're telling me you planned all of this, whatever it is"—McDuff's wave encircled the room—"merely to free your sister?"

"Yes." Tyler held McDuff's stare.

"No, there is more you're not telling me. Why was Lisette up on the moors? And where did you get the uniforms?" He leaned forward in his chair. "You are obviously in league with the resistance. You've had dealings with them. Come, now, Tyler. Tell me. Where did you get the uniforms? Who gave them to you, and what else have you planned?"

To that, he had no answer. He wouldn't reveal anything that might lead to the deaths of the Inverness Friends. He caught Hamish's emotionless glance.

"Tell me where this resistance cell is located, how you became aware of us here, and how you got these uniforms, and I will spare the women from the gibbets."

Tyler's gaze dropped, and he examined the swirls in the oak tabletop. They were trapped with no way out. He began praying silently.

McDuff sucked in on his pipe and grinned. "I have not yet mentioned the fate I'm pondering for you and Dougal, here. I could change my mind on this. It's something I don't have to do. It all depends on whether or not you cooperate. But perhaps hearing what could happen to you will loosen your tongue?"

Tyler again gazed at this man. Or was he a monster?

"You saw what happened when the demon had its way with the woman traitor. Some quality time with the demon beast, my friends, is what awaits the both of you if you don't tell me what I want to know."

The room seemed to swirl. The heat on his forehead seemed to fall in waves. He couldn't imagine a worse fate. But then, it was a demon, wasn't it? And all he had to do was utter the one name that, in the past, had vanquished the other demons he'd encountered. He forced himself to speak. "I can't . . . tell you . . . what you want."

For long seconds, McDuff stared at them. He shook his head and called Sloan to his side. He whispered something.

Sloan spoke to the four guards, and they handcuffed Tyler and Hamish. Then Sloan and the guards led them all into the courtyard.

As two guards pointed their weapons at Tyler and Hamish, Sloan and Ewan lowered the gibbets. The rotting bodies that had been hanging there ever since their arrival had already been removed. McDuff must have planned this.

Sloan forced a shaking Lisette into the first iron cage. Then Sloan went to Aurora. But before he shoved her into the gibbet, he whispered something in her ear.

When Tyler saw her expression of surprise, he wondered what the man had said—because in that glance, he imagined there was hope.

The men then worked the ratchets on both gibbets, one crank at a time. The rings at the top clanked and rattled. And when the iron cages hit the top and swung, Aurora gripped the bars and looked down.

Tyler cast her a last glance before Sloan, Ewan, and the four guards pushed them toward the castle, down the stone staircase, and into the dungeon. Sloan released Hamish's handcuffs and motioned him to enter a cell. Then he did the same with Tyler, locking him inside an adjoining cell.

Sloan shut the gate, and the lock clicked with an echo of finality.

But after Ewan and the other guards left, Sloan remained. Then he approached Tyler's cell. "The weather this evening will be mild, so do not fear. The women will survive the night. I will return in a bit to talk further." He looked both ways. "But first, I must make certain arrangements. You have a friend."

"What?" Tyler couldn't believe what he was hearing. What was he saying?

But Sloan had already turned on his heels and was walking away.

* * *

As a gentle breeze swung her cage, Aurora was thankful the night was warm. She remembered the sight of the last occupants and shuddered. Was that how they would soon end up?

"I'm a–afraid, Aurora." Lisette's voice shook. "We're going to die here, aren't we?"

"No, Lisette. We mustn't lose hope." Aurora said the words, but did she really believe them? There was a chance that Wallace could help them. What had he whispered a moment ago? "I'll do what I can, but there are no promises." Was he going to help them? Or was he just trying to ease his conscience? He was questioning everything here, but did he have the means and the will to actually help them?

She wriggled an arm, and she could barely get it past the iron to scratch her face.

Then she remembered how the birds had pecked at the faces and eyes of the last victims, and a shiver rippled down her spine. Would she eventually become so weak that she couldn't fend them off?

She mustn't lose hope. What was Eli always telling them? To put their trust in the Lord?

She prayed. She asked Jesus to save them, to help them out of this predicament. She ended with this:

But if it's your will that we die here, then . . . let me die with dignity.

PART V

JUDGMENT!

Zephaniah 1:14–17 (HCSB):

The great Day of the Lord is near, near and rapidly approaching. Listen, the Day of the Lord—then the warrior's cry is bitter. That day is a day of wrath, a day of trouble and distress, a day of destruction and desolation, a day of darkness and gloom, a day of clouds and blackness, a day of trumpet blast and battle cry against the fortified cities, and against the high corner towers. I will bring distress on mankind, and they will walk like the blind because they have sinned against the Lord. Their blood will be poured out like dust and their flesh like dung.

CHAPTER 51

A CHANGE OF PLANS

Castle Danger, Scotland ~ March, Year 3

Up in his room, Wallace wondered what he could possibly do to help. Whatever it was, it must happen soon. The women could last a few days in the gibbets, but McDuff's patience could run out at any time. And then—Wallace shuddered—the director could feed Tyler and O'Brian to the demon beastie. But Wallace could never let that happen. There'd been enough death at the director's hands.

He checked his watch. Twenty-one hundred hours. The evening shift change was happening now, and Ewan would be leaving for his quarters in the outbuildings. Wallace strapped on his pistol and headed for the dungeon.

Making sure the guard had already passed, he approached Tyler's cell—the same one Aurora recently occupied. "I've returned, Tyler."

Tyler rushed to the front and gripped the bars. "Yes? What did you mean when you said I had a friend?"

"I want to help you and O'Brian—"

"My name is really Hamish."

Wallace turned to see a grinning Hamish at the front of his cell.

"Will you help get us out of here?" asked Hamish. "Is that what I'm hearing, Sloan?"

"Aye. But you may call me Wallace."

"Aye, Wallace. First names. That's good." Hamish nodded. "But I interrupted you. Please go on."

"I want to release both of you and Aurora and Lisette." Wallace glanced at the floor. "You see, I had a vision last night. And I–I want to become a Christian. But no, I *am* a Christian."

Tyler beamed. "That's great, Wallace. Congratulations!"

"Now that I am with you, what did you have in mind when you came here in disguise and when Lisette was wandering on the moors?"

"How do we know we can trust you?" asked Hamish.

"I thought you might ask that, so this is what I'll do." He unlocked Tyler's and Hamish's doors and handed Tyler a pistol. "Will that ease your minds?"

"Aye, Wallace." Hamish nodded. "That will do."

"So what did you have in mind?" asked Wallace.

"We had a plan," said Tyler. "But it fell apart when they captured Lisette."

Then Wallace learned how Tyler had planned to create a diversion with the C-4 and free not only Aurora, but all the prisoners. After Tyler finished, Wallace shook his head. "It wouldn't have worked. What about everyone fleeing across the moors? How did you expect them to stay free?"

"There's a group in a nearby city waiting for my message," said Hamish. "If you have a plan, if we can free everyone tonight, then if I can borrow your phone, I'll give them the signal to be ready with transportation."

"McDuff suspected you were involved with some kind of resistance group. So you would rather be given to the demon beastie than betray your friends?"

"Aye."

"Admirable. But what you planned would never have worked. Yet . . . with my help, I think—it's still risky—but aye, I think we might be able to do it." Wallace rubbed his jaw and examined the floor. "I wish we had more time, but I fear what McDuff might do if we delay. We must act tonight."

"To free everyone?" asked Tyler.

"Aye." Wallace passed Hamish his phone. "Call your friends. Tell them we'll release the prisoners tonight. If the call comes from my phone, it won't alert the monitors."

Hamish's grin widened. He took the phone, but when he spoke to his friends, it was in Gaelic.

Meanwhile, Wallace mulled a plan.

Both Tyler and Hamish stepped out of their cells, but Wallace raised a hand. "For now, stay inside and pretend the doors are locked. Otherwise, you might raise the alarm. I'm still working this out in my mind. But I'll need your help to get the C-4. I also need to incapacitate the guards, but I can't do that until after twenty-three hundred."

He gripped Tyler's and Hamish's hands. "We can do this, my friends."

"We don't know how to thank you," said Tyler.

"Thank me after it works. Stay in your cells until I return. I'll only be a few minutes."

Then he left.

* * *

WALLACE HAD BARELY LEFT WHEN a man with a bushy red beard, wearing greasy overalls and carrying a ladder, stopped outside Tyler's cell. He climbed the ladder and replaced a string of LEDs hanging from the ceiling. But as he folded the ladder and was about to leave, he glanced at Tyler, still gripping the bars at the front of his cell. He shook his head and said, "How the mighty have fallen."

Then he, too, left.

CHAPTER 52

A NEW ALLY

Castle Danger, Scotland ~ March, Year 3

Moments later, when Wallace returned, he gripped his new coconspirator's hands. Tyler left his cell and hugged him. "You are a gift from Heaven, my friend."

"You are too kind. Here, put this on." Wallace held out a guard uniform and a cap.

Tyler returned to the cell, undressed, and put it on.

Then Wallace handed him an SA80 semiautomatic rifle. A similar weapon dangled from a strap around Wallace's neck.

After Tyler slung the rifle over one shoulder, he asked, "What's your plan?"

"You and I will go together to the cave and bring back the C-4. It will be dark, so let's hope the guards at the gate won't recognize you. They rarely get down to the dungeon anyways." Wallace reached behind him to slap the backpack he was wearing. "We can carry the contents of your cache in this."

"Right. Lead on." He patted the pistol in its holster.

"What about me?" asked Hamish.

"For now, it would be best if you remain in your cell. Less chance of raising the alarm."

"I understand. If that's the plan, then aye."

They left the dungeon, climbed the stairs, and entered the yard. Tyler glanced up at the women in the iron cages. As Wallace had said, the night was warm. They should be okay.

They exited through the portcullis and left the castle. Above, the stars winked in a darkly azure sky. A few clouds passed beside a three-quarters moon that had risen over the western mountains.

The gate was manned by two guards, also bearing SA80s. Each held a leash attached to a Doberman pinscher, and the dogs uttered rumbling growls at their approach.

"Keep your head down," said Wallace, "and pull your cap over your forehead."

Tyler did as ordered.

"What's happening, sir?" asked the tallest of the guards.

"We've had a report of an intruder on the moors."

"Funny," said the second man with a black mustache, "we didn't get any notice."

"It was from one of the motion sensors we put up there earlier. You probably haven't heard about that yet."

"No." The first man rubbed the stubble on his chin. "Well, happy hunting."

Tyler walked behind Wallace through the gate and released a deep breath. "You put sensors on the moors?"

Wallace laughed. "No, but they don't know that."

Smiling, they climbed to the ridgetop where Tyler led them into the forest. It was darker beneath the pines, and they turned on their flashlights. From somewhere nearby, an owl hooted. He shone his beam on fallen pines, tree trunks, and piles of rock. When the slope steepened, he warned that they'd gone too far, and they retraced their steps.

"There!" Tyler pointed to a rock outcropping with a hole.

Wallace began climbing in then quickly backed out. "There's something in here!"

An angry badger waddled out, growling, its teeth bared. It headed straight for Wallace.

Yanking his pistol from his belt, he aimed and fired. The shot echoed off the slopes and across the valley. The badger stopped moving.

"Didn't expect that." He holstered his weapon and reentered the hole.

Tyler followed through a cloud of gunpowder into the cave. The backpack was right where he'd left it.

When they were both outside again, Wallace examined its contents. "Wire. Blasting caps. C-4. A timer. Pliers. A bolt cutter. And two Glocks." He transferred everything to his own pack. "This should do it."

"Where can we set the charge?"

"The most damage would be in the power plant."

Tyler nodded, and they headed back.

Before they arrived at the gate, Tyler pulled his cap over his forehead and kept his head down.

As they neared the guards, the taller man stopped them. "We heard a shot. Is everything all right, sir?"

"Aye. Just a badger. It attacked us."

"We've seen the same with other animals. Lately, they've all become aggressive. Very odd." But now he was staring at Tyler. "Who is this? Haven't seen him around lately."

"A new man." Wallace laid a hand on Tyler's shoulder. "I'm giving him an orientation tour."

"As you say, sir." Then the guard waved them through.

They crossed the compound on the path between outbuildings. The power plant was the last building after the exercise hut and before the castle. Wallace veered toward the squat metal building, now throbbing and pulsing from the generators within.

He glanced in all directions then approached the door with its keypad. He punched in some numbers, but before he finished, a man in grease-stained overalls opened the door.

"What the—?" asked the man.

"Sorry, Finlay. I saw the door ajar and thought someone had forgotten to close it."

The one addressed as Finlay was the same man who'd seen Tyler in his cell a short while ago. Now, he turned widened eyes on Tyler. "I'm sure the door was closed. But this man"—he jerked his thumb toward Tyler—"he was a prisoner. W–why is he free?"

"Because I released him." Wallace's hand went to his pistol. "This is unfortunate, Finlay. I wish no harm to come to you, but unless you do as I ask . . ."

"What's going on?" Finlay's glance was wild now, bouncing from Wallace to Tyler.

"I'll give you a choice." Wallace's hand closed about the Glock. "Either you give me your word to go to your quarters in the worker's hut and keep silent, or . . ."

"Or what?"

Wallace sighed. "You and I both know what goes on here. I've seen how you look with pity on the prisoners in the dungeon. You must be as appalled as I am. So tonight, we're going to put an end to it. If you cooperate, we will free all the prisoners. As for Fergus McDuff and his people . . ."

Finlay spat on the ground. "They deserve whatever they get. I ken what you're about, sir, and as long as they can nae place the blame on me, more's the power to you. I'll go to my quarters, and mum's the word."

Wallace smiled and extended a hand, and they shook.

"Is there somethin' I can help you with?" Finlay pointed to Wallace's backpack.

"We're going to blow up the generators to create a diversion by cutting the power. We've got C-4."

Finlay gawked. Then he grinned and slapped a hand on a thigh. "Better to do the deed out back, on the diesel tanks, not in here. That'll make one grand explosion, sure and certain. Follow me."

The smell of oil permeated the power plant. Finlay opened the back door and led them into an enclosure where chain-link fencing surrounded two mammoth diesel tanks. Still grinning, he patted the first tank. "Put your C-4 on this one, and you'll make one heck of a bang."

Wallace passed the bag to Tyler. Hamish had trained Tyler how to do this, and he got to work. He molded the C-4 around the neck leading from the first tank to the generators inside. Then he stuck the blasting cap into the C-4 and ran a wire to the timer.

With his hand on the dial, he faced Wallace.

"Set it for twenty-three thirty." After staring at his watch for a moment, he lifted his head. "No, make it midnight. That'll give us plenty of time."

Tyler set the timer and stood.

Still grinning, Finlay again slapped his thigh. Were others on the staff of the same mind as him?

As if thinking the same thing, Wallace gripped Finlay's shoulder. "Do you know of others who might think as you do?"

"I fear that most have sold their souls to the devils whose names be Davato and Fergus McDuff." His grin turned down into a frown. "And there, I've said it, haven't I? I ken we both believe the same."

"That's right, Finlay," said Tyler.

"If you know of anyone," said Wallace, "and you trust them with your life, then at five minutes before midnight, tell them to flee for their lives as fast and as far from the castle as they can. But no sooner than that."

"Across the moors, sir?"

"Aye."

"What about the guards at the gate?"

"Don't worry about them. They won't be a problem."

Finlay cocked his head then nodded. "Then aye, there's a few I trust, and I will warn them."

"Good."

They exited through the power plant's front door. Finlay headed for the workers' hut beyond the guards' quarters, and Wallace led Tyler inside the castle to his tower room.

Again, Wallace checked his watch. "It's twenty after the hour. I've some errands to run." But after saying this, he smiled. "Aye, some *errands*. You should stay here until I return. We don't want anyone else recognizing you, do we?"

"Right. I'll wait until you've finished your . . . your errands." Tyler matched Wallace's smile, and Wallace left with an empty knapsack.

CHAPTER 53

WALLACE'S ERRANDS

Castle Danger, Scotland ~ March, Year 3

As his feet slapped the courtyard cobbles, Wallace didn't look up at the two women in their cages. If it were possible, he'd release them now, but of course, that would alert the guards. He had thirty minutes before the men received their first round of coffee, and his first stop would be Creig's lab. By now, the doctor should be fast asleep in his room. This should be a quick in-and-out trip.

He climbed the stairwell to the tower's fourth floor. He could open the doors to most places—most were electronic—and he unlocked the lab door. But when he pushed through into the lab, he froze.

The lights were on.

On the counter, a flame from a Bunsen burner was boiling red liquid in a beaker flask. Then Creig himself rounded the corner from the back room with a cigarette dangling from his lips. He stopped and stared. "What are you doing here, Sloan?"

For a moment, Wallace had no response. This wasn't supposed to happen. Why was Creig working so late?

"I said why are you here?" Creig dropped his cigarette on the floor, rubbed it out with a heel, then moved the beaker from the flame and set it on the counter.

Wallace had no choice. He yanked the pistol from his belt, drew back on the slide, and aimed. "Get down on your knees and put your hands behind your head."

"What? I will do no such thing." Instead of obeying, Creig approached. "Are you insane?"

"Down on the floor, Creig." Wallace waved the gun. "Now!"

"I will not!" Creig kept coming. "I don't know what you're doing, but when McDuff hears about this, I—"

"I said get down on your knees!"

Still standing, Creig stopped a meter away.

Wallace holstered his gun and reached for his handcuffs.

But the doctor lunged, and one hand reached for Wallace's belt. Somehow, Creig managed to pull the Glock from its holster.

Wallace's fingers closed, hard, around Creig's hand and squeezed.

Creig grimaced and dropped the gun. Metal clattered over stone.

Whirling away, Creig dropped to his knees and fumbled for the weapon.

Wallace fell on top of him. Strong hands flipped the man onto his back, and knees pinned both arms at his sides.

Creig was breathing fast. Angry, wild eyes bored into Wallace's. "Whatever you're doing, Sloan, you won't get away with it. I never trusted you. I never thought your heart was in the mission here. And now, you've revealed yourself as a traitor."

Wallace rolled the doctor back onto his stomach. With zip ties from his pockets, he bound Creig's hands together behind him. He yanked Creig to his feet and herded him into the back room where no one could hear him thrashing about. He dropped the man into the chair before his desk.

The room held two tall chests, and after rummaging in the drawers, he produced a length of plastic cord. As he tied Creig's feet to the chair legs, Creig continued his ramblings. "Do you know what they do with traitors, Sloan? Do you have any idea? They . . ."

But Wallace wasn't listening. Once the doctor's feet were secure, Wallace found masking tape in another drawer.

"It's too bad I won't be there to watch as they send you to—"

But tape covered the end of the sentence.

Standing to his full height, Wallace examined his work and smiled. "You are a monster, Creig. And I hope someday soon you'll receive what's coming to you."

Creig struggled against the bonds, but his only response was a muffled groan and a shaking of his head.

Back in the front room, Wallace searched the tall glass-fronted cabinet where the doctor kept his compounds and chemicals. He remembered the name of the opioid that Creig sometimes used to put a patient into a deep sleep, and he scanned the labels on the bottles.

There! An amber-glass bottle filled with capsules.

After placing it in his knapsack, he checked his watch. Twenty-five minutes left. Barely enough time. The kitchen was his next stop.

When he arrived, the night cook was making the coffee she would soon serve to all the guards. The smell of coffee permeated the room.

Again, he checked his watch. He had twenty minutes.

"Evening, Sophie."

"Evening, sir." Sophie was pregnant and needed a different blouse. What she wore tonight exposed a round, fleshy belly. "What can I do for you?"

"I need something from the larder. Back in a moment."

She nodded, and he opened the door to where they stored the canned goods, dry goods, wine, and spirits. The stone walls kept it cold here, and he shivered. He flicked on the light and found what he needed—whiskey. He grabbed two bottles.

From each, he splashed a bit of whiskey on the floor, enough to make room for the narcotic capsules that he dropped inside, one at a time, until the amber bottle was empty. After recorking the bottles, he shook them. But the narcotic was slow to dissolve, and he had to keep shaking until no residue was visible.

He glanced at his watch. Five minutes left! He rushed back into the kitchen.

The cook was placing empty mugs on a tray, and as she set the last one in place, he breathed out.

She hadn't filled the cups yet.

"When you serve the coffee this evening," he said with a smile, "make sure each cup gets a generous serving from these bottles. It's a special treat from me." He set the whiskey on the counter then put a finger to his lips. "But don't say a word to anyone where it came from."

"Aye, sir. Mum's the word." Sophie winked. "I'll see that each cup is half full of whiskey. The boys'll love it."

"More than you can imagine."

Then he left the kitchen and returned to his room.

CHAPTER 54

SIX MINUTES TO MIDNIGHT

Castle Danger, Scotland ~ March, Year 3

Shortly after eleven, Wallace opened the door to an impatient Tyler. "What kept you so long on your errands, as you call them?" he asked.

Wallace set his backpack on the desk. "It's time you learned my plan. But it's got a big hole in it."

"Let's hear it. Maybe I can think of something."

"I've drugged the guards on duty. Soon, they should all be asleep. We can block the doors for the guard's quarters, but by the time the bomb goes off at midnight, I'm afraid they'll find a way out before the prisoners—including all of us—can escape. That's the problem."

"I see." Tyler rubbed his chin. "If only we had something to keep them busy."

"I thought of releasing the demon beastie, but . . ."

"You could do that?" Tyler's heart surged. "You can let it out?"

"I can. But it would kill not only the guards who got out but also the prisoners. Everyone in its path. It would probably kill and keep on killing, not even stopping to eat." Wallace shuddered. "It's said as much to McDuff during what he called his communion with the thing."

"Ah, but I know how to keep it from harming the Christians. All they have to do is say the right word."

"What?" Wallace's eyes widened. "Are you serious?"

"I am. I've encountered demons before, and all you have to do is invoke the name of Jesus. The second the demon beastie hears Jesus's name, it will back off."

Wallace plopped into the desk chair, his gaze drilling into Tyler. "You *are* serious. And you think that will work?"

"It's a creature of darkness, isn't it? It came from the Dragon, and even Satan himself cannot stand up to the Son of God."

A grin parted Wallace's lips, and he slapped his knee. "Then I'll release it." He checked his watch. "I'll do it at midnight. It's twenty-three twenty. We've got to move!"

They left the room, and Wallace led them down the spiral steps to the basement where he opened the door to a maintenance room. After grabbing a shovel, he brought them up the steps to the courtyard.

They crossed the drawbridge and turned left to the power plant where a pile of lumber was stacked beside the building. Wallace selected two boards about two meters long and passed one to Tyler. They passed the exercise hut and went to the rear of the guards' quarters.

"Are all these huts the same?" asked Tyler.

"The power plant is the smallest," answered Wallace. "But all the others are longer. And they're all the same. Each has a row of narrow windows cut high in the walls—too tiny for an escape. Each hut has a single door in front and another in back, always opening to the outside. Perfect for what we're about to do."

He laid the first timber on the ground and slid it up under the door handle. Marking the spot where the board touched the ground, he dug a shallow hole. He placed the board in the hole with the top under the door handle and packed dirt into the hole at the bottom.

"There!" He stood back with a smile. "That should keep them inside for a bit."

Again, he checked his watch. "Thirty minutes to beastie. We've got to hurry. Now for the other door."

Tyler followed him to the front, but as Wallace was digging the next hole, the door opened, knocking the shovel from his hands.

Out walked Ewan, and Wallace stepped back.

"W–what are you doing, Sloan?" Ewan glanced at the board and the shovel. But when his gaze settled on Tyler, his eyes widened.

For one moment, both men stood, staring into each other's eyes, frozen in position.

Then Ewan's right hand shot to the sidearm at his belt, and his fingers fumbled to undo the snaps holding it in place.

Wallace lunged, and his hands closed over Ewan's.

Ewan tried to back away, and when Wallace's grip on the holster tightened, Ewan sent his left elbow smashing against Wallace's skull.

Wallace staggered and fell to the ground.

Ewan yanked the weapon from his holster.

Tyler started forward to help, but Wallace's feet wrapped themselves about Ewan's legs, twisted, and Ewan went down.

Wallace rolled on top of his opponent, and with one vicious yank, he wrenched the pistol from Ewan's grasp.

Ewan fought for the weapon, and his fingers closed over the barrel.

"Don't!" cried Wallace.

The gun went off. The shot exploded the stillness of the night, and Tyler feared it would wake the entire castle.

Wallace shot to his feet and stood over his opponent.

With effort, Ewan pulled himself to a sitting position. His eyes wide, his glance dropped to a wide swath of red spreading across his abdomen. "W–what?" He looked up at Wallace. "H–how?"

Then he fell backward, gasped, and stopped moving.

Tyler's gaze fixed on Ewan's body, on the blank, dead eyes staring up at nothing.

But shouts from inside the hut tore his attention away from the dead man.

Wallace grabbed the board and slammed it in place—one end resting under the doorknob, the other sliding into the shallow hole.

From inside, the door rattled against the board, but it didn't open.

Wallace threw dirt atop the hole and stomped it down.

Tyler glanced at his watch. "Eleven forty-two."

After an exchange of glances, they began running.

They sprinted across the drawbridge, into the yard, straight to the gibbets. While Tyler worked the ratchet for Aurora's cage, Wallace worked on Lisette's. After the cages rested on the ground, Wallace opened them with the key, and Aurora fell into Tyler's arms.

"About time you got us out!" She tried to stand on her own, but her legs gave way. "I need to sit for a bit."

They released Lisette, and they both sat on the bench a few meters away. Again, he checked his watch. "We're running out of time. Less than twenty minutes left."

"Twenty minutes until what?" asked Aurora.

"Until the power plant explodes." Wallace kept glancing toward the portcullis. "We've locked the guards in their quarters, but it won't be long before they escape. Can you walk?"

"I'm not sure." Aurora took a few unsteady steps then returned to the bench. "I need to sit for a bit first." Then she glanced at Lisette. "What about you?"

"Same here."

"Both of you, listen!" Tyler raised both hands. "We're going to release the prisoners and the demon."

"You're going to do—what!" Lisette's head jerked back.

"It will keep the guards busy, but if it approaches you, all you have to do is say the name of Jesus, and it won't bother you."

"Like back in Wisconsin?" Aurora nodded. "Okay, we'll do it."

"You two, wait here!" Wallace waved. "Tyler and I have twenty minutes to free all the prisoners and give them directions."

The two entered the castle and raced down the steps to the dungeon.

At the bottom, Tyler glanced both ways, hoping there were no guards. But Wallace's concoction must have worked, as the only guard he saw lay across a bench and was snoring.

"After I open a cell door, tell them what to do and where to go."

"We must get Hamish first," said Tyler.

"Of course."

They ran down the passage, past the bars over the demon's cage, around the corner, and stopped at Hamish's cell. As Hamish opened his cell door, Tyler explained all they'd done since they parted.

"And you left me here while you did all that?"

"Sorry, laddie," said Wallace. "Until I'd incapacitated the guards, it was risky enough walking in the open with Tyler."

"Other than Ewan," said Tyler, "it's working out."

"I should call the Friends and tell them what's happening." Hamish beckoned to Wallace. "Can I borrow your phone again?"

"Aye." He passed it over. "Keep it."

"We're going to release the demon," said Tyler. "But if you say the name of Jesus, it won't bother you."

"Seriously?" said Hamish.

"Yes! Believe me, it works."

Hamish called the Inverness Friends. After conversing in what must be Gaelic, he reported they were waiting at the gate before they went any further. But now they'd drive up the peninsula as far as their four vans could go. They'd be ready, he said, for anyone who crossed the moors.

Meanwhile, Tyler and Wallace began releasing prisoners. And each freed prisoner gushed their thanks and headed for the stairs to freedom.

At ten minutes before midnight, Wallace announced it was time to unleash the monster.

He gave his key device to Tyler. "Take this and keep freeing prisoners. We'll meet in the courtyard when you're done."

"Right," answered Tyler.

Tyler and Hamish continued opening cells and giving instructions. After freeing all the Christians, they worked on the control group. But too many of the latter stared in disbelief when they explained how to avoid being attacked by the demon.

But they'd done what they could for them. If they wouldn't listen, that was their choice.

By now, prisoners would be streaming out of the castle, and Tyler hoped the guards were still locked inside their quarters.

They had fifteen cells to go, and he checked his watch.

Six minutes to midnight.

CHAPTER 55

MIDNIGHT!

Castle Danger, Scotland ~ March, Year 3

As he climbed the steps out of the dungeon, the stream of fleeing prisoners slowed Wallace's progress. At the top, he turned off toward the kitchen and found the door to a room with this warning, "Authorized Personnel Only." He punched the combination on the keypad and entered the control room.

The guard on duty at the monitors was asleep in his chair, an empty coffee cup on the counter. Wallace wheeled him to the side and took a vacant chair.

He'd been trained on how to use the systems, but this was the first time he'd done this alone. A clock on the main screen registered 2356. Time was running out.

He found the icon for the dungeon controls. Underneath that were four others marked: Den Access 1, 2, 3, and 4. Two of them controlled the plexiglass doors used to give it food. The other two must be for the secret passage leading to the courtyard. But which was which?

Above the main console were three windows pointing at the demon beastie from different directions. All of them showed the creature huddling in a corner, as if brooding.

Holding his breath, he opened doors 1 and 2.

Warning icons popped up, and he pressed the buttons to ignore them. On the monitors, the plexiglass doors for the feeding gates opened.

The beast rushed for the open passage. Wrong doors!

Wallace's thumb slammed down on the icons, dropping the doors only moments before the demon beastie smashed into the plexiglass.

The clock now showed 2358. He opened doors 3 and 4. The monitors showed the metal door inside the den as it swung open. The demon beastie charged toward it.

The numbers on the clock rolled from 2358 to 2359.

Wallace sprinted out of the control room into the hall. He raced toward the courtyard.

The castle shook. A thunderous boom echoed down the hall from the passage leading to the courtyard. The lights in the hall went out.

He hoped Tyler and Hamish had freed the last of the prisoners, but now it was time to join the two women. They'd be in the courtyard when the demon beastie began its rampage.

He prayed that the name of Jesus would do its magic.

CHAPTER 56

A MEETING IN THE YARD

Castle Danger, Scotland ~ March, Year 3

Just as Tyler and Hamish were opening the last cell in the control group, the castle shook, and the lights went out.

"What's happening?" asked the middle-aged man they'd just freed.

Tyler switched on a flashlight, as did Hamish. "Follow us," he said. "We'll get you out of here."

Their flashlights shone on the last of the prisoners clumped ahead of them. They trailed the crowd down the passage and onto the stone stairs.

"What's going on?" came more than one startled voice.

"It's all right!" shouted Hamish. "We killed the power. Keep going!"

The crowd kept going, and they left the stairwell.

In the courtyard, some of the prisoners raised their hands to the sky in praise. Others ran toward the portcullis and the exit.

Waiting under the gallows, Aurora and Lisette waved.

Tyler and Hamish hurried over, and from somewhere behind, Wallace followed.

But they'd only gotten halfway there when the demon beastie threw aside the metal doors and emerged from the underground passage into the courtyard.

It stood between the men and the women.

The thing's green eyes seemed to pulse with eagerness and hate. Its slit of a nose opened, closed, opened, closed. Then it raised its simian arms and rushed toward them.

"Stop!" yelled Tyler. "In the name of Jesus, stop!"

The creature stopped as if confused. It backed up. It glanced toward the portcullis. Then it lumbered its way toward the gate. Escaping prisoners fled from it on both sides, and it disappeared through the portcullis.

For one moment, Tyler watched it leave, breathing fast.

"Good show, laddie!" Hamish slapped him on the back. "It really did work."

Nodding, Tyler ran to his sister and hugged her first. Then he took Lisette in his arms. His lips smashed into hers, and she kissed him back.

When they separated, Lisette clapped her hands. "You did it. I don't know how, but you did it."

Wallace brought up the rear, and before he could speak, Aurora threw her arms around his neck. Much to Tyler's surprise, her lips joined with Wallace's. The kiss went on and on. And when they parted, Aurora was holding his hands, Wallace was breathless, and his face seemed flushed.

"Well!" Tyler smiled. "I see you two have been introduced."

Aurora released Wallace, stepped back, and her face, too, seemed flushed. "I don't know why I did that. Forgive me, Wallace."

Wallace was grinning. "No need to, lass."

Hamish was also smiling when he nodded toward the exit. "Maybe we should get out of here."

"Aye," added Wallace.

They'd barely left the benches when McDuff rounded the pines bearing a rifle. "Stop right there!" He pointed his weapon at the group.

But Tyler, Hamish, and Wallace all wore sidearms, and their fingers reached for their holsters.

"What's happening?" McDuff stared at Wallace. "Why are these prisoners free?"

"It's over, McDuff." Wallace's hand undid the leather buttons and freed his pistol. "We blew up the power plant, and—"

"You did *what*!"

"That's right, McDuff." Wallace smiled as he brought his gun out. "And we've locked the barracks so no one can get out. All the guards in the dungeon and at the gate are asleep. And we freed all the prisoners."

"You did *what*? It's not possible. You're lying." The rifle in McDuff's hands was now shaking. "*You* did this? You are with them?"

"That's right, McDuff. And here's another thing I've been dying to tell you—I'm now a Christian. Just like these folks."

Aurora's and Lisette's gazes whipped toward Wallace.

"Traitor! You will pay for this. All of you!" McDuff's glance searched the yard, but it was empty. Everyone had fled. "Guards!" he cried. "Help!"

"I told you." Wallace waved his pistol toward the gate. "The guards are either asleep or locked in the barracks."

Still pointing his rifle at them, McDuff began backing up. "I'll check this out and bring an end to this. If you try to leave the grounds, I'll shoot. You won't get away with this."

"We have three guns to your one." Wallace aimed his weapon. "Go get your guards. We won't stop you."

McDuff glanced toward the exit. Then he turned and hobbled away.

After McDuff disappeared through the portcullis, Hamish grinned at Wallace. "You neglected to mention a certain detail, my friend."

"You mean about the demon beastie?"

"Aye!"

"He's always wanted to commune with the thing." Wallace's grin widened. "Well, now he'll get a chance to do that, up close and personal."

CHAPTER 57

JUST DESERTS

Castle Danger, Scotland ~ March, Year 3

Isaiah 3:11 (HCSB): *Woe to the wicked—it will go badly for them, for what they have done will be done to them.*

When McDuff passed through the portcullis and crossed the drawbridge, he was fuming. Sloan had betrayed him, and nothing the man said could possibly be true. How could all the guards inside the castle and at the gate be asleep? And if the barracks was locked, he would soon release everyone inside.

That would be the end of Sloan's traitorous escapade. Then he'd feed the lot of them, one at a time, to the demon. The very thought brought a smile to his lips.

But as he passed the place where the power plant had been, he grimaced. The building was gone. Its bricks were strewn everywhere, even on the path at his feet. The odor of burning diesel filled his nostrils. A tower of flame and smoke rose from one of the tanks in back, and he could feel the heat even here, fifty meters away. The explosion had also blown in one wall of the exercise hut.

He hurried on.

But on the path ahead were four bodies. Not just corpses, but arms, legs, and heads.

"No!" he cried out loud. "This cannot be."

Had someone released the demon? Who would do such a thing and why?

He arrived at the entrance to the barracks, but the door lay askew on its hinges. From the dark depths beyond came screaming. He took a step closer and peered inside.

Two large green eyes peered back.

McDuff froze. His heart pounded in his throat. A shaking began in his shoulders and inched down his back.

Trembling fingers raised the weapon to his shoulder, and he pulled the trigger. But he'd forgotten to put a bullet in the chamber, and there was nothing but a click.

The creature rushed out at him.

He turned and tried to run.

* * *

WHEN CREIG FELT THE CASTLE shake and heard the explosion, he realized events were out of control. Whatever Sloan was doing had to be stopped. He had to alert the guards and capture this lunatic. And when they did, he relished what they would do to him.

He tried to wiggle his hands out of the restraints, but, of course, that was impossible. If only he had a knife or a sharp instrument, he could free himself from these plastic ties. In the front room, on the lab counter, he had such an instrument. All he had to do was maneuver the chair into the other room.

There was no problem a man of his intelligence couldn't solve. Even in a predicament like this. That Wallace thought he could stop a man of Creig's caliber from escaping was, well, humorous.

He stood. By taking tiny steps, he discovered he could inch his way along, pulling the chair behind him. Minutes later, he was in the doorway between the two rooms. And yes! He'd left a scalpel on the counter next to the Bunsen burner. It would easily cut the plastic that bound him.

He inched his way to the counter. But his hands were tied behind him, and to reach the instrument, he would have to back up against the counter. Raising his bound wrists, he backed toward the goal. His fingers fumbled for the instrument. They grasped the handle but couldn't quite close on it.

If only he could get his fingers beneath it. He mustn't drop it, or he'd never be able to pick it off the floor again. But he'd be careful. He'd be diligent and methodical. Only a man of intelligence could prevail in circumstances like these.

Carefully, his fingers searched for purchase.

And yes! He had it. Then he jerked away from the counter.

But something crashed behind him. There was a whoosh, as of flame, and he twisted his head to see what was happening.

He'd knocked over the beaker, and flame was spreading across the counter. Fire was surrounding a container of highly flammable acetone.

Heat touched his back. Was it from the counter? He began inching the chair away.

But no! He smelled burning hair—his hair!

It wasn't possible. How could such a thing happen? That he, Dr. Albert Creig, the premier researcher in charge of the Decency Inquiry Project, chosen from hundreds of candidates for this task because he'd risen above them all—in intelligence, accomplishments, and vision—how could this possibly be?

The last thought that raced through his mind before the acetone exploded was this:

He was on fire here on this earth. And if the Christians were right, he was headed for another realm where the flames never stopped.

CHAPTER 58

AFTERMATH

Lochbroom, Scotland ~ March, Year 3

John 6:47 (NLT): *I tell you the truth, anyone who believes has eternal life.*

As they were climbing the ridge beyond the castle, Aurora heard, or rather felt, a huge explosion and glanced back. The second diesel tank behind the power plant must have exploded. Fire and smoke rose high above the towers. And were those flames now shooting from a window in one of the towers beyond?

She followed Wallace as he led their group onto the moors. Above, a three-quarters moon splashed silvery beams over the heather and rocks, casting gray shadows.

She breathed in the scent of heather and pines on the slopes. Just being outside and breathing the dry, warm air without the smell of rusting iron bars was invigorating. But what buoyed her more than this was that her prayers had been answered.

God had not abandoned them. And the whispered promise she'd received that first day in her cell had been fulfilled—in the end, there *had* been a purpose for her imprisonment. Because she'd been captured and subsequently freed, many other innocents, both Christians and non-Christians, had also been freed. She hoped the Friends of Inverness could get them all to safety.

Lisette came up beside her and whispered. "What's with this thing between you and Wallace?"

Aurora smiled and turned toward the path ahead. "I'm not sure. We'll see how it plays out."

Lisette returned the smile. "This has all been so amazing—how everything finally fell into place to get us out. When we were up there in those iron cages, I nearly lost all hope."

"I almost did too. Then I remembered what Eli was always telling us."

"To put our trust in the Lord?"

"Right."

Lisette stepped around a boulder and returned to Aurora's side. "I–I have to admit that God exists. After seeing what I've seen, how could I deny it?"

"And Jesus?" This came from Tyler, who had caught up and now walked beside her. "Do you believe in him?"

"You've been listening?" She gave him a playful slap on the shoulder.

"Only to hear that you believe in God. So what about it? Are you ready to become a Christian?"

"I–I . . . yes! I am."

Aurora stopped, forcing Lisette and Tyler to stop. Then she spoke so everyone could hear. "Everyone, listen! Lisette has decided to become a Christian!"

Wallace came back, extended a hand, and they shook. "You and me—we're both Christians now."

They all broke out in applause.

"I'm proud of you, Lisette," said Tyler. "I knew one day you'd come around." Then he hugged her.

* * *

THEY CONTINUED ACROSS THE HEATH to the trail that led down to Alltnaharrie. Below, the waters of the loch gleamed in the moonlight where the boat was waiting. They descended, and there, on the rickety dock, stood the fisherman, Brett, and Maeve.

When the fisherman saw them, the engine began its deep, throbbing rumble.

Brett hugged his sister and Lisette, and Maeve hugged everyone.

"We didn't know if you'd make it back here or not," said Tyler.

"After I led the Friends to the dirt track, I came back so Maeve and I could bring the boat here for you."

The black-bearded fisherman coughed, and Tyler approached.

"What happened at the government facility up yonder?" The man nodded his head toward the cliff. "We heard explosions."

"There was a castle and a compound holding dozens of prisoners." Then Tyler broke out in a grin. "When we left, the prisoners were fleeing, and the castle was on fire."

The fisherman slapped a hand on one thigh and matched Tyler's grin. "And I suppose you dinnae ken who did the deed, hey?"

"No, we don't," said Hamish.

"It's all right by me. All right, indeedy." Grinning, the fisherman motioned them toward the boat. "It's mighty late. Let's get you back to Ullapool."

They piled into the boat and motored across the bay.

* * *

BRETT HAD KEPT ALL THREE rooms at the hotel. Tyler and Brett would share one. Aurora, Lisette, and Maeve would take the second. And Hamish and Wallace had the third.

But as they mounted the stairs and stood in the hall, Wallace faced the others. "I have something to ask you folks. Aurora has told me some of what you're about, but now that I'm a fugitive from the Unitum Imperium, I have no place to go. They'll be hunting for me, and—"

"And you're wondering if you can join us?" asked Tyler.

"Aye."

Tyler glanced at the others, and by their expression—especially Aurora's—he knew the answer. "The consensus, Wallace Sloan, is yes! We'd be glad for you to join us!"

The others clapped. Aurora approached him, and, for the second time that day, she kissed him on the lips.

Before they entered their rooms, Tyler addressed them. "Tomorrow, at breakfast, we'll decide what to do and where to go next."

Then Lisette added, "Aurora, you can have the notebook back. Maybe it will give us some guidance."

"Aye, the notebook." Wallace's eyes widened. "Is it true that knows the future and tells you what to do?"

"It is, Wallace." Aurora nodded. "But it's God who's been guiding us through the notebook."

"Amazing! I cannot wait to see what it says next."

CHAPTER 59

THE BAPTISM

Venice, Italy ~ March, Year 3

Acts 2:37–39 (NLT): *Peter's words pierced their hearts, and they said to him and to the other apostles, "Brothers, what should we do?"*

Peter replied, "Each of you must repent of your sins and turn to God and be baptized in the name of Jesus Christ for the forgiveness of your sins. Then you will receive the gift of the Holy Spirit. This promise is to you, to your children, and to those far away—all who have been called by the Lord our God."

It was Sunday, and the sun had dispelled the clouds, warming the alleys and bridges as Carlita led Nick and Brooke on a winding path over the cobbles and canals.

"Our group is small," said Carlita over one shoulder. "And the service is all in Italian, but I will ask if we can speak English today, just for you, Brooke."

"I can pick out half the words," she said. "Nick promised to begin lessons. If we're going to live here, I need to become fluent."

Carlita threw her a smile and kept walking. At a house with yellow bricks, she knocked. Someone opened a peephole then the door.

A twentysomething woman with ink-black hair, wide black eyebrows, and an infectious smile waved them inside. "Welcome, Carlita. And you've brought guests!"

"They want to be baptized, Maria. Can you ask Pastor Alberto if we could speak English today?"

Maria clapped her hands and gave a little jump. "Oh, how exciting!" she said in English. "I'll tell the pastor. What a wonderful day!" Then she ran on ahead.

Carlita followed in her wake, down a narrow hall to a back room with a view of a canal. Present were fifteen people of varying ages before a music stand, behind which sat a white-bearded man in his sixties wearing jeans and a sports jacket.

"Welcome, Carlita." Speaking English, the pastor stood. "And who are these two who wish to join the family of God today?"

Carlita introduced everyone, and Pastor Alberto announced that, since they all spoke English, they would conduct the morning's service in Brooke's tongue.

Then a young man left a front row seat, picked up a guitar from its stand in the corner, and stood before the gathering. "Let's sing some golden oldies today, starting with 'Amazing Grace'."

He began to play, and the group began to sing. Song sheets were on the seats, and Nick sang along with the others. The music was joyful, and now that they'd both read the Bible, it was meaningful and uplifting. The second song was "How Great Thou Art". Then Pastor Alberto thanked the youth and took the front.

"As Maria announced with great enthusiasm a moment ago, our two visitors have become Christians and want to be baptized." Alberto faced his audience. "Today's message just so happens to fit perfectly for two souls wishing to join God's flock. It's from the book of Luke, chapter fifteen, verses four through seven." He picked up his Bible and read.

"'If a man has a hundred sheep and one of them gets lost, what will he do? Won't he leave the ninety-nine others in the wilderness and go to search for the one that is lost until he finds it? And when he has found it, he will joyfully carry it home on his shoulders. When he arrives, he will call together his friends and neighbors, saying, "Rejoice with me because I have found my lost sheep." In the same way, there is more joy in heaven over one lost sinner who repents and returns to God than over ninety-nine others who are righteous and haven't strayed away.'"

After closing the Bible, he gripped the stand with both hands. "Everyone in this room is like our two visitors today. Before Christ came to earth to take his people home, none of us knew him. We were *all* lost sheep. And today, since Nick and Brooke have given their hearts and minds to the Lord of lords and King of kings and want to be baptized, the angels in Heaven will shout for joy, even more than our Maria here."

At that, everyone in the room broke out in wide smiles.

He went on, describing the joys and wonders that awaited Christians when they entered the kingdom of God, not only here on earth, but when they passed from this life to the next.

"Not only will we receive eternal blessings, but also, in the trying times ahead, we will be spared some, but not all, of the terrors that await!"

He finished with a prayer, asking that, though they all came late to faith, everyone here would be spared the wrath God had stored up for unbelievers.

"Now, Nick and Brooke, we have swimsuits for you, and Maria will lead you to rooms where you can change. We dare not use the canal for fear some of our neighbors will report us, so we use a bathtub. Not ideal, but it will have to do."

"Thank you, Pastor."

They changed, and when they reappeared, they climbed to an upstairs restroom where a tub had been filled with cold water. The congregation followed, crowding into what little space the room and the hall offered.

Pastor Alberto led Brooke to the tub, and she stepped into it. At his direction, she sat.

"Do you, Brooke Barkley, give your belief, your trust, and your heart to Jesus, the Son of God?"

"I do."

"Then I baptize you in the name of God the Father, God the Son, and God the Holy Spirit."

He grabbed her head, and while she held her nose, he gently dipped her under the water.

She emerged, dripping and smiling.

"Welcome to the family of God!" cried Alberto, and everyone burst into applause.

As she dried off, Nick took her place, and when the pastor repeated the phrases for Nick, he went under and came back out, again dripping and smiling.

But something had changed. He could feel it. Such a feeling of joy and comfort and strength now filled every part of him. Was it because he could feel the Holy Spirit now living inside him? Is that why he felt he could float to the ceiling?

He dried off, and after both had changed into their street clothes, they descended to the kitchen where Mary, the woman of the house, had made coffee, tea, and muffins.

They talked and mingled, but even as it was time to go, Nick was still floating on air.

Halfway back to Carlita's, in the middle of one of the bridges that arched over yet another canal, Brooke stopped them. "Carlita, you asked us a question earlier, and I never gave you an answer."

Carlita cocked her head. "What question was that, Brooke?"

"Whether Nick and I would stay here and run the safe house."

Nick's heart sped up. He was hoping she'd come around.

"And what is your answer?" asked Carlita.

"Yes! If Nick still wants to do it, I do too."

Carlita broke into a wide smile. She rushed forward and hugged Brooke and then Nick. "Both of you have made me so happy. This is a wonderful day, indeed! Tomorrow, I'll teach you what you need to know."

CHAPTER 60

NEW ORDERS

Edinburgh, Scotland ~ March, Year 3

On their second night at the Hilton Edinburgh Carlton, Aurora sat at one of the restaurant's large round tables, listening to the hum of conversation and the clatter of dishes coming through the kitchen door. Even now, two days later, she reveled in her newfound freedom and in how they had helped to free all the prisoners. The revelations from Wallace and Lisette, that they were now both Christians, also warmed her heart.

But once again, they were being hunted.

The news reported that a mysterious creature was on the loose across the Lochbroom peninsula, viciously killing everyone in its path. But a unit of the UI army had been dispatched with high-powered rifles to take care of the problem, and citizens should not be alarmed.

The internet and television were now replete with warnings that the region should be on the alert for dozens of prison escapees, promising big rewards for anyone who turned them in. Even before they left Ullapool, the television and internet blasted Aurora's, Tyler's, Hamish's, and Wallace's pictures.

So before they drove further, they stopped at the Inverness Friends' house where Wallace, Hamish, and Aurora received disguises. They dyed Wallace's hair red, gave him brown, plastic-rimmed glasses, and a fake mustache to paste over the real one he was now growing. For Aurora, they dyed her hair black and gave her black, wire-rimmed glasses. Apparently, the castle hadn't had time to take Lisette's picture. The media had only a poor sketch of her. And since the picture for Tyler showed his Gavin Roberts disguise, he removed his fake mustache and goatee, and they dyed his hair black, returning to his Tyler Carter, alias Greyson Ross, visage.

"I'll come up with something in a few days," he said. "For now, I'll be myself."

269

They had just ordered, and everyone remarked how the menu items had dwindled by half and how the prices for everything had nearly doubled. But they still had plenty of Greyson Ross's cash, and the hotel was glad to take it.

The only fly in Aurora's otherwise savory soup was uncertainty about what they would do next. Now, she voiced her thoughts to the others. "We've done everything the notebook told us to do. We freed an entire group of Christians and even non-Christians from the clutches of evil men. Most of them got what they deserved. But have you ever completed some lengthy project, and after it was finished, you were left with a sense of emptiness?"

"Aye," said Wallace. "I, too, have felt that sometimes. Why do you ask?"

"Because that's how I feel now."

"Like we need a new purpose?" asked Brett. "Something to work toward?"

"Exactly." She lifted her wine glass and drank.

"I, for one, would like to go back to Minnesota." Tyler glanced at Lisette, who nodded. "Things have been so crazy for so long I could use some peace."

"I second that," added Lisette. "There's been too much excitement lately for me."

"But how would you get there?" Brett raised an open hand. "The ocean trip here was crazy dangerous. Then there's the problem of traveling through Canada again."

Tyler sighed. "I suppose you're right. It's out of the question."

Aurora's gaze wandered to the far end of the room. "It has been rather hectic lately. I wouldn't mind a break from all the craziness."

"Aye, lass." Wallace placed a hand on top of hers. "And if you don't mind, I'd like to join you."

"I don't mind at all." She brought his hand to her lips, kissed it, and released it.

The others at the table smiled and looked away.

"Now that we're out of danger," said Brett, "assuming the UI doesn't find us, that is, I wonder why the notebook hasn't said something."

"I've wondered too, and I've been checking it twice a day." Aurora scooped her purse from the floor, removed the notebook, and opened it before her. She flipped to the end, expecting the same blank page she'd seen this morning, but—no!

"There's a new message!"

"You're kidding!" Wallace leaned forward. "This is for real?"

"Aye, laddie," said Hamish. "Believe it or not, I've seen it for myself."

But as she read the new message, her brows wrinkled.

Greyson Ross and Briella Hall must return at once to Jerusalem, leaving for Paris by train and then for Jerusalem by airplane. The rest must seek the safety of Friends in Italy and wait on the Lord. John 15:13.

Her first thought after reading it was for Tyler. He would not be happy about this. She passed the book to the rest so they could read it. Then she pulled her Bible from her purse and looked up the passage.

No one has greater love than this, that someone would lay down his life for his friends.

That, too, was scary. She read it aloud.

"What!" Tyler slapped the top of his head. "It wants me to go back to Adam Turner in the Clal Center, pretending that I'm Greyson Ross again? And what's this warning about laying down one's life? I don't like it."

"Oh no!" Lisette was shaking her head. "This cannot be. I don't like it either."

The others looked away and said nothing.

Tyler dropped his head in his hands. "Why this? Anything but this."

Brett laid a hand on his shoulder. "You don't have a choice, brother. Everything it's told us we have to do."

"The message comes from God," added Aurora. "Who knows what might happen if we disobeyed it."

For a time, Tyler seemed to examine the tablecloth. Then he took a deep breath. "You're right, of course. We have no choice." Then he faced Lisette. "We have to do it, Lisette."

For several seconds, she held his glance. Then she nodded. "You're right. I don't like it, but, of course, you're right. But what's this about laying down a life?"

Aurora breathed out. Who knew what would happen if one of them took a different path than the one God had laid for them? "Hamish, can you arrange tickets? It appears everyone is traveling somewhere."

"Aye, that I can. Tonight before I go to bed." He refilled his wineglass. "But now I have an announcement. Though the rest of you will leave, I must stay. I was waiting to tell you, but now is as good a time as any. This morning, I, too, received orders to be in London in two days' time."

"Then we are all going our separate ways." Brett raised his glass of wine. "Here's to safe travels and to fulfilling the missions God has in store for us, wherever and whatever those may be."

Aurora hoisted her glass, as did the others.

But after she drank, she wondered what adventures or dangers they might encounter next.

AUTHOR'S NOTES

APOSTASY WILL PRECEDE THE ANTICHRIST

One of the precursors of the end is a great turning away from God. Many mainline churches are losing their way and preaching what we call apostasy. But a similar turning away from God is also happening in the culture at large. For we are living in an age that has abandoned the Lord, embracing and promoting everything God hates. Listen to the words of Isaiah 5:20–24 (HCSB):

> Woe to those who call evil good and good evil, who substitute darkness for light and light for darkness, who substitute bitter for sweet and sweet for bitter. Woe to those who are wise in their own opinion and clever in their own sight. Woe to those who are heroes at drinking wine . . . who acquit the guilty for a bribe and deprive the innocent of justice. Therefore, as a tongue of fire consumes straw and as dry grass shrivels in the flame, so their roots will become like something rotten and their blossoms will blow away like dust, for they have rejected the instruction of the LORD of Hosts, and they have despised the word of the Holy One of Israel.

What Isaiah condemns is what the culture not only accepts but insists that we promote. Truly, we are living in an age of apostasy and godlessness.

And the result?

It's preparing the way for the Antichrist. Before the man of lawlessness appears to reign in evil, a great apostasy must precede it. Before Christ returns, before the Rapture and the end times, there will also be a turning away from and a rejection of God in the culture at large. Listen to the words of Jesus in Matthew 24:10–12 (NLT):

And many will turn away from me and betray and hate each other. And many false prophets will appear and will deceive many people. Sin will be rampant everywhere, and the love of many will grow cold.

And from Apostle Paul in 2 Thessalonians 2:1–3 (HCSB):

Now concerning the coming of our Lord Jesus Christ and our being gathered to Him: We ask you, brothers, not to be easily upset in mind or troubled, either by a spirit or by a message or by a letter as if from us, alleging that the Day of the Lord has come. Don't let anyone deceive you in any way. For that day will not come unless the apostasy comes first and the man of lawlessness is revealed, the son of destruction.

THE SIGNS OF APOSTASY

What are the signs of this "apostasy" and this turning away from God?
* An increase of false prophets and teachers of apostasy in the church, such as the "health, wealth, and prosperity gospel".
* A great rejection of God and especially of Jesus in the culture at large.
* A worldwide intolerance of Christianity leading to what some are calling, today, the worst persecution of Christians ever recorded.
* A mindless, demonic hatred of Israel and the Jewish people.
* A passionate insistence on murdering the unborn in the womb.
* An embrace and promotion of every kind of sinful lifestyle abhorrent to God, such as LGBTQ.
* A confusion of genders and sexuality.
* An explosion of lawlessness, crime, addiction, and homelessness.
* A desire and a push toward globalism and one-world government.

Truly, we are living in the shadow of the end times, in an age where speaking the Word of God is called "hate speech", where evil is called good, and good is called evil.

SO WHAT ARE CHRISTIANS TO DO?

But what about us? How do Christians live in such a world? What should we do?

First, we must reject the lies of an evil, corrupt culture. We must live according to the advice from the great novelist Alexander Solzhenitsyn, who lived under the repressive, atheistic regime of Soviet Russia. "Live not by lies," he said. For when people accept the untruths of an atheistic, immoral culture, those lies begin to eat, bit by bit, at their souls. They become desensitized to the evil surrounding them. Then they become unwitting allies of the Adversary, the Prince of Darkness.

But we are not like that. Within each of us lives the Holy Spirit. We have no choice but to resist.

Second, we must fortify our souls with God's revelation to mankind, the Bible. We should read it and imbibe its truths, for until we get to Heaven, God's Word is our water of life.

Third, we must engage with and be committed to a local church, for only by living and praying and worshiping with other Christians can we strengthen and nourish our souls and resist Satan and his demons.

Finally, we must not let the times in which we live become a millstone that drags us down to despair and hopelessness. We have a great hope that nonbelievers do not. We have been saved by a God who gave up his life for us, who loves us more than we can imagine, and who promises an eternal future so filled with happiness, joy, and love, the prospect is beyond our comprehension.

Knowing all that, we should be filled, not with sadness, but with joy—not with despair, but with hope. Because the first event on the end-times calendar is the Rapture of the Church, a moment when, in the blink of an eye, all who have put their trust in Jesus will be swept out of this earth and up to Heaven.

Lord Jesus, tarry not. Lord Jesus, come soon!
Maranatha!

APOCALYPSE MISSION 3

NEWSLETTER INVITATION #2

**The shadow of the Tribulation already darkens our world.
Stay true to the faith and seek refuge in Christ.**

Subscribe and keep abreast of new releases and receive these free gifts:

1. 10 Reasons Why the End Times Could Come Tomorrow
2. How the Green Agenda Prepares the Way for Earth Worship and the Antichrist
3. Prophecy and the Book of Revelation: What Is Its Blessing?
4. The Rapture of the Church: Time Is Running Out. Are You Ready?

To sign up, go to: www.MarkFisherAuthor.com/newsletter

SCRIPTURE REFERENCES

* Preface: Our salvation and our hope come only from God. 62:1–2, 5–21
* Part I: The opening of the fifth seal brings persecution to Christians. Revelation 6:9–11
* Chapter 1: Woe will fall upon evil people. Micah 2:1
* Chapter 3: God will help those who wait on him. Psalm 40:1
* Part II: Put on the armor of God against the strategies of the devil. Ephesians 6:10–13
* Chapter 15: Invoking the name of Jesus casts out demons. Luke 10:17
* Chapter 16: The coming of the beast, who is the Antichrist. Revelation 13:1, 5–7
* Part III: Avoid the path of the wicked. Proverbs 4:14–19
* Chapter 21: In the end times, there will be lawlessness and cold hearts. Matthew 24:3, 12
* Chapter 25: Thinking God does not exist, the wicked plot evil deeds. Psalm 10:1–2, 4, 7–9, 11–12
* Chapter 29: God did not appoint us to wrath but to salvation. 1 Thessalonians 5:1–11
* Part IV: The existence of demons: Jesus drives out a demon. Matthew 12:22–28
* Chapter 35: A call to sing songs of thanksgiving and praise. Psalm 95:1–2
* Chapter 37: God will have a day of judgment against the plots of the wicked. Psalm 37:12–13
* Chapter 39: Sorrow awaits those who plan evil deeds. Micah 2:1
* Chapter 43: There is a time for every activity under heaven. Ecclesiastes 3:1–3

* Chapter 48: God will judge people for what they have done, for ill or for good. Romans 2:6–8
* Chapter 49: Those who belong to Jesus hear his voice, and no one will snatch them away from him. John 10:27–30
* Part V: The judgment that awaits on the Day of the Lord. Zephaniah 1:14–17
* Chapter 57: Woe will fall on the wicked. Isaiah 3:11
* Chapter 58: All who believe will have eternal life. John 6:47
* Chapter 59:
    – Peter tells new believers what they must do next. Acts 2:37–39
    – The parable of the ninety-nine and the lost sheep. Luke 15:4–7
* Chapter 60: The greatest love is laying down one's life for a friend. John 15:13
* Author's Notes:
    – Woe to those who call evil good and good evil. Isaiah 5:20–24
    – Many will turn away from God, and their hearts will grow cold. Matthew 24:10–12
    – Before the end times, there will be a great apostasy in the church. 2 Thessalonians 2:1–3

MARK'S BOOKS

Christian Historical Fiction:
* Book 1: The Bonfires of Beltane: Following St. Patrick Across Ancient, Celtic Ireland
* Book 2: The Medallion: An Epic Quest in A.D. 486
* The Slaves of Autumn: A Tale of Stolen Love in Ancient, Celtic Ireland

General Market Historical Fiction:
* Death of the Master Builder: Love, Envy, and the Struggle to Raise the Greatest Cathedral of the Italian Renaissance
* The Sun Shines Even In Winter: A Novel of Invasion and Espionage in World War I

The Scepter and Tower Trilogy, an Epic Fantasy for Young Adults of All Ages:
* The Stolen Scroll, A Novella Prequel (eBook only)
* Book 1: Quest for the Scepter
* Book 2: Into the Druid's Lair
* Book 3: Return to the Tower

Days of the Apocalypse, a Bestselling Series of Christian End-Times Thrillers:
* Book 1: The Day the End Began
* Book 2: Days of War and Famine
* Book 3: Days of Trial and Tribulation
* Book 4: Days of Death and Darkness
* Book 5: Last Days of the End

Apocalypse Mission, a Series of Christian End-Times Thrillers:
* Apocalypse Mission 1: Chaos, War, and the Antichrist
* Apocalypse Mission 2: Plague, Peril, and Passage to Prophecy
* Apocalypse Mission 3: A Demon, a Dungeon, a Den of Evil

* Apocalypse Mission 4: New Babylon, the Beast, and the Refuge (April 2026)
* Apocalypse Mission 5: The Rescue, the Blood, and the Abyss (October 2026)
* Apocalypse Mission 6: The Fire, the Ice, and the Second Coming (April 2027)

THE DAY THE END BEGAN

Days of the Apocalypse, Book 1
By Mark E. Fisher

First of a Bestselling Series of Christian End-Times Thrillers

Margot's paintings are stunning, terrifying, and prophetic. Within months the world will end—but few believe her.

The end times predicted by the Book of Revelation are about to crash down upon the world. One woman, gifted with divine prophecy, foretells a time of terrible trial and divine judgment. Are her visions a gift from God? Or a trick from the Great Deceiver?

When Dylan discovers her prophecies, his life and the lives of his brother and sister change forever. He flies from Chicago and joins Margot in Belgium. But then people begin vanishing. And Margot's paintings send them both on a divinely-inspired mission to thwart the Antichrist.

Days of the Apocalypse is a five-book series closely based on the biblical prophecies in the books of Revelation, Matthew, Daniel, Ezekiel, and others. It brings to life the tale of the Rapture of the Church, the coming of the Antichrist, and the seven terrible years of Tribulation.

See: https//www.MarkFisherAuthor.com for more details.

THE SUN SHINES EVEN IN WINTER

A Novel of Invasion and Espionage in World War I

By Mark E. Fisher

It's 1914, and few hear the rumblings of war, only months away.

When Dieter Jaeger is diagnosed with a fatal heart defect, he leaves University before final exams and returns to his wealthy, aristocratic family of Prussian descent in Lille, France. Fearing to saddle the woman he loves with someone who could die at any moment, he breaks his engagement in a tearful parting.

Days later, his uncle, a highly placed general in the Prussian army, comes to visit. His uncle warns the family of a coming war, but Dieter's father, a pacifist, refuses to listen.

After the invasion, Dieter and his family are imprisoned. Now he faces a choice: Work for his uncle as a spy for the Kaiser. Or let his family and fiancée rot in a German internment camp.

Then the French resistance gives him a third choice—spy for Germany, but as a double agent!

A gripping, gritty, but clean novel of historical fiction, written for a general audience.

See: https//www.MarkFisherAuthor.com for more details.

ABOUT THE AUTHOR

Mark E. Fisher wrote his first twelve pages at the age of ten, complete with drawings of a prairie fire, Indians, and a stampede. Since then, he's authored novels of epic fantasy and historical fiction for the Christian and the general market. He's also written Days of the Apocalypse, a bestselling series of Christian end-times thrillers, closely following the biblical prophecies in the books of Revelation, Matthew, Joel, Ezekiel, Daniel, and others.

He's now working on Apocalypse Mission, a six-book series of Christian end-times thrillers with new characters who will sometimes intersect with the characters from Days of the Apocalypse.

At various times, Mark has welded rails for the railroad, inspected glass in a glass factory, given aid checks to welfare clients, and programmed micro-code for IBM. He has a bachelor's degree in anthropology/sociology, and Masters' degrees in both computer science and ministry. He once helped plant a church. He has played acoustic guitar in a church band. He is the treasurer of New Gospel Frontiers, a 501(c)(3) organization dedicated to funding missions opportunities for the unreached peoples of Central Asia and Africa. He is also on the board of the Lord's Discipleship House, a 501(c)(3) organization with a goal of providing a gospel-oriented living center for recovering addicts. He has led small groups and sometimes preaches.

He and his wife enjoy traveling with recent, weeks'-long trips to Mexico, Japan, the Dominican Republic, Ireland, France, Italy, Portugal, and Switzerland. If not traveling, he's at his desk writing, eating out, or walking his miniature Australian shepherd around the neighborhood.